By JASON HUFFMAN-BLACK

Snakes Among Sweet Flowers

Published by DREAMSPINNER PRESS
www.dreamspinnerpress.com

SNAKES AMONG
SWEET FLOWERS

JASON HUFFMAN-BLACK

Published by
DREAMSPINNER PRESS

5032 Capital Circle SW, Suite 2, PMB# 279, Tallahassee, FL 32305-7886 USA
www.dreamspinnerpress.com

Snakes Among Sweet Flowers
© 2016 Jason Huffman-Black.

Cover Art
© 2016 Angsty G.
http://www.angstyg.com
Cover content is for illustrative purposes only and any person depicted on the cover is a model.

ISBN: 978-1-63477-235-8
Digital ISBN: 978-1-63477-236-5
Library of Congress Control Number: 2016901403
Published June 2016
v. 1.0

Printed in the United States of America

This paper meets the requirements of
ANSI/NISO Z39.48-1992 (Permanence of Paper).

To Ethan and Mark for believing in me.

I also want to thank my friends and family who encouraged, read, reread, and helped me make this novel into reality.
I couldn't have done it without you all.

AUTHOR'S NOTE

ALTHOUGH THERE is an actual Hog Mountain, GA, in relatively the same location mentioned in the book, the town in this novel is fictional.

CHAPTER 1

CAMDEN SANDERS stood from where he had been leaning over the engine of the year-old Honda. Out of the corner of his eye, he took stock of the car's young owner. Not more than twenty-one, the boy looked panicked at the sight of smoke coming from under the open hood. Although the car wasn't anything special, the clothes and particularly the watch the young boy wore told Cam what he needed to know. Probably still living at home, maybe fresh out of college, and trying to show his father he could take care of his own problems, even if he was living off his dad's dime.

Cam sighed, curling his top lip as he sucked his front teeth, staring at the engine a moment longer. "Okay, John." Cam always used his customer's name. It helped give the impression they were friends and that Cam had their best interest at heart. "I can see this car is your baby, and I know how that is. It's why I'm gonna help you out here. We're gonna fix her up right."

He nodded his head until John nodded along.

"Now, on jobs this complicated, I would normally have to charge over a thousand. See, when I worked in the city, they set the prices, you know? Out to take all the money they could get. But I ain't like that. I just wanna help people and make a livin', not a thievin', right?"

He locked eyes with John, making sure John was following along. And the boy was right there, looking at Camden like he was his savior.

"I'm sure you're savin' money for something besides handin' to some mechanic like me. That's why I'm gonna do you a solid, man." Cam leaned over the engine again and pointed to the area around the end of a black hose that had a small amount of white residue. "Now I learned this trick from the old man that trained me. See this white here? It's calcification from the pH being all wrong in your motor oil.

It'll destroy a car faster than lettin' the water deoxygenate in your radiator. But don't expect them city mechanics to tell you that. They fix the damage, don't tell the owner the *real* cause of their problem." He stood back. "Immoral the way they do."

The boy was just smart enough to be stupid, the way Cam liked them. He'd moved out to the small, recently upwardly mobile community of Hog Mountain on the far outskirts of Atlanta in hopes of finding people with more money than sense, and so far, he had hit pay dirt. The old country town had attracted a class of people who could afford the gas for a long commute back into Atlanta. Lots of upper middle class, kids getting money tossed at them to keep them out of the hair of Dad and the new trophy wife, divorcées using alimony and child support to fund their yoga and club memberships, living in a near-rural area where they trusted all the local businessmen to be honest and fair.

By the end of the day, Cam had made a simple repair of a leaking hose, charged John more than ten times what it should have cost, and had the boy promising to bring the car back monthly for a "free" check of the oil's pH.

After watching the little Honda drive off, Cam pulled the garage doors closed on the former gas station he'd paid cash for several weeks ago. The pumps were no longer operational, but he only needed the garage area and a place to sleep anyway. It had come with the dilapidated farmhouse behind that he now lived in. It had been a smart move, getting away from the city and his former associates, cutting ties with a group of thieves that were making good money but also becoming increasingly violent. Camden liked his con games light on danger and high on rate of return. He'd already done prison time twice and was finally done with parole and off the books. He wasn't going to push his luck again.

Camden stripped himself of his stained work shirt, exposing his inked skin as he walked back toward the industrial-sized sink. He dropped his shirt to the floor near the back door. Most of the tattooing on his arms were prison tats, which he'd gotten colored and enhanced once he was out, but the one on his chest was the only one that had been there before his first stint in prison.

Over the left side of his chest was a blackened anatomical heart with a leather strap squeezing it tightly and crimson blood dripping to create a puddle beneath. Scrawled in what looked to be the blood were the words *Et tu, Brute?* He'd had it put there as a reminder of the pain of betrayal, although, at the time, he hadn't known what real betrayal was. Having a friend run and leave him to take the rap for shoplifting was pretty mild when it came down to it.

Camden scooped some of the orange stuff beside the sink and lathered up his hands and arms to the elbows, then frowned as he took a small brush to work on the black around his nails. It was what he hated about being a mechanic. He enjoyed working on machinery, liked fixing things and the solitude of working without someone else there with a running commentary, but he hated the way it left behind a stain on his skin to announce his unworthiness. Then again, didn't he have plenty of those? Life had a way of doing that to him.

Once Cam washed the soap from his arms, he grabbed a clean shop towel and stood back from the sink, taking a moment to examine himself in the little mirror that hung above it. He dried himself as he studied the face in the reflective surface. The blue eyes, which had always helped him earn the trust of others, were starting to come off more as cold. The pretty-boy looks were sharper and light on the "boy."

At thirty-six, he could see the marks of hard living on his skin, but not near as hard as some others he'd known. For the most part, he'd stayed away from the drugs he'd pushed to others, kept his drinking to the weekends, and worked out when he could, at least while in prison. Cam had always been in the scams for the money, not as some way to self-destruct, but he'd seen his fair share of those who chose each and every aspect of their lives as a way to destroy themselves.

There were lines at the corners of his eyes and one between his eyebrows, likely from holding his "I will cut you" frown firmly in place while serving time. That face had just been for show, though. He didn't have violence in him. At least not without some just cause, he supposed. Cam ran a hand over his closely cropped hair. It looked black when cut so short and there wasn't a hint of gray. His beard and mustache were trimmed just as closely, but still visible. He'd always been concerned with appearances. There was no need to look scruffy, even if he was a grease monkey.

Movement around his legs distracted him from his thoughts, and he glanced down with a grin. "All right, Tom, we're almost done here." The orange cat had adopted Cam not long after he had moved in and now spent most of the hot July days lazing close to the box fan that kept a breeze circulating in the unair-conditioned garage. Tom had now insinuated himself enough into Cam's life that he knew Cam's standing in front of the sink heralded the end of the day.

Cam dropped the towel back to the counter next to the sink and took a moment to make sure the place was all locked up, the fan unplugged, and the lights switched off before scooping up his shirt. When Cam opened the back door of the shop, Tom led the way out. Cam had yet to let the huge cat in the house, although he had made the mistake of putting a bowl of water on the porch.

He made his way across the littered backyard of the garage toward the small white clapboard house that sat behind it. He had bought a swing blade and cut the grass down to about calf height, but that had only revealed all the old tires, engine parts, and beer bottles the higher grass had been hiding. The property had sat empty for a while before Cam bought it, and he felt sure that during that time both the yard and the house had been an unofficial site for teenaged parties and trysts.

The old house looked as worn-out as he was feeling that evening. The place could do with a coat of paint, new roof—some tender care, for sure. If he planned to stay there, which he hoped he would, Cam was going to have to do some work on the little cottage.

It was the first home he'd ever owned. Although for the people around these parts, it wasn't much to write the family about, he felt some pride for it, like he was finally coming up in the world.

On the first floor, it had three small bedrooms and a large country kitchen in the back—although he didn't consider himself much of a cook—but the best part was the large second floor—"the attic" was what the realty agent had called it. It was under the gables and the entire length and breadth of the house, but the last owner had finished the area into a large master bedroom with attached bath, which Cam had claimed as his room.

He headed up the steps to the front porch. They were a bit wobbly and so was the handrail. Another for his list of projects. At some point, he was going to have to start on that list before the house fell in around him. As he made it to the door, he took the handle in one hand while leaning and putting the other hand out in front of Tom, knowing all too well the cat would make a try to scamper inside with him.

"Sorry, boy. I'm sure you got fleas or ticks or something I don't want in the house."

He slammed the door closed behind him, but then turned to peek out the window at the cat as he slumped down right in front of the door in the shade of the porch. *God, I am such a sucker.*

With a grumble, Cam stripped off his shoes and socks before making his way into the kitchen, tossing his shirt and socks into the washer as he passed it. "Tom survived just fine before you came to town. He's playing you," he mumbled to himself. He'd read an article about how cats had domesticated themselves in order to take advantage of the perks related to being a pet. "The damn thing is running a scam and you are falling for it."

Shaking his head, Cam opened the refrigerator and pulled out a bucket from KFC along with several styrofoam containers. The last five pieces of chicken went on a plate, and then he emptied the other containers of green beans, mashed potatoes, and brown gravy. While his dinner spun in the microwave, he made himself a huge glass of iced tea and placed it on the little kitchen table along with the final styrofoam container, the last of the coleslaw. Then he leaned against the counter next to the microwave in eager anticipation.

Although there were several fast food selections in the small town, the KFC was out near the interstate. Before moving to Hog Mountain, five miles of driving had seemed pretty standard to get somewhere, but that had quickly changed once he'd relocated. Everything in the small town was much closer, in more ways than one. And country miles seemed so much farther than city ones, so when he'd made the drive out to the interstate a couple of days before, he'd bought the biggest barrel of chicken KFC offered plus several cartons of each side, even though he would be the only one eating from it. He'd finally worked through to the last of the food, and without the large red-and-white bucket in his refrigerator, it was pretty bare. He added a trip to the grocery store to his mental list of activities for the weekend.

A ding sounded as the microwave stopped, and Cam pulled the plate out and gingerly took it to the table along with a fork from the drawer. The chicken was always better fresh, but even heated over, it was better than anything he could have whipped up on his own or the shit he'd eaten while incarcerated. He scooped the rest of the coleslaw onto his plate and then dug into the meal.

Fried chicken always reminded Cam of his grandmother. She used to cook for him when he was younger and spent the weekend, or months on end during the summer, with her. She had been his savior while growing up, taking him out of a home with a drunk for a dad and a mother with her own survival—and her "stories," as she called her TV shows—to worry about. His grandmother had put him in piano lessons, encouraged him to get good grades, and supported him, even when he had come out to her. She would have loved his farmhouse's big, airy kitchen with all its counter space and windows. He wished she'd been around long enough to see it.

While gnawing on a chicken leg, he got up from the table, grabbing a napkin to wipe his hands, then took the cereal bowl from the dish drainer before settling back in front of his plate. Cam stripped the meat from the final piece of chicken and shredded it into the bowl, rolling his eyes at himself as he did. Once the bowl was filled, he took it to the front door, opened it, and knelt to place it beside the orange beast lounging there.

"Gotta keep your strength up for all that tomming, right, boy?" Damn, he was going soft.

He scrubbed the cat between the ears as it dug into the food, and was just rising to go back inside when a blue Ford Taurus pulled into his driveway and stopped in front of the old house. Cam couldn't control his body's reaction to the unexpected visit, his heart pounding and hands growing clammy.

An older lady stepped out from behind the wheel, giving Cam a smile that looked a bit unsure before leaning back into the vehicle. He glanced down to realize he was shirtless and barefoot. Well, wasn't this embarrassing? With no time to run upstairs to rectify that, he simply stood and waited as the lady made her way up onto his porch with a linen bag full of something. He could only hope she wasn't somehow in cahoots with Harold. It would be just like him to get some little old lady to do his dirty work.

"Hello, dear. Sorry to interrupt your evening and another apology for taking so long gettin' over here. I've been meaning to stop by for weeks, but life has a way of foiling even our best intentions." She smiled, and Cam couldn't help but smile back, while also attempting to cover his bare chest with crossed arms. He had no idea what the woman's intentions were, but if she was there to kill him, he would simply have to stand there and let her. She was way too sweet to ever disrespect by putting up a fight.

"I… uh…." Cam did a little wave at his chest and feet, words failing him for a moment. "Yeah, I woulda been dressed if I'd known. Um…."

"Oh, I'm Dotty Calhoun." Dotty stepped closer as she spoke. "I wanted to welcome you to town and bring you a pie. And don't you worry none about how you're dressed. Men like their comforts."

"Camden Sanders." He held out his hand and shook the one she had free, then suddenly realized he was being impolite to his guest. "Would you like to come in? The house isn't much right now, but it's clean… fairly, at least."

Dotty smiled as she followed Cam to the door. "My sons aren't homemakers, so I'm not expecting Martha Stewart. Hope you like pecan pie."

Cam hummed in approval as he held the door for Dotty to enter. If his death was coming by pecan pie, all he could say was *what a way to go*! "It's one of my favorites, but I insist you stay and have a piece with me. I can make coffee."

He led Ms. Calhoun into the kitchen, then rushed to throw away all the containers from his dinner and place the plate and utensils in the sink. "Sorry about the mess. And uh… let me grab a shirt to put on. My work shirt was too dirty to wear inside."

Dotty nodded and began setting out the pie and other items from her tote as Camden left the room and ran up the stairs. He had wanted to take a shower before putting any other clothes on, but it didn't look like that was going to happen. Once in his bedroom, he grabbed a white tank-top-style undershirt from the top drawer of his dresser and yanked it over his head, then shoved his feet into a pair of shower shoes that sat beside the piece of furniture.

The habit of wearing the sandals had come during prison. When not required to wear the nasty slip-on tennis shoes that were part of his uniform, he'd changed to sports socks and the sandals, which were much more comfortable. There was never a moment while on the inside that he had allowed his bare feet to touch the floor, during a shower or otherwise. He'd seen too many guys who'd made the error. He shuddered at the memory. It had taken months once he got out before he had been able to walk around barefooted again.

The journey back down the stairs was slower due to the sandals, and much louder on the scuffed hardwood. When he reentered the kitchen, he found the table set with two small plates, each holding a piece of pie with a healthy dollop of whipped cream on top, and mismatched cups full of milk. Cam frowned and looked up from the table to find Dotty at the sink drying her hands, his dinner plate and utensils now sitting in the dish rack next to the sink.

Cam opened his mouth to protest, but Dotty beat him to it by saying, "Not a word. I did it because I wanted to. Now let's sit and have some pie, shall we?"

He sat without speaking, but then took another look at the glasses of milk. "If this came from my refrigerator, I'm surprised it isn't solid, ma'am. We might want to skip on drinking it."

"I brought a half gallon along with me, and whipped the cream fresh. I have three sons, darlin'. I understand more than you know. And it's far too late for me to drink coffee, even decaf." She smiled and lifted her glass of milk for a toast.

Cam clinked his glass against hers and took a sip. Yeah, he needed to get to the store; milk tasted wonderful. Before taking his first bite of pie, he asked, "So have you and your husband always lived here in Hog Mountain?" Then he hummed loudly in approval as he savored the still warm, obviously homemade pecan pie with *real* whipped cream on top.

Dotty canted her head to the side. "Sort of. We started out here, married when we were right out of high school, but then James joined the Navy and we traveled around until he retired. After that, he got a job with the post office here in town and we took up again like we had never been away. Now tell me about you. Have you always lived in Georgia?"

"I was born and raised in Atlanta, ma'am. Your husband still working at the post office?" Cam said around another bite. Dotty was sweet, and it wasn't that he was trying to be rude, but his entire goal in this situation was to keep the conversation off himself. Cam knew eventually people were going to learn some things about him, but that didn't mean he was going to make it easy.

"No, darlin'. James died three years ago in March. He had a heart attack in his sleep and went like that." She snapped her fingers, then picked up her glass for another sip.

"I'm sorry, ma'am. I didn't mean to—"

"Now don't you dare. He lived a good life and went the way we all hope: fast and painless. As much as I miss him, life goes on." The kitchen grew quiet then, both of them focusing on their pie, and Camden felt he needed to get the conversation going again.

"You sure make a mean pie, Ms. Calhoun. I don't think I've tasted anything this good in years." When he glanced across the table, Dotty was looking at his uncovered arms and the tattoos there. He felt confident the fact they were prison tats was covered up by the re-inking and added color, and he wasn't at all sure someone as sweet as this woman would recognize they were done while on the inside, but he still worried.

Dotty lifted her gaze to his, obviously proud he enjoyed her cooking, but Cam spoke before her. "I should have put on something with sleeves. Hope I don't offend you."

She waved a hand. "My husband had some, but they were all anchors and military stuff. Yours are prettier." She pointed to the flower in full bloom on the back of his right hand.

He raised a brow, since the back of his other hand had a skull, which she probably didn't find "pretty."

"Okay, *that* one is prettier," she corrected.

Cam chuckled. "You like blue roses?"

"I love all flowers," she said, passion clear in her voice.

He nodded and traced the flower tattoo with his finger. "My grandmother did too. I think you two would have gotten along just fine."

The flower had been a signature design for his grandmother. Her china pattern and even the wallpaper in her bedroom had borne the dainty blooms. The image of his grandmother and the flower were so intertwined, he couldn't think of one without the other coming to mind. The tattoo on his hand was a permanent reminder of the woman who had been there for him when he felt no one else was.

Both of them had finished their pie by that point and Dotty rose to clear the table, but Cam stopped her. "I can get that, Ms. Calhoun."

Dotty pulled her hand back from the plates with a guilty expression but did take the pie and leftover whipped cream to the refrigerator. While putting them away, she said, "You can call me Dotty, dear. But I have to get going. My eyes aren't what they once were, and roads can get dark as sin out here in the sticks."

As Cam took the plates to the sink, she patted his shoulder, then scooped up her now-empty linen bag. He followed her to the door and opened it for her. "Thank you again for the delicious pie and the nice visit."

"Out here can get awful quiet when you live alone. You ever need another pie or a visit, you just call, you hear?" Dotty handed over a flowery piece of stationery with her name and number carefully printed on it, and Cam took it and nodded.

They each waved good-bye as the Taurus left his driveway, and Cam sighed as he closed the door. What had just happened? Shouldn't he feel put out by the visit? But he'd actually enjoyed the company, although it still was a bit odd to have anyone treat him as anything other than a criminal. Weird is what it was.

Back in the kitchen, he used a dish towel to wipe off the table before washing the plates and forks in the sink. When the dishes were drying in the rack, he started the washing machine since it was finally full with the week's work clothes. As the water filled, Cam shed the tank top he'd just put on, his underwear, and his jeans, pausing to dig into the pocket of his pants to retrieve his earnings for the day, then tossed everything in and closed the lid.

The sloshing and rattling of the old machine could be heard as Cam made his way into one of the first-floor bedrooms. They were usually closed off since there was spray paint on the walls and he didn't have furniture for the rooms, or even any use for the space at the moment. *Well, other than this.* He knelt in the corner, and with a butter knife from the kitchen, he worked loose one of the floorboards. Underneath, a glass mayonnaise jar lay sideways, cradled between two boards underneath. The jar was full with wads of cash, and Cam added most of his haul for the day, only keeping back enough for the errands he needed to run.

Once the floorboard was returned, Cam went upstairs, leaving his spending money on the dresser in his bedroom before entering the attached bathroom to take a long shower.

In a pair of basketball shorts and with a towel around his shoulders, Cam returned downstairs to refill his tea glass before heading for the living room.

The space was filled with mismatched furniture he'd found at yard sales in the area. Cam reached for the remote to turn on the TV but paused when he noticed the pulsing hum of crickets and other night creatures outside. When he'd lived in Atlanta, he'd never really noticed the evening sounds before, but here in Hog Mountain there was little else to hear. Maybe it was because he didn't have any assholes around who didn't know how to shut up, but Cam found it peaceful. He sat back on the sofa and dropped the remote beside him. Taking a sip of his tea, he relaxed and enjoyed the country. He hoped Dotty had made it home safely.

Cam considered going back out to the porch to sit with Tom, but when he looked out the window in the door, the cat was no longer there. With nothing else to do, he decided to turn in for the night. Before bed, Cam took his glass to the sink and then moved the clothes from the washer to the dryer. It all seemed so normal that at times he felt the very real need to pinch himself.

CHAPTER 2

THE NEXT morning, Cam rose with the sun. He stood beside the bed once it was made and stretched his arms over his head, working out the kinks and soreness that had appeared overnight. He'd gotten used to getting up early and making his bed while in prison and had kept the habit going by refusing to hang curtains in his second-floor bedroom.

Being locked up had not been a treat by any means, but since he'd spent a good portion of his adult life there, it was a bit hard to break the habits made while incarcerated. Some he wanted to keep, others he would be glad to move past.

Cam padded downstairs once his teeth were brushed and face was washed. He considered his options for the day as he pulled clean clothes from the dryer and dressed. He probably wouldn't get any customers at the garage for at least a few hours and there was nothing in the house but pie for breakfast. With those thoughts in mind, he settled on driving into town and getting something. He could bring whatever he got back to the garage and spend the time searching through some of the back cabinets in the bay areas of the old gas station.

Once dressed, Cam turned toward the front door and grabbed his work boots from where they had been placed just inside, then took them out onto the porch and sat on the front stoop to put them on. He found Tom sitting there, as if waiting for him, and reached over to scratch behind his ear.

"Man, I don't know who you banged last night, but it must have been epic. I've never heard anybody that loud during sex. If you do that chick again, I suggest a ball gag or something. People are trying to sleep, you know?"

Tom seemed unconcerned and gave a large yawn that showed sharp fangs to convey his sentiment.

"Look, I feed you, asshole. At least act embarrassed that I had to be privy to your man-whorin'," Cam scolded without heat and offered another scratch before getting up and heading down the steps toward the banged-up Silverado beside the house.

He'd paid cash for the old pickup when he moved out to Hog Mountain, leaving his previous car sitting in front of his mom's house. It wouldn't keep Harold from finding him, but it might make it a little harder and help add credence to the lie his mother was supposed to tell if Harold came looking.

The engine turned over easily on the twenty-year-old vehicle. Cam hadn't cared much about what it had looked like, but he needed it to run well. What had needed fixing on the truck had been his first priority. He turned out toward town, considering his options for breakfast food. The local Hardee's was the first restaurant he came to and seemed as good as any, so he pulled in.

Since there were already four cars in the drive-thru line, Cam opted to go inside the restaurant to order and found the counter clear of any customers. The employee working the register looked to be fresh out of high school, a nice-looking guy with wavy brown hair sticking out from under his uniform cap.

"Good morning, sir. What can I get for you?" Sean, according to his name tag, asked.

"Hey, man." Cam nodded while checking out the menu, even though he had been there enough times that he didn't really need to. "Give me two sausage biscuits, a large hash rounds, and the biggest coffee you have."

Sean paused before ringing the meal up and leaned over to Cam. "You know, if you order two of the sausage biscuit breakfast meals, it's cheaper. You get the two biscuits, two small hash rounds, and two small coffees. Two smalls in both the coffee and the rounds combine to more than one large in either, and it's less expensive."

Cam frowned through this long speech, then canted his head in curiosity. "Why are you telling me this? Aren't you supposed to be making money for the business?"

"Well, yes, sir, but I'm just offering what's on the menu. It's only neighborly to make sure you get the best deal."

For some reason, Cam didn't like the guy. Why would someone want him to spend less money in their business? It just seemed suspect. "All right, give me two of the meals, then," Cam conceded after a moment, digging in his pocket for his money. "And no scrimping on the cream and sugar for the coffee." He smacked a twenty on the counter and took his change and his food once it was ready.

Cam left the restaurant with a grumble at the unexpected customer service. Sean called out a sincere "Have a great day!" as the door was swinging closed behind him. What was wrong with these people? Not that it wasn't great to have an entire town full of suckers who thought being neighbors meant they should be neighborly. But did they have to be so nice about it?

When Cam parked his pickup in front of the pumps at his station, he was surprised to find a local police cruiser waiting by the closed garage door. A tall blond cop leaned leisurely against the front bumper, staring directly at him as he took his time getting out. The frown on the policeman's face was at odds with his stance, and although Cam didn't think he had much to worry about, he couldn't help the hammering in his heart, the constricting of his chest.

He'd dealt with cops and guards enough to know there wasn't a one of them that wasn't a sadistic asshole. They thrived on making people like Cam suffer. Cam had yet to deal with the local law and had hoped his lucky streak would continue. He had to admit the officer knew how to wear a uniform, though, with broad shoulders and slim waist accentuated nicely. Too bad he couldn't sit in the truck all day and ogle the man instead of having to deal with whatever he wanted. With a sigh, Cam gathered his wits and opened the truck's door, stepping out, then turning back to grab his breakfast. Well, shit. Wasn't this morning starting off with a bang.

Instead of walking toward the officer, he aimed for the front door of the gas station. He'd turned the area attached to the garage into a waiting area with mismatched office chairs and an old coffee table from the Goodwill. Cam had to jiggle the key in the lock a few times before the cylinder turned, and as he opened the door, he heard footsteps approaching.

"What can I do you for this morning, Officer?" Cam asked as casually as possible. "Your cruiser giving you trouble?"

Cam sat his breakfast on the counter that ran along the back wall, then stepped over to the window-unit AC and pushed the button to get it going. It wasn't that hot yet, but it wouldn't take long to get there. When he still hadn't gotten an answer from the cop, he turned to find him doing a thorough visual inspection of the area, then stepping over to the glass door leading to the garage and doing the same, canting his head to get as much of a view as possible without entering. Cam frowned.

"Is there a problem, Officer?" Now he had a reason for concern. What was the cop looking for? Cam had a sudden itch to run for it, although he had no idea what he was running from.

The officer turned, and Cam squinted to read the name Jackson Rhodes above the pocket of his uniform. When Officer Rhodes's hand came to rest on the butt of his gun, it was all Cam could do not to flinch. "Who is the second coffee for, Mr. Sanders?"

Cam glanced over to his breakfast and back to Rhodes, his nervousness kicking up a notch. "I... uh...."

"Is anyone else here, Mr. Sanders?" Officer Rhodes took a step forward.

Shit! Cam was going into a full-out panic. His gaze darted around the room, looking for some way out of the situation, but then just as suddenly, his subconscious gave him a metaphoric kick in the ass. *What the hell?* Was he going to let this asshole come into his place of business and fuck with him? He had nothing to hide. Well, okay, that wasn't exactly true, but he wasn't going to simply crumple over one question.

Cam slipped into his I-give-not-one-fuck persona and looked Officer Rhodes in the eye. "I don't see where that's even a little bit of your business, Officer. Want to tell me what this is about?"

Officer Rhodes took a few more steps closer, until he was crowding Cam against the counter in front of his food. "I've been hearing tales on your methods of auto repair. From changing the winter air out of tires to replacing dissolved halogen crystals in headlights or the deoxygenized water in a radiator. A quick background check shows you've served time in the past."

Fuck it! Cam thought. He took a step forward too, coming chest to chest and nose to nose with the officer. "Yeah, I done time, and I paid my debt. I'm here making a fresh start and I won't have you bad talking my business. I have a logbook of work done, signed off by the customers. It shows I did legitimate work, no matter what you hear."

"I'd like to see this log, if you will," Officer Rhodes responded. Damn, the man was fine. Light brown eyes sparking with challenge, blond hair cut short in a crew cut. *He looks so clean-cut, you'd think he would squeak when he walks.*

Instead of pulling out the log, Cam turned toward his breakfast. "Coffee, Officer? I do have two. Might as well share. It was like I knew I was going to have company this morning." He busied himself by pulling out the creamer and sugar packets from the bag and placing them where Rhodes could get to them, then pulling out the rest of his purchase and divvying up the food as if he'd meant to buy the cop breakfast.

When Cam glanced over, Rhodes was looking around again as if making sure no one else was in the shop. Then he shrugged and started doctoring his coffee to his satisfaction. Cam did the same and took a sip before opening one of the cabinet doors below the countertop. He pulled out a receipt book and pushed it over to the officer, then scooped up his breakfast and coffee and settled into one of the chairs to eat.

While Officer Rhodes leaned over the counter and flipped through the receipt book, Cam took the opportunity to admire the fine backside on display. The cop was built like a brick shithouse and would make a great addition to his spank bank. No doubt Rhodes had a gaggle of cheerleader-esque girls in town who giggled when he walked by. And that was too bad. Cam wouldn't mind giving the fine officer a strip search.

The sound of a throat clearing brought Cam back from his thoughts. He glanced up to find Officer Rhodes staring at him with a frown on his face. *Oops.*

"Everything in order, Officer?" Cam smirked. He had made sure the work he'd noted on the receipts was legit-sounding, even if his sales pitch to the customer might be questionable. "Check and service headlights" instead of "replace dissolved halogen crystals," "oil change" instead of "correct oil pH," etc.

Rhodes leaned against the counter and sipped his coffee before answering. "For the moment. Tell me, Mr. Sanders, what brings you to Hog Mountain? Your record notes you have a few known confederates. Did they make the move with you?" Rhodes glanced down at the counter and added, "Is this for me too?" He gestured to the biscuit and hash rounds.

"Of course they are, Officer. It's only right to be neighborly." Cam gave him a greasy smile, then took another bite of his own biscuit, chewed, and swallowed before answering his other question while picking at the wrapper.

"You should know that the worst thing an ex-con can do is fall back in with his old crowd. I'm out here changing my ways, and I hope those sons of bitches have no idea where to find me." That last was more truth than he probably should have told, but it was the God's honest, for more reasons than he planned to share with the local law enforcement.

"Mm-hm," Rhodes agreed sarcastically around a mouthful of biscuit. "I get the distinct feeling you haven't changed one stripe. And you are in my jurisdiction, scamming the residents of my town."

Cam narrowed his eyes. "So what's next, Mr. Law? You gonna get a warrant? Come in here and tear up the place I bought with hard-earned money? Maybe turn the community against me? Some late-night hooded visits? Odd accidents until I up and leave? You think I don't know your kind?" Cam was getting louder, thinking back to the way guards had taken care of anyone they didn't like. How police treated men like him. He stood up and stepped toward Rhodes as he continued, his anger making him tremble. "You think it's easy for an ex-con to find a job? Find a place to live? Find a way to go straight? Not when assholes like you take the law in your own hands, decide who is innocent and guilty without the need for any evidence. And who is going to stop you? Who is going to believe a two-time ex-con over the town golden-boy cop? HUH?"

Cam had only paused for breath, his passion blinding him until he heard the sound of a gun cocking in the silence. He froze, eyes widening as he looked up at Officer Rhodes in true abject fear.

"I'm going to need you to step back and take a seat, Mr. Sanders."

The gun wasn't pointed at him; Rhodes simply held it at his side, ready if needed. Cam realized how close he had gotten to the officer and quickly did as directed, taking a deep breath and blowing it out.

"Look," Officer Rhodes continued, "I don't know what kind of law enforcement you have dealt with, but they sound unsavory. In Hog Mountain, we don't take the law into our own hands, but we do protect our citizens. Right now, you are one of them, but don't think I won't be watching you. If you're cheating people, I *will* catch you, Mr. Sanders."

Before Cam or Rhodes could say more, there was a sharp rap at the service station door. Both of their heads quickly swiveled in that direction. At the sight of a customer, Cam stood and Rhodes quickly holstered his gun. Hesitantly, an older gentleman opened the door and peeked his head around the frame.

"Am I safe to come in?"

Cam nodded and Officer Rhodes smiled and said, "Hey, Jim. Come on in. I was just having breakfast and a chat with Mr. Sanders here."

Jim glanced between the two. "With your gun out?"

Cam dove into the conversation then, ready to be done with the officer and get his balance back. "Welcome, Jim. I'm Cam. What can I do you for this beautiful morning?" Cam glanced out the front door and added, "Ain't that fine ol' truck, is it?"

When Cam walked outside, both Jim and Rhodes followed him. "No, not the truck. I was just checkin' to see if you fixed bike tires. I got one in the back needs air and a patch."

"Sure thing," Cam said. "Let me take a look."

From the truck bed, Jim pulled a blue boy's bike, a colorful flag on a long flexible pole attached behind the seat, and handed it to Cam, who set it down and went to open the garage. While he was jiggling the lock on this door—it had become such a regular occurrence that he was sure he would automatically start jiggling the key in any lock he tried to turn—he heard footsteps and turned to see the officer and Jim close in on each other. *Great!* Rhodes was even going to ruin a cheap tire repair.

"Taking up biking, Jim?" Rhodes quipped.

"Nah," Jim said with a chuckle. "I been collecting old bikes I see at garage sales and secondhand shops, then taking 'em over to the Arcadia House. Ain't much I can do for those kids, but...."

"That's awful nice of you, Jim. I'll keep an eye out too. Maybe I can get the department to do something for them."

Cam kept an eye and an ear on the pair as he patched the tire and then filled it with air from his compressor. Their chatting never moved to a warning about Cam's business practices, and Cam wished the officer would just leave if all he wanted was to stand around and gossip.

"It's holding air now, and no signs of dry rot on either of the tires," Cam announced as he carried the bike back out to Jim.

"How much do I owe you?"

"It's on the house. Just remember me if you ever need some repairs done on that fine vehicle." That should show Mr. Lawman a thing or two. In fact, Cam turned to the officer and lifted a brow. Rhodes returned the expression, then scooped up the bike and placed it in the back of Jim's truck.

"Will do, young man. And thank you." Jim shook Cam's hand and patted Rhodes on the shoulder. "Thank you too, Jackson. See you at church on Sunday."

As Jim drove off, Cam turned to Rhodes. "What is Arcadia House?"

"It's a home for kids out on 365. Mostly deaf or blind." Rhodes steered the subject back to Cam. "Don't think that freebie changes anything, Mr. Sanders. I have my eye on you."

Still standing in front of the garage, Cam watched Officer Jackson Rhodes get into his cruiser and drive off. When he looked down, he found Tom rubbing against his leg and smirked. "Nice timing. I guess you're allergic to the cops too, then, huh?"

CHAPTER 3

BEFORE OFFICER Jackson Rhodes pulled out of the small parking lot in front of Camden Sanders's garage and took a left toward town, he drew in a deep breath, held it for a moment, then let it out in a whoosh of air. Jackson might have attempted calm while Jim Barnes had been there, but in fact, Mr. Sanders's outburst and his own reaction had really done a number on him. The way the man's ice blue eyes had burned with hatred in them had honestly frightened Jackson, but the things he'd yelled, what he'd expected to happen… from a man of the law, at that. It made Jackson wonder, that was for sure.

Jackson had made a trip out to Sanders's garage after several comments in the last week about the type of work done to their car. Not one of the people had complained, but in explaining the type of work performed, they had clued Jackson in on the nature of the man's game. He hadn't known what to expect upon his visit, but Camden Sanders had not been it.

Covered in tattoos and… smarmy. Well, up until that outburst. All Jackson was sure of was that Camden Sanders was bad news…. That, and he seemed to push all of Jackson's buttons.

And then Jackson had pulled his gun, although he hadn't aimed it at Sanders, thank God. That was the first time his weapon had come out of his holster in the line of duty. He'd completely lost control of the situation. Jackson thumped his open palm against the steering wheel in utter frustration.

As he accelerated, Jackson reached over for the handset to the radio and keyed the mic. "Jennifer, this is Jackson. You there? Over."

"Brian here. Jennifer took a break. She had to go to a conference at the school. Anything going on? Over."

"Nah. Heading down Sullivan toward town, gonna stop over at Ruby Mae's to make sure she's okay. I hear tell Junior went on a bender last night. Is Jennifer's son giving her trouble again? Over."

"It's a shame he's off the wagon. Tell Ruby we can keep some kids if she needs them gone for a bit, you hear? And yes, it's Jennifer's son again. The school called this morning and asked her to come in. Over."

"Will do, Brian. And I talked to Jim Barnes. He's collecting old bicycles for the Arcadia House. I told him maybe the force could do something to help. Wanna pass the word? Over." He wasn't sure what to say about Jennifer's son. The kid stayed in some kind of trouble all the time.

"Sure thing. I think we may have one that needs a new seat. I'll put something up in the break room. Over."

"Thanks, Brian. I'm pulling into Ruby's driveway. Over and out."

When Jackson stepped out of the police cruiser, a handful of half-dressed children were already running around the side of the house and heading right for him. He laughed at the dirty but happy faces on the children and knelt down in preparation of the collision sure to come.

Jackson took his time talking to each child, mussing the boys' hair, smoothing down the girls'. Ruby had a gaggle of kids. Six crowded him for attention, and he was pretty sure she had one or two more that weren't old enough to be running around yet. When he looked over the tallest of the kids' head, sure enough, there was Ruby Mae on the front porch. She had a baby in her arms and a toddler hanging on to the hem of her ragged dress.

She gave a weary smile. "Howdy, Jackson."

He nodded and rose, patting children as he waded through them to get to their momma. "Good mornin', Ruby Mae. How're you doin' today?"

She gave a shrug and bounced the baby at her shoulder. "He's sleepin' it off. I appreciate you comin', but it wasn't too bad this time. Wanna glass of tea?"

"Yes, ma'am. That would be right fine. It's the start of a hot one today." It was hard for Jackson to treat Ruby as a contemporary, hard to believe anyone his age could have so many kids. She'd dropped out of school in the tenth grade and married Junior when she'd found herself pregnant with the first one. Jackson went on to be the star quarterback his senior year. By then, Ruby Mae had two kids and a husband who got mean when he drank too much. In the next ten years, she had given birth to six more and watched her husband go sober and fall off the wagon more times than he could even remember.

Ruby led the way into the kitchen with the entire brood following. As he sat at the old table, much too small for a family of their size, he took the opportunity to look around. The place was clean, even if everything looked as worn-out as Ruby Mae.

When one of the eldest opened the pantry, she hissed, "Galen, close that door." But he wasn't quick enough to keep Jackson from seeing how bare the shelves were within.

"Thank you kindly." He smiled and took the mason jar of iced tea, then sipped it with appreciation.

"I'm out of lemon. Sorry," Ruby said as she sat across from him.

"This is fine how it is," Jackson assured and gazed past her to the six hungry stares watching him sip the tea. As much as he wanted to offer them a cup, he bit his lip and turned back to Ruby. "How old is the baby now?"

She patted the child on her shoulder as if just remembering it was there. "He'll be seven months soon...." She frowned, her eyes cutting up to the ceiling. "No, eight. He'll be eight months soon."

Jackson was no expert on babies, but this one didn't look near big enough for eight months yet. He tried to look clueless, although he did have friends and coworkers with kids. "So that means he should be eatin' table food soon, huh?"

"Naw. I mean, I ain't even given him baby food yet. I ain't got none to give him so I'm still breastfeedin', you know?"

Jackson nodded. What he wanted to do was go into the bedroom and beat the livin' hell out of Junior, tell the useless fuck to get his ass to work so his family could eat. Instead, he said, "Brian told me to tell you that some of the kids can come stay a few days if you need a break."

She smiled at that. "Tony and Galen been wantin' to go back fishin' with Brian. That would be nice."

"Can I go too?" came a chorus of voices.

"Luanne, you can go play with Alisa, but now, Mr. Brian don't need all of you over there."

There were moans from the other three, and Jackson felt right sorry for them. "I'll step outside and call Brian to let him know," Jackson said. "Get your things together." He pointed to the three who were going so they knew he was talking to them, then walked back out the screen door before dialing Brian.

"I got three of them coming with me when I leave," Jackson said as soon as Brian answered.

"I already told Linda. Can you just drop them to her on your way out?"

"No problem. They're hungry, Brian."

"Yeah, usually are. We'll take care of it."

"Thanks." Jackson hung up and took a moment to stare off in space before dialing another number.

"Gordon's Market," greeted a perky female voice.

"Paula, is Gordon around?" Matthew Gordon was the owner of the local grocery and one of the elders at the Hog Mountain First Baptist Church where Jackson and most of the locals attended. The majority of the people in town called him Gordon, although Jackson couldn't have said when that started.

"He's right here."

There was some muffled talking and then a male voice came on the line. "Gordon here."

"Gordon, it's Jackson. Listen, I'm out at Ruby Mae and Junior's this morning."

"I hear Junior's back to drinkin'."

"And from what I can see, back to not workin' too. None of these kids are eatin' and Ruby is trying to keep breastfeeding a baby with no food in her belly."

"How many of them are there now?"

"There's eight kids. The youngest needs baby food. Do I need to pay? You know I will if I need to."

"Nah, the church fund'll cover it. I'll set 'em up with a bunch. Has she got a workin' refrigerator?"

"She had the tea in it, but let me go see if the freezer is coolin'." Jackson headed back through the screen door and into the kitchen, opening the freezer and sticking his hand inside the empty space. "Yep, and lots of room inside too."

"What are you doin'?" Ruby asked, still at the table.

Jackson ignored her for the moment and continued talking to Gordon. "Want me to come get it?"

"Give me an hour to get it together."

"You got it." Jackson hung up and tucked the phone back in his pocket. Then he went to the cabinet and pulled down three plastic cups and a sippy for the toddler. Since the house had no air-conditioning, there was little reprieve from the heat of the summer. He pulled out the one ice tray that was still frozen and dropped a few cubes in each cup.

"Jackson Rhodes, what are you doin'?" Ruby asked again, louder this time.

Next Jackson pulled the pitcher of tea from the refrigerator and poured each cup full.

"That's for Junior's dinner! He don't like it when we don't have cold tea." Jackson heard the scrape of Ruby's chair as she got up, but it didn't stop him from giving each of the kids their cup.

Then he turned his full attention on Ruby Mae. "You more worried about that drunk in there than your own kids? Has he pushed you that far, Ruby, that you don't even care your kids are starvin'?"

She sobbed and fell back into her chair. The baby she held began a weak cry too, and Jackson felt a bit guilty for bringing more sorrow into the woman's life.

"I'll be back with food. Enough for the month. But, Ruby, if Junior touches any of these kids while he's drunk, I'll get the county to come get 'em. You hear?"

She nodded and continued to sob. When Galen, Tony, and Luanne came back down the stairs, Jackson waved to the other three, still in the kitchen but looking much better for having at least the little cup of tea in them—even the toddler seemed to have more life in his eyes—then took the older ones out to his car and buckled them in the backseat.

When Jackson lifted the handset for the radio, it gave a squawk, and in the rearview mirror, he saw three pair of wide eyes appear as they strained to look over the seat. There was a chuckle in his voice as he called in to say he was on the road. While most kids were excited to be anywhere around a police car, these three stared out the window as if the world away from their front door was something they rarely saw. Jackson knew the kids went to Brian's house once in a while, but wondered how often they went anywhere else. These were all old enough to be in school. Maybe they were just happy to be away from the heaviness that pervaded their home.

Once on the main strip of the town, he pulled into the McDonald's and queued the car in the line for the drive-thru. His three passengers didn't say a word but glanced back and forth as if wondering if they would get anything.

When it was Jackson's turn to order, he called out, "I need seven cheeseburger Happy Meals. Can you give me fries and apples with them? And um… Cokes."

"Girls' or boys' toys with those?"

Jackson huffed as he tried to remember, but then Luanne's quiet voice came from behind him. "Four boys and three girls."

Jackson repeated that into the speaker, then smiled back at Luanne. He was pretty sure she played second mama to her brothers and sisters much of the time. At the window, he paid and collected the large amount of food, then pulled into an open parking space long enough to give the three their meals.

He almost encouraged them to eat up, but it wasn't necessary. Before he pulled out of the parking spot, the boys had already inhaled their sandwich and were stuffing handfuls of fries in their mouth. While Luanne wasn't being quite so voracious, he could see her hands quaking with hunger as she ate.

After dropping the three oldest of the Watson clan off with Brian's wife, Jackson picked up enough groceries to fill both the trunk and backseat of his patrol vehicle. As he pulled back into the dirt driveway of Ruby Mae and Junior's house, three kids ran to meet the car. Jackson handed them their meals, and they dropped to the grass to eat and examine their toys.

Grabbing up the remaining meal and as many bags of groceries as he could carry, Jackson headed into the house, calling over his shoulder to the kids, "Bring in some bags when you finish eating."

He sat the toddler down with his meal, then sat Ruby down with a bowl of rice cereal to feed the baby before unpacking frozen food to put in the freezer.

The kitchen grew quiet as everyone focused on their task, except for the smack of the screen door as the children began to bring in the rest of the groceries, making little squeals when they noticed goodies in some of the bags.

When a gravelly voice bellowed from upstairs, his three helpers scattered. "Ruby. Where's Galen? Tell the boy to get his ass to the store and get me some cigarettes."

Jackson turned from his focus on the freezer to look at Ruby, who kept her head down and continued to feed the baby. He wiped the frown from his face and softly said, "Just don't answer him."

Ruby nodded but never looked up, and soon the sounds of heavy footsteps could be heard coming down the stairs.

"Goddammit, Ruby. Where the fuck are you? I need my tea and—"

Jackson knew, without turning from the refrigerator, when Junior discovered they had company. "Afternoon, Junior" was all he said as he spun to face the big man.

Junior took less time to recover from the surprise than Jackson had expected, not even seeming shocked at the bags of food scattered across the kitchen floor. "Mmm, bomb pops. My favorite," Junior said as he leaned over and grabbed the box off the counter, then ripped it open and took out two.

"Those are for the kids," Jackson said with a frown.

Junior shrugged as he stuck one in his mouth, then spoke around it. "In my house, makes 'em mine."

Instead of arguing the matter, Jackson countered with "So, Junior, you sending a minor to buy cigarettes now?"

Junior glared at him. "So, Jackson, you gonna cook me dinner too, or you just helping my lazy wife with the housework?"

Jackson took a step toward Junior, causing him to take a step back. "You are pushing your luck right this minute, Junior Watson, and I'd advise you to take my words to heart. If you touch one hair on these kids' heads while you're trying so hard to prove whatever it is you have to prove, I'll take them all out of this house so fast your head'll spin. And you touch Ruby, and I'll lock your ass up and make sure that the state files charges so Ruby can't drop 'em. Hear me, tough guy?"

Junior gave another shrug but was no longer looking Jackson in the eye. Jackson felt sure he had gotten through to the man, at least for the moment.

Turning his attention to Ruby, he nodded to the groceries still to be put up and said, "All the cold food is put up. The rest you can put up when you have time. There are two pans of frozen lasagna in the oven so they'll be ready by dinner. Salad in the fridge and french bread to go with it. You and the kids need anything, you know my cell number, right?"

Ruby nodded and said, "Thank you, Jackson. I don't know what we woulda done."

Junior looked like he was going to say something to that, but Jackson frowned at him and he shut his mouth. Jackson then stepped around him and walked out of the house, patting each of the three kids on the head as he passed them on the porch steps, heading to the car. He waved as he pulled out of the driveway and turned toward town. He hoped that Junior would be nicer to his family after being confronted, but knew that was probably not going to happen.

Jackson grabbed the handset again. "Jennifer, you there? Over."

"Still Brian. Jennifer took the rest of the day off. Is everything okay out at Junior's? Over."

"As well as can be, I guess. Is Daddy in? Over." Jackson felt for Jennifer and her husband. They seemed to be good people.

"Your daddy was here this mornin', but he had a meeting with the mayor this afternoon, Jackson. I can leave him a message if you want, but I don't know if he's comin' back or not. Over."

"No, I'll drop by the house tonight and see the chief. No problem. Any calls I need to respond to? Over." Jackson's father had been chief of police since Jackson was in middle school. He was getting close to retirement now, and most of the town expected Jackson to replace him when the time came.

"Hate to tell you, but Mrs. Montgomery out in that new subdivision called again. She reported someone down from her house for parking on the street without *special permission* and also mentioned that Mr. Jordon still hasn't trimmed his tree where it hangs over her fence. Over." There was amusement in Brian's voice as he reported this to Jackson. The entire force hated getting calls from the woman. She seemed to have little to do other than watch her neighbors and report even the smallest problem to the police. Jackson had told her several times that the rule about parking on the street was not a law and needed to be reported to their homeowners' association, not to the police, but it still didn't seem to sink in.

Jackson sighed. "Then that's where I'm headed now. If something more important comes up, let me know. Over and out."

CHAPTER 4

CAM CURSED to himself as he closed up the garage for the day. No other customers had come by, which was not completely unusual but did make him wonder if that cop had warned people off of doing business with him. He went out the front way instead of the back door, since his truck was parked there and he still had some errands to run.

Tom slinked off around the building before Cam cranked the engine and headed out. He turned toward the interstate since he'd seen a sign for a neighborhood yard sale starting Friday afternoon in one of the new upscale communities in the area. There was still some stuff he needed for his house, and Cam figured he'd find some bargains this way.

A staked sign with glittery letters let him know he was at the right place. At first, he tried to drive through and look at what each homeowner had to sell on their lawn, but he soon found that was hard to do with so many people wandering around as well as cars parked everywhere. So he found a place to park and started out on foot from yard to yard.

At one house, he bought an old toaster for a dollar, tucking it under his arm as he headed on. At another, he found a stack of sheets and blankets that he managed to talk the lady into taking five dollars for. He asked her to hold on to those until he could bring the truck around.

When he found a stylized iron bed complete with mattress and box springs sitting out on the driveway of a house way bigger than any one family could ever need, he stepped closer to take a look. A small tag hanging from the headboard had a price of one hundred dollars. Cam frowned and leaned in to make sure he had read correctly.

"Can I help you?" asked a thirty-ish lady dressed in a tennis dress, hair and makeup done as if she was going to the club and not selling odds and ends in her front yard. The rock on her finger was bigger than anything Cam had ever seen in his life, and he wondered how she didn't pull her knuckle out of joint just lugging that thing around.

"How much for this bed?" Cam asked, hoping he would get a different answer.

"The tag says one hundred dollars. It's from Arhaus in Buckhead, but we—"

Cam stopped her right there. "Lady. This is a yard sale. If I could afford Arhaus, do you think I would be looking at the furniture sitting on someone's lawn? How much will you take for it?"

"I… uh…." Cam was sure the woman had never had anyone talk that way to her. "Well…."

"What if I take all them lamps and the end tables?" Cam started walking and the lady followed. "I could use that ceiling fan, and how old is this paint?"

"Um… the paint is from last season. I bought more than I needed, but it was a special mix so I couldn't return it."

"I need them dishes and those glasses. Tell you what. I'll give you two hundred for the lot." Cam pulled out his wallet as if it were all settled.

"That's—those dishes alone are worth that much."

"Do they go in the dishwasher?"

"Well, they can, but—"

"Good to know. Here ya go." Cam shoved the money at her and she took it, then tried to hand it back. He didn't take it. "I'll go get my truck. Get your boy to start taking that bed apart for me."

He turned and wandered back toward his truck but down the other side of the street, looking for more bargains. The lady was left speechless, holding the two hundred in her well-manicured hand.

About three houses down, Cam noticed a police car in the driveway and a familiar police officer walking toward it with an uppity woman following him down the sidewalk talking to his back. By the set of Officer Rhodes's shoulders, Cam could tell the policeman was not enjoying the encounter. Cam wondered if this was the officer's house and he had a nagging trophy wife. That made him smile and hurry his step.

"Well, if it isn't Officer Rhodes, and this must be your beautiful wife," Cam exclaimed with a pinch of sarcasm as he neared the pair, taking the lady's hand in his and giving a put-on smile.

"What the…?" Rhodes said.

"Excuse me?" the woman said, pulling her hand away from Cam as if he were a leper. "I am *not* married to a policeman," she added with indignation.

That snotty, entitled answer really got his goat, so Cam decided he enjoyed messing with the lady more than Officer Rhodes and turned his full attention on her. "Well, he ain't gonna marry the cow if he's gettin' it for free, my momma always said. Now, can you help me with a purchase over here?"

The policeman stood there for a moment, then saw his exit strategy and turned on his heel and got in his car. The woman looked back and forth between the two and seemed to realize her time with the policeman was at an end as he fired up the engine and began inching out of her driveway. She followed Cam as he meandered through her yard, picking up items and setting them back down.

After a few minutes of following Cam, the woman finally asked, "What *exactly* did you need my help with?"

"Does this vacuum cleaner work?" Cam asked as he examined where the cord attached to the plug.

"It works, but the maid brings her own so I don't really need one anymore."

"I'll give you fifty cents for it," Cam said without looking up.

"I'm asking twenty dollars."

"All right, two dollars, but that's my final offer. I can see here that the cord needs to be replaced and that's a fire hazard." He showed her a small black mark just below the plug.

She squinted at it, then shook her head. "Fine, take it, but I won't accept less than five."

"Sold." Cam pulled out a five-dollar bill, tossed it to the lady, and scooped up the vacuum before heading on his way. When he'd made it back to his truck, he placed his treasures in the front seat, then drove carefully up the road to pick up his other purchases.

On the way home, he grabbed a cheese pizza and then stopped at a convenience store to fill up his tank. When he ran into the store to pay, he grabbed a cheap prepay cell phone off the rack next to the register along with a card good for a couple of hours' worth of calls and added those to his purchase. He ripped open the packaging around the phone when he was back in the car and dialed a number he knew by heart, from having to actually memorize the full telephone number while in prison.

"Hello?" a woman's voice answered.

"Hey, Mom. It's me." Cam slumped back in the seat. He definitely didn't have the closest relationship with his mother. He blamed her for a lot of things that went wrong in his childhood, but still, she was his mom and the only real family he had. She'd even sent money to his account while he was in prison. That was a lot more than anyone else had done for him.

"I was beginning to wonder if you were even going to let me know you were okay," she said. He could hear her take a puff off a cigarette and could just see her sitting on the couch in the living room, a big glass of iced tea on the coffee table and the entire room filled with the haze of smoke and the flicker of a television. It had been that way as long as he could remember. Even worse before his dad had died of cancer. The son of a bitch.

"I just wanted to lay low for a while, you know? Anyone coming around asking for me?"

"Yeah, a few. I told 'em what you said and they seemed to believe it."

He nodded even though she couldn't see it. "Good." It was a plausible lie. He had rarely gone to see his mom, so it was believable she didn't know where he was, and that since his car had been left in front of her house, she could only guess he'd gone back to jail.

"Where are you? Are you okay?" She didn't sound too concerned, more curious. She never had been overly concerned about him, even when his dad beat him as a kid. But she had at least let him go over to his grandmother's house to keep it from happening as often as it might've otherwise.

"I'm okay, Mom. But no need to know where I am. Just save this number under some weird name and call me if you need to."

"Okay. You take care now."

"You too, Mom." He hung up and tucked the phone in his pocket, then cranked the engine and headed toward home.

Later that night, Cam lay on some of the softest sheets he'd ever felt, in his new—well, new to him—bed, but getting there hadn't been easy. He'd come straight in the house and put the sheets in the washer, then unloaded the entire truck by himself, washed dishes and glasses, and placed end tables. Then he'd taken apart the bed already located upstairs and moved it along with the mattress and box springs down the stairs and into the largest bedroom on the first floor. After that was done, he'd moved the sheets to the dryer and started toting the heavy-as-living-hell iron bed, plus a king-size mattress and box springs, up into his bedroom. He'd had to run over to the garage twice for tools but finally got the job done. He'd then taken a shower, gone down and eaten his cold pizza, and finally got his clean sheets, which just happened to be the right size, to make his bed.

He'd definitely made up for not doing much during the day. It felt good to just lie on the bed and relax, although he couldn't much lie still, since he was having trouble getting over how soft the sheets were. Cam finally got up and took off his sleep shorts, underwear, and T-shirt, then dropped back down on the bed in nothing but his bare skin.

Cam sighed. He was in heaven. He could not only stretch his arms and legs out as far as they could go and still be completely on the bed, but he also could do it in such luxury, he couldn't quite believe it. He began moving his arms and legs like he was making a snow angel, enjoying the feel of the sheets against his skin.

"Okay, ultimate test," Cam announced to no one but himself, and turned over onto his stomach. He lay still a moment, then thrust his hips forward against the smooth sheets. "Oh God, that's nice." He laughed. "But no, I ain't messin' up these fine sheets."

Cam rolled back over and got comfortable against his pillows, then took himself in hand and gently stroked from base to tip of his hard cock. "Yeah, that's nice." Closing his eyes, he searched for an acceptable image in his mental spank bank, only to jerk his eyes back open when his brain regurgitated a familiar image: that of Officer Jackson Rhodes, complete with khaki and dark green small-town cop uniform.

"Shit. What am I gonna do? Jack off to him beatin' me with his baton or something?" But Camden's cock had not gone down a bit, even at his disgust at himself. "Okay, I admit, he's a fine man, but no, no, no." Despite his reproof, his hand again started stroking his straining cock.

With a groan, he closed his eyes again, imagining Rhodes slowly taking off his uniform. Revealed beneath his shirt were wide shoulders and narrow waist, bulging pectorals, defined six-pack, a smattering of golden hair—then the utility belt came off and his pants unbuttoned.

Cam gasped for air, giving a gentle twist of his wrist on each upstroke. "Oh shit. He wears tighty-whities." It took no more than that and Cam's hand was speeding over the velvet skin of his cock, no longer needing instruction from his brain. A good thing too, since the thought of sexy Officer Rhodes in nothing but his BVDs and SWAT boots had short-circuited any higher intelligence he'd had.

Cam gulped and grunted, his hips arching up as he cupped his hand around the head of his cock, deftly catching his release before he made a mess of his clean body and nice soft bed. At least he'd had that much of a mind left. He lay there a moment or two, gasping for breath and trying to make sense of what had just happened.

After he'd cleaned up, he found himself feeling especially dirty for using the officer to get off to. There was a strange sense of being betrayed by his own body, but mostly he just felt really good, so he went with it, pulling up the covers, closing his eyes, and then drifting off.

CHAPTER 5

CAM WAS in a good mood as he walked through the sliding doors of Gordon's Market. It was still pretty early, so the day hadn't turned hot and the store was fairly empty. Just the way he liked it. After testing a few buggies, he settled on one that didn't have a crazy wheel but still pulled to the left a bit. Cam was pretty sure they made the things that way just to annoy people like him.

He'd done the one thing he'd always heard not to do. He had come to the grocery store while hungry, and he was struck in that moment with what a bad decision he'd made. His stomach growled loudly. Making a detour from the usual path shoppers were encouraged to take, he headed straight for the cereal aisle, never even slowing as he grabbed a box of Cap'n Crunch and kept walking. He was munching from the open box as he went back to the starting spot in the store, not sure he knew how to shop if he didn't follow the right path.

Several employees frowned as they passed, seeing him also opening a pint of milk to wash down his cereal, and finally a young lady in the store's uniform approached. Her name tag identified her as Gladys, a rather old-timey name for someone her age.

"Excuse me, sir. You'll need to pay for those items."

"Don't I have to pay for all of it, Gladys?" Cam asked sarcastically, but Gladys didn't seem to catch that.

"Well, yes, but...." Her words stumbled to a stop.

"Now that we have that settled, I need you to show me where I can get something cheap for a cat I know who has fleas or whatever bugs live on a cat."

She seemed to struggle with the need to continue the prior conversation but finally nodded and led him off through the store to the aisle with all the pet supplies. She stopped about halfway down and searched through her options, then pulled a small box down with a picture of a cat on the front, wearing a white collar around its neck.

"A flea collar is what you want." She pushed the box at Cam, who took it and considered.

"I don't think he'd like this," Cam said after a moment, shoving the box back into her hand.

"What? Lots of pets wear them. After a while, they forget they're on."

"But he's not really a pet. See, he's more just a friend and um...." Cam pulled at the collar of his T-shirt, just imagining wearing the thing. "H-he doesn't like feeling fenced in, you know?"

Gladys narrowed her eyes, surely wondering if Cam was all there in the head. "Okay, well.... Your other options are more expensive. Like this one...." She pulled down a package with a small dropper bottle inside and showed Cam how to apply it and explained how often.

"That. He'll like that better." Cam glanced up and down the aisle for a moment, then back to Gladys. "And what kind of food would he like? I mean, if he comes to visit."

"There's wet food and dry food." She walked farther down and pointed out the different brands, told him what she knew about them. "You know, if you found some stray, you need to get him wormed too, right?"

"Worms?" Cam exclaimed more loudly than he had intended.

"Yeah, you should take him to the vet." She paused, then added, "Even if he's just a friend, you know? He'll appreciate it and they can give him a flea treatment there. Hog Mountain Animal Clinic is in the same parking lot as this store and Dr. Moore is good. He's my dog's vet."

"How the hell am I gonna get him there? I'm pretty sure Tom isn't going to be up for a car ride. We aren't on those kinda terms yet."

Gladys took back the flea treatment and pulled down a small animal carrier.

Cam shied away from it as if it were the plague. "Oh no, not using that thing."

Now she looked at him as if he was completely crazy. "It's just for the ride, and it's to keep him safe. I always give my dog treats for having to go in the carrier." She pulled down a few bags of cat treats and handed those to Cam too.

By the time Cam was done shopping, his cart was overflowing, both with food for himself and purchases for his non-pet. He stood in line, still munching from his box of cereal, behind an older couple with their own full cart.

After a moment or two of waiting, the woman patted her husband on the arm and pointed toward a bench at the front of the store. He hobbled over and slumped down, looking worn-out from the shopping trip.

Once she made sure he was safely seated, the woman turned to Cam with a smile. "He has COPD," she confided, as if Cam had wanted to know.

He nodded and pushed another handful of cereal in his mouth. He didn't feel like getting into a conversation with the woman, but she didn't seem to care one way or the other.

"He worked hard all his life," she continued as she unloaded her buggy onto the conveyor belt, "and now that he's retired, he's just too sick to do all the things we dreamed of doing. Even the little things like shopping for groceries."

Cam nodded absently and chewed. He hoped the woman got the message that he wasn't in the mood to chat, but she still seemed oblivious.

"Are you new in town? I don't think we've met. I'm Ida Evans, and that is Charles. We've lived here all our lives."

He considered not answering, but then a miraculous thing happened. Mrs. Ida Evans became the most interesting person in the world when she pulled her wallet from her purse and opened it wide, displaying an impressive stack of cash as she counted out the amount owed to the cashier.

Cam spoke up after quickly swallowing his mouthful of Cap'n Crunch. "Camden Sanders, and I'm new to town, ma'am. Bought the garage and fillin' station over on Sullivan a few weeks back. Started working on cars, living in the old house out behind it." He wiped his hand on his pant leg, then offered it to her. "Do you need help out to the car? I hate to see you and Mr. Evans having to do all that by yourself."

She reached back, shook his hand, and then patted Cam's arm. "You are a sweet boy. That would be right nice of you."

Cam smiled and turned to the clerk. "Can you ring these things up while I take their bags out?"

The clerk nodded, but Cam's attention was on Mrs. Evans as she haphazardly placed her wallet in her purse, where it wobbled as if it would fall out at any moment. Cam helped Mr. Evans off the bench and together they walked out to a big boat of a car parked in the handicapped space in front of the store. He had to wonder how either of the old couple could see over the steering wheel, but at least they lived in a small town where everyone knew to get out of their way.

After Cam planted Mr. Evans in the passenger seat and popped the trunk, he loaded the groceries as Mrs. Evans watched with a smile. When he was done, she shook his hand and tucked a dollar bill into his fist. "Bless you for helping."

Cam's return smile was syrupy sweet, and he took her arm, leading her around to the driver's side door. As she leaned to get in the huge land yacht, her wallet finally made the plunge from her purse and Cam placed his size-ten foot over it as he closed the door and watched her drive away, waving to the pair and chuckling to himself at the dollar in his hand.

Obviously, from the wads of cash in the woman's wallet, the pair was loaded. She probably wouldn't miss it at all, Cam told himself as he scooped up the wallet and shoved it into the back of his pants before strolling back into the store.

WHEN CAM pulled up in front of the old farmhouse, he caught sight of Tom lazing in the shade of the porch. He immediately felt guilty about the pet carrier in the back of the truck and decided to leave it for last when unloading.

He piled his arms full of grocery bags before heading up the stairs to the front door, then curled around his load to keep it steady as he fought with the key and lock. Tom's gaze followed him each time he made a trip out to the truck and back into the house, but the big orange cat never moved from his spot, even when Cam paused to grab his empty water bowl, then brought it back filled on the next trip.

Cam unloaded the groceries once he had them all in the kitchen, tripping over the plastic bags as he tried to find places for all of it. It wasn't that the cabinets were full but more that he just wasn't sure what was a reasonable spot for any of it to go. He'd bought a tiny frying pan he'd seen in one of the aisles, and decided to hang it on a nail that was already sticking out above the stove.

Mostly he'd bought sandwich fixings and ready-made items, but he could make a mean grilled cheese or fried egg sandwich. Maybe someday he could expand his culinary repertoire.

He dug into the last bag and came up with the prized possession he'd gained from this trip. A supersized bottle of Hershey's chocolate syrup. Cam's mouth watered just looking at it. He turned to the counter and pulled down a glass from the cabinet, then the milk from the fridge.

Oh yeah! That's the stuff! he thought as he stirred the mixture, then licked the spoon.

He washed out the glass once he'd downed the entire thing, then pulled the wallet from out of the back of his pants and flipped open the snap. He counted the wad of cash with the deftness of a bank teller, fifteen hundred dollars. Why would anyone carry that much cash around with them? Old and nutty, he guessed.

He flipped through the various pockets in the wallet and found nothing else he wanted, but as he went to toss it on the counter, he noticed the fabric covering was a pattern of blue flowers, roses. *Shit.*

He jerked open the back door and threw the wallet as far as he could, as if it were covered in some plague germs or something, then took the cash to the back bedroom to stash away.

When that was taken care of, he took a deep breath, readying himself for the task of loading up Tom for a trip to the vet's office. Cam scooped up a package of treats and headed out the door, locking it behind him.

"Listen," he said to the cat. "I gotta do this and you aren't going to like it." He jumped down the stairs and grabbed the carrier, turning with it in his hand. Tom still watched him with no overt concern. "But nobody wants worms, right?"

Cam sat the carrier down a few feet from Tom, then ripped open the package of snacks and tossed a few inside. The cat seemed more interested and sniffed the air before climbing to his feet and wandering toward the open cage door. Even after Cam had closed the door behind him, Tom simply lay down and ate the snacks scattered around him.

"Huh. I really saw this going much differently," Cam confided. "Okay, let's go."

CHAPTER 6

BACK IN the same parking lot as Gordon's Market, Cam pulled up in front of Hog Mountain Animal Clinic at the other end of the strip mall. On the glass door, written in white letters under the stylized name of the business, was *Dr. Grant Moore DVM.*

Camden shut down the engine but made no move to exit the truck. He glanced over at Tom, who was watching him from his spot on the other side of the barred door of the carrier. "You ready for this? I'm not sure what they do for worms, but I'm pretty sure I never want anyone to do it to me." He paused and considered. "I mean, I guess I would if I had worms, but... yeah. Just rather not, you know?"

Tom didn't answer so Cam stuck a finger through the bars to scratch Tom's head, and after a few more minutes of sitting in a quickly warming truck cab, he opened the door and decided to go inside.

The bell jingled as he opened the door, and the receptionist looked up from her spot behind a high counter. "Hi. Can I help you?"

"Yeah. Well, not me. I mean...." Cam placed the carrier on the counter. "This is Tom and he has bugs and maybe some worms. You know what to do for that?"

She peeked into the carrier and smiled. "Hi, Tom. I'm Regina, and we'll get you all fixed up." She handed some forms to Cam along with a pen and a clipboard, then directed him to the waiting-room chairs while she popped into the back, he assumed to tell the doctor they had a patient.

While filling out the form, he could hear whispering coming from the back, and once or twice when he looked up, Regina was peeking around the doorframe but pulled back as soon as she saw him looking. Cam frowned and wondered if he'd done something wrong and they had called for the vet police to come get him. Maybe he would be charged for illegal capture of an endangered local species or something.

About the time he finished filling in all the information they needed on the form, Regina came back and called out, "Tom?"

Cam glanced over at the cat in the cage, then to Regina in confusion. "Want me to come back with him?"

"Of course," she said on a laugh.

"Good, 'cause I'm not sure how he'd do on his own." Cam followed as she waved him down a hall and into a small exam room, where she closed the door and left them alone again. Cam sat in the chair beside a table, on which he'd set the carrier, and tapped his fingers on his thighs as he waited, finally standing and pacing back and forth in the almost claustrophobically small space.

After a few minutes, an extremely attractive man in a white coat entered the room with Regina following behind. Cam knew immediately that Dr. Moore was gay. There was no doubt in his mind. It wasn't that the man was obvious in his mannerisms, but the tell came from the way the doctor's gaze swept over Cam from head to toe, pausing dramatically at the crotch.

"Camden Sanders?" the doctor asked, then turned to the carrier on the table. "And this must be Mister Tom."

When Dr. Moore met his eyes, Cam lifted a brow to let the doctor know he was reading him loud and clear. "You can call me Cam and him Tom."

"Regina, I think we've got it in here. You can man the front desk for me." Dr. Moore never glanced away from Cam as he spoke.

Once Regina had left the room and closed the door, Dr. Moore busied himself getting Tom out of the cage and placing him on the table. "I'm Grant," he introduced, "and what is going on with Tom here?"

Cam stepped up next to the doctor and looked down at Tom where Grant held him down. "I think he has fleas and maybe worms." Cam noticed what looked like a wedding ring on the doctor's finger and wondered if the little town of Hog Mountain was up to handling a gay married couple in their midst.

Grant nodded and began searching through the cat's fur, looking in his mouth, and generally feeling him up. "How long have you had Tom as a pet?"

"Well, he ain't my pet. He umm… hangs around and toms it up out behind my place. I leave water out for him and sometimes food."

"If you feed him, he's yours," Grant said with a chuckle, then stopped short, froze, and cut his gaze over to Cam.

"What?"

"Who told you Tom was a boy?" Grant started to smile and it got bigger and bigger.

"What? Well, of course he is. Look at him." Cam sputtered. "He's big… and manly."

"He's also pregnant," the vet announced with a smirk.

Cam dropped into the chair and stared off into space. "Fuck." For a moment, he felt responsible. Not like he'd got the cat pregnant, for God's sake, but maybe if he'd known she was a girl, he could have kept her safe or something. He was a fucking idiot.

Grant patted him on the shoulder in compassion. "Okay, we are going to run some tests. Make sure she doesn't have feline leukemia and worms, generally make sure she's healthy. Then we'll give her a treatment for fleas. You sit here and come up with a girl's name for your cat." Grant laughed as he turned away and started pulling open cabinet doors.

"My cat," Cam mumbled to himself. "Leukemia sounds serious."

"It's like AIDS for cats, so yeah, pretty serious. And highly contagious too, to other cats, that is. So if she doesn't have it, you should keep her indoors to make sure she's safe."

Cam huffed but didn't answer. This visit to the vet was getting more involved by the minute.

While his back was to Cam, Grant said, "I like your tattoos. How far do they go?"

That got Cam's attention, and he grinned slyly. "How far you willing to look for 'em?"

Grant turned and walked back to the table, where the cat still lay, appearing unconcerned with the entire process. "I've always been known to give a quite thorough exam." He gave a mischievous glance to Cam, then added, "Come help me hold her while I draw blood."

Cam stood and positioned himself beside the doctor, gently taking hold of the animal and again spotting the wedding band on Dr. Moore's hand. He nodded toward it. "What's with the ring, doc?"

"Well, it's what you wear when you're married… and have two kids." When Cam raised a brow, he added, "Mrs. Moore is quite content and it keeps the neighbors from asking questions." Cam didn't reply, not sure what to say to that. Thankfully, Grant changed the subject. "You bought the old place over on Sullivan?"

Cam nodded and tightened his grip slightly as the cat began struggling a bit. "I still have a ton of work to do. The yardwork alone could take me a month or more."

"You should hire a couple of the local kids to help. It's cheap labor and most of them are excited to have something to do. Now Tommasina isn't going to like me much, but I have to get a fecal sample too."

Cam cringed at the thought, but then was caught by something else the doctor had said. "Tommasina, huh?"

"Yeah, you didn't tell me what you decided to call her, so I went with that." Grant grinned.

"I like it," Cam announced with a nod of finality. "Tommasina it is."

While waiting on the results of the tests, Grant stayed in the room and chatted with Cam. Cam found himself learning more about the residents of Hog Mountain than he ever wanted to know.

"I guess you know everyone in the town, having grown up here and all," Cam commented, not sure what else to say at that point.

"Oh yeah, all the dirt. I've either fucked 'em or someone close who knew their secrets." Grant waggled his brows.

"Wait." That got Cam's attention. "You fucked someone in this town?"

"Well, I fuck both male and female, but if you're asking if there are other gays around Hog Mountain, the answer is yes."

"You people have perfected the art of suburban camouflage for sure. I would never have guessed anyone around here was gay." Cam wasn't convinced he liked this kind of gossip, not for moral reasons so much, but because it was a double-edged sword and he had secrets he didn't want spread all over.

Grant smirked. "How about our own Jackson Rhodes?"

Cam coughed and slapped his chest. "No way!"

"Way. But he's so far in the closet, he knows what people in China are getting for Christmas. We used to hook up from time to time, until I got married and he decided fucking a married man was against his morals." Grant rolled his eyes.

Cam grew quiet, giving thought to that revelation. Officer Rhodes was gay....

After the results came back from all the tests, Grant scooped up Tommasina and placed her back in the carrier, then turned to Cam and said, "She seems pretty healthy. All you'll need is a litter box and she should make a fine house pet."

"*Litter* box?" Cam was taken aback.

Grant chuckled. "Where did you think she was going to go to the bathroom?"

Okay, yeah, that makes sense, Cam decided, but this was turning out to be a lot of trouble.

"And a bag of litter. You can get both of those over at Gordon's."

As Cam took the carrier from Grant, Grant leaned in and spoke low. "So, how 'bout I come around on Tuesday and check on Tommasina, her being pregnant and all."

Cam's brows rose and he grinned. "That would be right neighborly, doc. How about around seven in the evening?"

Grant returned a bright smile. "I look forward to it."

ANOTHER VISIT to Gordon's Market later, and Cam was on the way home again. Too lazy to even make a sandwich at home, he had grabbed a sub sandwich at the deli counter and was already eating it as he drove.

The first fat drops of rain hit the windshield as he was pulling into the driveway, and he hurried to get the carrier and his other purchases in the house before the bottom dropped out. Then with the soothing sound of a downpour on the tin roof of the porch, Cam set up the litter box in the downstairs bathroom, a food and water bowl in the kitchen, then let Tommasina out of her cage. He was a bit worried that he should be doing something special for the pregnant cat but couldn't think of anything in particular to be done.

It took no time before the cat went off exploring her new home and Cam plopped down on the couch with the rest of his sub and a big glass of iced tea to consider the fact that Officer Rhodes was gay.

CHAPTER 7

JACKSON PULLED the last table into place in the basement room of the Hog Mountain First Baptist Church, where in less than an hour, the first of the congregation would begin gathering to share breakfast before Sunday morning services.

"What else you need me to do, Momma?" He and his parents had always been the first in the doors and the last to leave each week, unlocking the building, getting coffee started, and making sure hymnals were in place and the attendance card racks were filled. Even as an adult living on his own, he still made sure to meet his parents and help them with the tasks.

Mrs. Pamela Rhodes came out of the kitchen area, which was attached to the banquet hall. She surveyed the setup, her dress covered with a white apron, and then gave her son a sweet smile. "You could reconsider taking Jenny Miller to the Optimist Club's Sadie Hawkins dance. Daddy said he'd give you the time off."

"Why are you so all-fired convinced of a sudden I need to go out with Jenny?" Jackson had been lucky in the past years that his momma hadn't pushed him to date. That seemed to have changed for some reason. Jenny Miller had popped the question a week before about the dance, but he had told her he didn't think he'd be able to make it. Obviously her invitation and the answer he'd given had already made the rounds back to his mother.

"Jackson Lee Rhodes, when was the last time you took a girl out? You need a little pleasure in your life. All you do is work." It looked like his momma was going to hold onto this like a dog to its bone. Jackson knew his mom just worried about him being alone, but he really didn't need her to start trying to fix him up with dates.

"Pamela, leave the boy be. He's old enough to decide who he wants to take out and when," his dad cut in from where he stood by the door to the large room. As if to be sure the conversation was over, he turned to Jackson and asked, "Did you hear Ida Evans lost her wallet yesterday? And she'd just cashed her social security check and Charles's too."

Jackson frowned. "Any ideas where she might have lost it?" Charles and Ida had never liked banks. They had a savings account at the local bank, but preferred to keep cash and use money orders for their regular expenses. While most everyone in town knew that, he couldn't imagine anyone stealing from them.

"She paid for groceries at Gordon's and had it then. It was gone from her purse when she got home. Gordon had the bag boys search the lot and the store. I went through her car myself and helped her look around the house." He shook his head.

"She can't remember anything different, somewhere else she might have stopped?" Jackson felt heartsick over the loss. The couple didn't have a lot to live on at the best of times.

"No. They had help loading the groceries and she tipped a dollar. That's the last she remembers of seeing the wallet."

"Was Barry bagging or Sean?" Jackson couldn't help pushing the subject. He wanted desperately to find the one clue that could turn this all around for the two.

"It wasn't them. Ida said Mr. Sanders helped Charles out to the car and then loaded up her groceries. The mechanic who bought the old service station south of town. Didn't you drop by there recently?"

Jackson felt his blood pressure go up at just the mention of the name. "Camden Sanders. Yeah, I met him…. Might need to meet him again right soon." Jackson scowled.

THE DAY had dawned nice and cool thanks to the previous night's rain, and Cam decided to go ahead with his plan to work on the yard even though the ground was wet. He placed a note on the door to the garage, letting anyone that stopped by know he was out back if needed, then got busy transporting old tires, engine parts, and empty oil drums from behind the shop to the street.

When he'd first headed outside for the day, he'd tried to convince Tommasina she should stay inside, but the cat was having none of it and now lounged on the porch, watching him slave away from her spot in the shade. He'd brought her food and water out in case she got a hankering, but so far she seemed far more interested in lying under one of the rocking chairs and flipping her tail back and forth. He wondered if that meant something in cat language.

Cam would never have expected before moving to Hog Mountain that his daily life would come down to something so mundane as an activity like this one. In fact, this was his first experience in living alone. He'd lived at home until his first trip to the Fulton County Jail on charges of shoplifting. That's where he'd met Harold, and at the time, he'd felt the meeting was advantageous, since his mother had tossed him out on his ear when she learned of his arrest. Harold had taken him in, letting him sleep on the couch of an apartment already housing four other people. Harold had seemed so worldly to Cam, and it hadn't taken long before he'd had a pretty mean crush on the guy.

One night, a few months after he'd taken up living in Harold's living room, Cam had wakened to find Harold leaning over him and pulling back the ratty blanket that covered him. Harold wasn't what anyone would call classically good-looking. He had one milky eye, caused from an accident when he was a kid, which definitely gave him the creepy factor. But somehow, when added to the sharp lines of his face, gloriously long dark hair, and lips that truthfully belonged on a girl, he made it work for him.

Cam had looked up into Harold's face and was mesmerized, felt fortunate to have the seductively charming man's full attention. Harold was completely nude and unashamed of the fact that there were others in the small apartment who might see him. All the tattoos on his firm chest looked more like the drawings of a psychopathic preschooler, or maybe the machinations of a shattered mind. They added to his creepiness, but still something drew people to Harold.

And Cam wanted him. Had wanted him since Harold had bailed him out of jail and brought him home. Their first meeting of lips was not what Cam expected, however; "brutal" was a good description. Cam could feel the hardness of Harold's teeth through the kiss, threatening to bruise or even break the tender skin. Cam grunted and tried to pull away.

As Cam was crushed under Harold's weight, powerful hands squeezing and holding him down, Harold chewed at Cam's bottom lip, ripping an involuntary cry from him.

"Not so rough." Cam squirmed and attempted to express to Harold what he needed, but Harold only boxed his ear and bit harder. Then Cam's legs were twisted to the side and held so that his hole was exposed and just that quick, Harold's cock was there. Cam panicked at the insanity sparking in Harold's eyes and fought harder to get out from under his heavy weight.

"No," Cam said firmly. This wasn't going anything like he had envisioned. It was as if Harold was raping him, but how could that be? Cam wanted this, didn't he? But they needed to use condoms! He had no idea if Harold was safe or had any diseases.

"No!" He yelled this time, hoping it would halt this whole crazy mess, but Harold grabbed his balls and twisted. Then he grinned at Cam, the expression soaked through with evil, and shoved his hips forward.

At first, Cam didn't think Harold would get inside. Cam was fairly new to anal sex, and he'd had no preparation at all, no lubricant either. But Harold wasn't giving up. He pushed harder, even though that kind of pressure on his cock had to hurt him as much as it was hurting Cam.

Cam screamed as he was filled to bursting. The pain was like nothing he had ever felt, and tears streamed down his cheeks.

"Scream for me, baby," Harold murmured as he immediately started pumping. "Tell everyone how good I'm fucking you." Between terror-filled screams, Cam realized no one in the apartment was coming to see what the noise was about. This must be a common occurrence and they were simply glad it wasn't them this time.

The next morning, Cam had barely been able to walk, yet Harold had joked and laughed with him like they were best friends or lovers. Something about the attention had Cam making excuses for Harold's behavior and kept him from leaving the tiny apartment, but Cam never forgot the evilness he'd seen that night. And he'd made a trip to the free clinic to be sure he hadn't caught anything.

Other than his stints in prison, he'd lived with Harold and a changing mix of others until his rushed exodus from Atlanta, but early on, he'd decided to stay far away from Harold's "love life." Harold had no preference for men versus women. His only mandatory ingredient was pain, and Cam made sure Harold knew he would be gone if there was ever any more of that crap.

Cam had hopped between jobs, always planning the next scheme. Harold was the ringleader, and slowly but surely became more and more sadistic and controlling, expecting others to follow his lead in all matters, never questioning. He'd been charismatic and Cam had finally come to realize Harold was much like a cult leader in the way he sucked people in and made them believe his bullshit.

For the last four years, it had been him and Harold and two women, Detra and Cally. Detra and Cally, however, never seemed to learn, and there had been some kind of drama going on in the apartment at all times. Most of it because of Harold's need to stir the shit and his increasingly violent nature.

Cam missed Detra the most. He wondered if it was safe enough for him to call her, just to make sure she was okay. When he'd left, he'd begged her to come with him, but she was sure she and Harold still had some chance.

Cam sighed and wiped his forehead. Thinking about the past wasn't going to change anything and it was getting hot out. Dragging a recyclables bucket around the yard was becoming harder since the thing was slowly being filled with old beer bottles. Turning in a full circle, he realized how little of the yard he had actually cleaned. *Shit!* He would be eighty before he got this place in any sort of order.

THE LAST notes of "Abide With Me" still ringing in the cavernous auditorium of Hog Mountain First Baptist Church, the congregation began gathering their things and heading up the aisle toward the large double doors in the back. Two of the ushers propped the doors open and the after-service greeting and mingling began. Pastor Jimmy Brown was already waiting in the foyer for at least an hour of palm-pressing and fellowship, the elders and deacons scattered around as well.

Jackson had found himself having trouble paying attention to the sermon that morning, his thoughts on Ida Evans's wallet and Camden Sanders. He felt a bit guilty for automatically assuming the ex-con had taken the money, but then again, Mr. Sanders did seem a bit too slick. And if he had taken that wallet, Jackson would have to work hard to hold back his anger. But there was no proof that Sanders had done anything more than help an old couple to their car. But... Camden Sanders was all-fire infuriating, and Jackson had no business having the handsome man on his mind in the middle of a church service, especially with some of the thoughts that had come up. And didn't that just make him even angrier at the man.

As he weaved through the crowds, waiting to say a few words to the preacher, he felt a hand land on his shoulder and turned to find Grant Moore giving him a smarmy smile full of bleached white teeth.

"Mornin', Jackson," Grant said without removing his hand from where it rubbed between Jackson's shoulder blades.

"Grant," Jackson greeted with a nod, then turned to the beautiful woman at Grant's side. "Suzanne, nice to see you."

Suzanne smiled, then turned to corral two nicely dressed children who were now climbing on hands and knees under the pews.

Once Suzanne was distracted, Grant leaned in closer to Jackson's ear and spoke softly. "How's the hunt going?" It never failed that Grant wanted to make some mention of their common sexuality whenever he could find even the smallest chance.

Jackson ground his teeth, then shrugged his shoulder to remove the offending hand. "Grant, I think your wife needs some help," he said and tried his best to leave the annoying man behind. Jackson had once felt strongly enough for Grant to consider coming out to the entire town, only to be blindsided when Grant announced his engagement to Suzanne. Grant had been shocked that Jackson had a problem with it, since in his opinion, it wasn't meant to affect their relationship at all.

That had been years ago, and Grant seemed oblivious to the emotional upheaval he'd left in his wake. Since then, Jackson had moved on, focusing on his career instead of a love life. He'd also come to learn that Grant Moore cared for no one other than himself.

Grant wasn't allowing the escape, grabbing hold of Jackson's bicep and pulling it against his chest. "I met someone yesterday. Going out to his house Tuesday night," he whispered.

Jackson scowled. "Why do you feel the need to tell me your business?"

Grant appeared unperturbed by the question. "You know him too. And he lives here in town."

Okay, that piqued Jackson's curiosity, and it must have shown because Grant continued without any comment from him.

Grant appeared smug as he dropped his voice even lower to say, "Camden Sanders."

Jackson could have spit nails. He was beyond sick of hearing that man's name. "Get away from me, Grant," Jackson growled. Jerking his arm away, he pushed through the crowd and away from Grant as quickly as possible, an uncontrollable need boiling in his gut to bust Camden Sanders in the nose.

CAMDEN WAS slumped on the front steps sipping from a large glass of iced tea when a fairly new blue Mustang pulled into his driveway. He was pretty sure whoever was driving it would take that kind of vehicle to the dealer for any repairs, not his shop, so this must be a social visit. Just his luck.

The sight of Jackson Rhodes climbing out from behind the wheel, tailored suit emphasizing his wide shoulders, thick chest and thighs, and slim waist, was enough to make Cam's throat go dry. *Fuck! The man cleans up nice!*

Attempting to hide the fact that he felt like a bitch in heat when he looked at the officer, Cam turned his gaze out to his front yard and spoke loudly to Jackson as he came across the lawn toward him. "Know any kids around here that would like a job helping me clean up this yard?"

When Cam looked back over, Jackson appeared to have been derailed by the question. He'd pulled up short, now staring at Cam but no longer moving toward him. "I—Maybe." Jackson shook his head and looked down. When his gaze came up to meet Cam's again, there was steel in those expressive eyes. "You know anything about what happened to Ida Evans's wallet?"

Cam's throat constricted. *Well, shit.* And the wallet in question was out in his backyard at that very moment. "Who?" was all that Cam could come up with, but he could tell from the look on Jackson's face the response had only made him sound guilty instead of innocent.

"So you steal from so many old ladies that you can't keep them straight anymore?"

"You here to arrest me for something, Officer?" Cam stood after placing his iced tea glass down on the porch, making sure to stay on the first step of his house to give him a height advantage.

Jackson huffed out a breath and rubbed his palm roughly over his face, then put his hands on his hips and turned to look out over the yard for a moment as if composing himself. "Look, Mr. Sanders...."

"You can call me Cam," Cam cut in, hoping to stir Jackson up even further.

It appeared to work somewhat, since Jackson frowned a moment, then turned back to focus on Cam's face. "I hear your name on the daily, and it's already twice today. Ida and Charles are good people who have very little to call their own. That money is pretty much the teetotal of their monthly income, and since her wallet came up missing, they have no way to pay for Charles's oxygen or their electricity. But I guess that doesn't matter to a man like you."

"A man like me?" Now Jackson had returned the favor, saying just the right thing to stir Cam up. "And just what kind of man would that be, Mr. Lawman? Just what does your churchgoing, thou-shalt-not-judge ass know about Camden Sanders other than I paid my dues and served my time? You think you got me figured out? You think you know me?" Cam was off the stairs and in Jackson's face before he could think better of it, poking some quite impressive chest musculature with each jab of his finger.

Jackson balled his fists and Cam prepared for a fight to begin in earnest. Cam might not be as built as Jackson, but he had a wiry strength that was usually underestimated, not to mention that he was scrappy and saw winning as the goal, not fighting fair. He was sure Jackson was tensing to send the first punch when a horn honked, bringing them both up short.

Their heads turned in unison toward the driveway where another car now sat behind Jackson's Mustang. A huge car that at first appeared to have no one inside. But then Cam noticed the top curls of an old lady hairdo peeking above the curve of the steering wheel. In the passenger seat, a bald pate glowed with the afternoon sun glinting through the windshield. There was another honk of the horn and then the driver's side door opened.

Jackson immediately headed toward the vehicle to help Ida Evans out, and Cam stood there watching until the passenger side door opened. At that point, he was compelled to rush to help feeble Charles Evans before he ended up facedown on the dirt drive.

"We aren't staying but a minute, so don't let us interrupt," Mrs. Evans announced, not seeming to realize that she had just broken up what could have easily become a scuffle across the front lawn. "I had no idea you were friends with Jackson Lee, Mr. Sanders. I used to watch Jackson when he was a baby and his momma worked over at the pharmacy. Ain't that right, Jackson?" She patted Jackson's arm, and Cam noticed the blush as Jackson nodded, surely grinding his teeth at being mistaken for Cam's friend.

"Oh yes, ma'am," Cam assured her as he helped Mr. Evans around the front of the car. "Jackson and I are getting closer by the day, ain't that right, Sheriff?"

"I'm not a sheriff, Camden." Jackson said the name as if it tasted bad in his mouth. "I'm with the city police department."

"And I'm so proud of you, Jackson," Mrs. Evans declared, still not noticing the tension. "I just wanted to come by—" She turned to Cam and smiled. "—to invite you over to supper tomorrow night." She took Cam's hand in hers and patted it. "You are such a good boy and I would love to get to know you better. Charles and I used to be very active in the community, but this getting old stuff gets in the way something fierce, let me tell you."

Jackson and Cam both chuckled with Ida. Charles tried but ended up coughing instead, which brought everyone a step closer to him in case he needed help.

Cam felt his stomach turn as he thought of the blue rose wallet lying out in the mud behind his house, having been rained on the night before. Why were these people being so nice to him? He'd almost like it better if everyone treated him like Jackson did. It would definitely feel more familiar, and it wouldn't bring all this crazy guilt with it. And how could they afford to feed him if they had just lost all their money? Cam glanced over at Jackson, who was frowning deeply. The good officer didn't seem to want him to go to dinner with Ida and Charles. Well, didn't that just cinch it?

"I'd be honored, ma'am. What time and where do you want me?" Cam smiled at Jackson as he answered.

CHAPTER 8

"BUT, IDA, that man may be the one that has your wallet. You know that, right?" Jackson had followed Charles and Ida home when they'd left Camden Sanders's house and now paced around their living room as the pair watched from their perches on the couch. He felt compelled to save them from Camden, who seemed to be seducing everyone in the town. At times, Jackson felt drawn to him as well, and didn't that just piss him all to hell.

"Jackson, honey, my mind isn't going... yet," Ida said with a smile. "And you've told me he's been to prison. But he moved out here all on his own."

"Moving doesn't change a man," Jackson pointed out. He didn't like the idea of the older couple hosting Camden Sanders in their house alone. He'd begged to be invited too, just to make sure all went well, but Ida had refused.

"Sweetheart, he bought a house here. He's fixing it up. That means he wants a home, that he plans to stay. Change doesn't come all at once. Sometimes you want to change long before you become who you want to be. But nobody can change if they aren't allowed to, if everyone still expects you to be all the things you once was."

"Ida, I-I'm not a judgmental man. I try to be fair." Jackson was trying to explain but couldn't seem to get it across.

"No, Jackson. You are a good man and a fair man. But you have only ever had to deal with the same people in this little town. You already know what every one of us is going to do before we do it. But now you've been dealt a wild card. That's what Camden Sanders is. You can't predict him like you can everybody else." She stared at Jackson for a moment, shook her finger. "Now... he's coming to dinner and you are going to go about your business and stop worrying about Charles and me."

Charles put his hand on Ida's and nodded at Jackson in solidarity.

"Ida, I don't mean to—" Jackson started.

"No more, honey. It's all going to be fine. You'll see." Ida led Jackson toward the door. "It's time for our afternoon nap, so if you don't mind...."

"Of course not." He nodded back to Charles and stepped out onto the porch. "Y'all have a nice nap."

JACKSON SLAMMED his car door and then huffed, staring out at the street from where he sat in front of the Evans residence. Was he being unfair to Camden Sanders? Expecting him to be what his record said he was, instead of keeping an open mind? Or was the man so slimy he was now making even Jackson question his gut instincts?

Jackson cranked the car and pulled away from the curb, his mind in a whirl.

It took him no time before he'd pulled into a narrow driveway and waited for the door of the one-car attached garage to slowly trundle open. His house was small, what most people called a starter home, and even that was more than he really needed. But it had been a good buy and his dad had encouraged him to invest in a home instead of throwing his money away renting.

He entered the kitchen through the garage door and tossed his keys on the counter, then opened the refrigerator to grab a beer. He twisted off the cap and took a healthy swig before leaning back in to collect the fixings for a sandwich. Once his meal was made, completed with a handful of Barbecue Lay's chips, he dropped onto one of the stools next to the island and pulled out his cell phone.

"Why didn't you come over for lunch? You have plans this afternoon?" his dad asked in lieu of a greeting upon answering the call.

"Nah, just having a sandwich at home," Jackson responded.

"You missed your momma's roast, boy. What's wrong? You feeling poorly?" His father could always read Jackson more clearly than a billboard, and now didn't seem any different.

"Dad, can I ask you something?"

"You just did." There was a chuckle in his dad's voice, but then he cleared his throat and answered, "You know you can."

"Am I judgmental?"

There was silence on the line. Jackson had been unsure if asking his father this question was the right course of action. But then, he'd known better than to ask his mother. She would have immediately told him he was the best man ever and then asked who she needed to tell off for saying any different.

After a moment, the sound of a voice clearing came again over the line, then his father said, "Son, what's this about?"

"I just…. Can people change, Dad? I mean, really change?"

"Well… sometimes it sure doesn't look that way, does it? But I have to believe a person can. God teaches it, doesn't he?"

Jackson smiled. Walter Rhodes was the best man that Jackson had ever met. He wasn't in other's faces about his faith, but Jackson knew he fell back on it and truly believed.

"Yeah," Jackson said as he thought that over.

"But," his father continued, "as a policeman, we have to try to predict the actions of others. We have to use our gut. It's hard to mesh those two sometimes. Who you judging?"

"I—" Jackson huffed.

"Spit it out, boy," his dad encouraged.

"What do you think of Camden Sanders?" Jackson asked.

"Never met the man. Should I? And even more to the point, what do you think of him?"

Jackson sighed. "I don't know, Dad. He seems nice enough most of the time, but he's got a record. And sometimes, I don't know, sometimes there is something…." How did he describe the feeling he had? And was that feeling justified? He sure didn't know how to rationalize it, even to himself.

"So you don't know. That doesn't sound judgmental. It sounds more like you're withholding judgment. Get to know him better. If your gut is telling you something, son, listen to it. You're smart, and a good policeman. Don't ignore your instincts."

"Yes, sir. Thank you." Jackson meant it. His dad had indeed been the right person to talk to.

"We are about to head back over to the church to get it cleaned up before evening services. You coming?"

"No, I think I'm gonna sit it out tonight. But can you do me a favor? If you see Ruby Mae, can you tell her that I'm gonna pick up the oldest tomorrow morning to do some yard work in town?"

"Yeah, I'll tell her. You have a good evening. I'll see you tomorrow."

"Night, Dad. Tell Mom I love her." Jackson hung up and went back to eating his sandwich with much to think about.

CAM WAS back on the front steps, surveying the relatively small amount of improvement he'd managed to his front lawn. It had taken most of the day and he still wasn't even to a point where he could mow. At least the long list of work he needed to do around the house kept his mind off all the worrying he could be focused on.

And speaking of worrying. What had he been thinking to accept an invitation to dinner from Ida and Charles? How was he going to sit at the table and look them in the eye after stealing all their money? Yeah, that was going to make for a pleasant evening. But Jackson Rhodes had clouded his brain or something, and all he'd been able to think about was showing the policeman that he could do whatever he wanted. No matter that what he'd agreed to do wasn't even close to anything he wanted.

Tommasina approached and nudged his arm with her big knotty head, and Cam scrubbed behind her ear. "I can't just not show up. I mean, they know right where I live. What am I going to do, Tom?" The cat looked at him, and Cam corrected, "Tommasina." He was a fucking idiot.

After a few minutes of staring off into space, Cam had a sudden idea and pulled his phone from his pocket. It was a dumb idea and he knew it, but it didn't stop him from punching in the phone number and listening to the ring as the call connected.

A soft voice answered just as he'd about given up, but he lost all use of his tongue and simply sat there as the voice again said, "Hello?"

The line went quiet except for breathing, then finally the voice said, "I'm alone."

Cam breathed a sigh of relief. "Are you okay?"

He could imagine Detra nodding on the other end of the line, finally realizing he couldn't hear and answering, "Yeah. He's mad, but he doesn't know I had anything to do with it. Are you okay? Tell me you are halfway around the world right now, Cam."

"I'm halfway around the world right now."

"You are such a fucking liar. And stupid as hell too. You are still in Georgia, aren't you? He isn't gonna play if he finds you, Cam. Get on a plane and get gone."

"I found a place to settle, Detra. It's pretty good here, quiet and nice. You should run too. It's a little town called Hog Mountain. You could come and—"

"Shit! Cam! Don't tell me that. Don't call here again. He'll find out. Just be happy, okay?" Detra didn't wait for an answer before the line went dead.

Cam felt the sting of tears as he stared at the phone in his hand, wondering if he had just made the biggest mistake of his life.

CHAPTER 9

THE SUN lit up the entire bedroom early the next morning, and Cam covered his head with a pillow to ward it off. It wasn't like him not to get up immediately, but he'd had a lot of trouble sleeping the night before as his mind continuously played over his phone conversation with Detra.

Although Detra still held out hope that her love would somehow change Harold, Cam would feel better if she gave up that entire life and move out to Hog Mountain with him. He could see her fitting in and enjoying the slow, easy life in the country. He could also see her blossoming without Harold around to keep her under his thumb. But Cam couldn't force her to leave. So all he could do was worry.

While Harold was the one in control, other people had come and gone from their little band of thieves. Cam supposed Harold would have let him do the same except for one small detail. Cam had left with a huge chunk of change, most of which belonged to Harold.

Cam finally threw back the covers and climbed out of the bed. He straightened the sheets and pillows quickly and headed toward the bathroom. He was going to need an extra-large cup of coffee to make it through the morning, that was for sure. And he had a long day ahead of him, too, what with his dinner at Ida and Charles's that evening. He sighed at the thought and stepped under the shower spray.

Cam was just stepping out the front door, second mug of coffee in hand and cat under his feet, when a familiar police cruiser pulled into his driveway. Cam couldn't think of a less welcomed event. What the hell was he doing back again today? Had they not had enough of each other already? Or was Rhodes back to finish the fight they had almost started the day before?

Cam waited on the top step until the policeman stepped out of his car, then called across the lawn. "Mornin', Officer Rhodes. To what do I owe the pleasure?"

To Cam's surprise, the policeman smiled and returned the greeting. "Morning, Mr. Sanders. I brought the manual labor you requested yesterday." Rhodes opened the back door to his squad car and three kids piled out.

Cam frowned and glanced between the children and Rhodes. "What—"

Seeming to understand what Cam meant, the officer continued. "Give them the tools they'll need and tell them what you want done. They'll require a little supervision, but they are good kids. You should feed 'em, though, and make sure they don't get too hot out here, drinks every once in a while. You can pay 'em what you see fit at the end of the day when I come back to get them. This is Galen, this is Tony, and this is Luanne. I expect you to be good to 'em." Then he turned to the children. "Listen to Mr. Sanders and work hard for him, okay? And we'll go to Walmart like I said."

"Look," Cam started. The last thing he wanted was a bunch of kids in his yard all day. "I have enough to worry about without babysitting."

The three kids all frowned, and the oldest—Galen, wasn't it?— said, "We ain't babies, mister."

Cam held up his hands in surrender. "Fine. I got trash cans out back behind the house. Pick up all the trash in the yard, front and back. Then gather all the rocks big enough to get thrown by a lawn mower and make a pile of them over here." He pointed to a dry creek bed over to the right of the house. "I'm gonna be in the garage, but Tommasina, here"—he gestured to the lazing cat on the porch—"is watching every move you make. Don't make her tattle on you."

The kids snickered and started to head for the trash cans. Cam glanced at Officer Rhodes and saw he was grinning too.

"I'll keep an eye on them," Cam assured him. "Thanks for bringing them."

"They're good kids," Rhodes said, then seemed to search for something more before simply nodding and opening his car door. "I'll be back this afternoon."

Cam watched him leave, then headed for the garage to open up for the day. He had plenty of cabinets in the garage area to clean out. It would keep him busy between the trickle of actual paying jobs that came in. None of which he happened to have at the moment.

Throughout the morning, he found himself peeking out the back window at the children on his lawn. For the most part, they stayed busy, but from time to time, they chased each other across the yard or sat on the porch to pet Tommasina, who seemed quite pleased with their attention. He had expected them to be trouble, but he had to admit they seemed like good kids and it wasn't as horrible as he had thought to have them around.

When the day started heating up, Cam opened the back door and headed across the lawn for the house. The trio quieted and tried to look extra busy as if nervous he would be mad at them for something, which Cam thought was funny since they had been working hard enough as it was. He waved them over as he passed.

"Come on. Let's make some iced tea and sandwiches, why don't we?" Cam directed the kids toward the house.

WHEN JACKSON pulled into Mr. Sanders's driveway about three in the afternoon, it was to find the trio of kids laid out on the porch. They looked completely worn-out but each had a smile on their face and money in their hands. The yard still had tall grass, but there were large bins full of all kinds of trash, so Jackson figured the kids had done a good job.

Galen and Tony stood up when they saw him, but Luanne had a large orange tabby in her lap and seemed content to stay where she was. He heard the back door of the garage open and close as he made it to the stairs.

"Did y'all get a lot done today?" Jackson asked the three, but Sanders answered from behind him.

"They were a big help."

"He paid us ten dollars apiece," Tony exclaimed, waving his money to stress the point. Luanne and Galen waved theirs too.

"I guess that means you're all ready to go to Walmart, then?" Jackson grinned at the kids. He was pretty sure they had never had that much money to call their own, and he loved to see the happy grins on their faces.

"Gonna get a new toy?" Camden asked curiously.

Galen and Tony got quiet and looked at each other as if unsure how to answer. Jackson didn't want to embarrass them by saying more than they wanted Camden to know so he decided to let them decide on how to respond.

Luanne spoke up. "We all need new school clothes, Mr. Sanders, and we figure we ain't gettin' 'em otherwise."

Camden glanced over at Jackson, his expression serious, then mumbled, "Ain't getting much for ten dollars, even at Walmart."

"All right, kids, to the car so we can get going," Jackson ordered and watched as the three clambered down the stairs and to the patrol car. After they had gotten into the backseat, Jackson turned to Camden. "I figure this trip will cost me money, but they are good kids, and they do without more than they should."

Camden nodded and turned to look toward the patrol car again. "Can you bring them again tomorrow?"

Jackson was surprised by the request but nodded. "Yeah, I can manage that."

"Then let's tell 'em they still have work to do." Camden started across the lawn toward the car and Jackson followed behind. Camden opened the back door to the patrol vehicle and announced, "There's still work to be done, and I need a reliable crew to do it. How do you three feel about staying with this job for another day?"

Galen and Tony cheered and Luanne nodded happily. Jackson was sure they would do just about anything for the chance to get away from their house, sad as that fact was.

"Okay, then," Jackson said. "Why don't we put off our trip to Walmart 'til tomorrow afternoon?"

The cheering subsided and the backseat got awfully quiet. Finally, Luanne spoke up. "Is it all right if we leave our pay here 'til tomorrow, sir?"

Shit. Jackson hadn't even thought of what would happen if the kids brought home thirty dollars cash. That money would surely not be in their possession by the next day if it even stayed there for ten minutes. It seemed Camden had gotten at least an inkling of the problem too from the frown on his face.

Jackson held out his hand. "Tell you what. I'll lock up your money in the glove compartment of the police car. We can get it out tomorrow, okay?"

All three nodded in unison, and the money was quickly handed over for safekeeping.

When they backed out of the driveway, all three kids waved good-bye to Camden as he stood on his porch steps, and Jackson found himself raising a hand as well.

CHAPTER 10

CAM WASN'T looking forward to his evening with Ida and Charles. He'd scrubbed himself until he nearly shined, and he'd put on the only pair of dress pants he owned, a pair he'd worn when going to appointments with his parole officer. They fit better than they had then, and he turned around to check out his own ass in the mirror.

"Not bad, if I do say so myself. Only, I doubt the old folks are going to appreciate my fineness." Cam frowned. "God, I hope not...." He shook off the disturbing thought and pulled on a white button-up shirt, then sat on the end of the bed to put on his socks and shoes. None of the clothes were the latest fashion, and to be honest, Cam thought he looked like nothing more than a convict dressing for a court appearance.

Tom hopped up on the bed to inspect Cam's unfamiliar clothing, sniffing, then rubbing her head on his arm. "Okay, no orange hairs on the clothes. I already look goofy enough." He patted Tom on the head before standing and clomping across the room. Dress shoes were as loud as his damn shower sandals.

At his dresser, he pushed his wallet into his pocket and scooped up his keys. He turned a three-sixty in the room to make sure he hadn't forgotten anything, then headed down the stairs. Did people take a present when they were invited to eat at someone's house? Hell if he knew. And unless he wanted to take a half-empty squirt bottle of Hershey's syrup, he wasn't sure what he'd bring. He shrugged and headed out the front door.

As Cam passed the small park in town, he noticed a group of men gathering for what looked like an impromptu game of football. Some had already taken off their shirts as a way to designate their chosen team, and Cam debated pulling over to watch. Probably not a good idea, he decided and kept on his way. Damn, he needed to get in on one of those games.

It was only another couple of turns before he pulled up in front of a tiny white house with bright green shutters. The flowers around the matching mailbox and along the walkway to the front door were in full bloom and looked to be well taken care of. The huge land yacht in the driveway told Cam he'd found the right place.

Before Cam made it up the walkway, the front door swung open and Ida pushed open the screen door. "You're just in time! We can sit right down to eat."

Cam smiled at the energetic little lady. Ida didn't stand any higher than his elbow, but he had no doubt she could take charge of a room full of Vikings if she had a mind to. "Thank you for inviting me. It smells delicious," he said as he stepped past her and into a house that had nothing out of place. Charles stood in the doorway between the living room and the dining room, smiling and waving Cam in that direction.

And it did smell delicious. Cam felt his stomach gurgle with pleasure at the mere thought of the home cooking he was in for that evening.

Ida followed behind Cam and pointed out his spot at the table before she sat and busied herself with putting her cloth napkin in her lap. "We have always loved company, Camden—may we call you Camden?"

Cam nodded his consent, but Ida didn't give him a chance to say anything before she continued.

"We used to have dinner parties all the time, but now it seems either we are too tired or our friends are."

Charles made a noise somewhere between a grunt and a laugh, then passed his bowl to Ida. She took it and scooped out a helping of chicken and dumplings with big white dumplings that looked more like ping-pong balls floating in the thick broth. Cam's bowl was next to be filled and then he dived right in, not worrying about if he should wait for anyone else first. He hadn't had chicken and dumplings in years and hadn't had *homemade* chicken and dumplings since his grandmother had died.

Cam hummed his approval at the savory flavor. "This is better than my grandma's, Mrs. Evans," Cam confided. "But I wouldn't have ever said that to her. She could cook like you wouldn't believe."

Ida smiled. "Thank you, honey. Sounds like you loved her. And please call us Ida and Charles. We've never stood on formality."

"Yes, ma'am. My grandmother was a special woman." Cam ducked his head and went back to shoveling in his food. Talk of his grandmother could make him emotional, but thinking of her love for blue roses and the blue rose wallet he'd taken from Ida's purse made his heart hurt something fierce.

Ida served up cucumber salad to each of them, then tucked into her own food. The room quieted for a time as they each enjoyed the delicious dinner.

When Cam had finished his second helping, he pushed back his chair and patted his belly. Ida seemed pleased with the gesture, as did Charles. "I have dessert, but maybe we should let dinner settle first," Ida said. "Let me start the coffee and then we can relax in the living room for a bit while it brews." Ida started collecting plates and Charles tried to help.

"Please, let me do that. It's the least I can do," Cam said, taking the plates from both of their hands before carrying them into the kitchen. He ended up washing the small amount of dishes while Ida got the coffeepot set up and started, and then they both met Charles in the living room and Ida sat Cam between them on the long sofa.

Ida leaned forward and pulled out a photo album from the lower shelf of the coffee table, then sat back, placing the heavy book on Cam's lap. Cam felt a bit trapped in the situation. The last thing he wanted was to go on a walk down memory lane with two people who probably had enough photo albums to keep him busy for weeks. He looked down at baby pictures and realized this was going to be a nightmare.

"This is Charles when he was a baby, and this is me," Ida began. "But I won't bore you with all of that. I just wanted to show you something."

Charles reached over and flipped the pages, obviously knowing what she was looking for. More toward the middle, they found the page they sought and Cam looked down at pictures of a teenaged couple, the female fresh-faced and beautiful, the male virile and handsome. Both had huge grins, arms around each other and dressed as if going to a party. Cam stared in shock.

"We weren't always old, you know," Ida said with a chuckle. She tapped her finger on the picture. "We loved to dance back then, never missed a party." She flipped the page and there was the same couple doing some out-of-date dance step surrounded by a crowd of other young people in what looked like a gym. "Charles could really cut a rug. All the girls wanted to dance with him."

Cam glanced over and Charles grinned at him. He could see the handsome teen buried under the wrinkles age had wrought. The discovery shocked Cam for some reason, and he turned away quickly before Charles saw the expression he was sure was obvious on his face.

"When we were seventeen, we'd been dating over a year and thought we were so worldly." Ida turned the page again and the couple held a trophy between them. "We won the dance contest at the Optimist Club dance," she explained. "Then I found out I was in the family way." Ida looked up then, staring at Cam to be sure he understood.

Cam had no idea what to say. He glanced away, not wanting to look at Ida's sincere but sad expression, and not at all sure why she was telling him this. There were no pictures of children on the walls, and he was pretty sure Officer Rhodes had said they had no kids to help them out. Didn't he say that?

"There was a doctor in the next county over. He did procedures in the back rooms of his office, and a friend of mine took me there because I didn't want anyone to know what I had done." She continued to stare at him, and Cam fidgeted. He couldn't seem to think of a thing to say. He glanced over to Charles, who now looked down at his hands. *Shit!* What the fuck was happening here?

"It was the most traumatic thing I have ever gone through, and within a day of visiting the doctor, I knew something was horribly wrong. My parents rushed me to the hospital, and I spent the next week there. I almost died, Camden."

Why had she said his name? What did she want from him? He stared down at the picture of the two happy people with their trophy to keep from looking into Ida's intent gaze. He heard Charles sniffle and gritted his teeth.

"When the hospital released me, I was told I would never be able to have children, and by that time, the entire town knew what I had done. Not only did I have to deal with regret for the decision I'd made, but with the shame of knowing everyone else knew. Charles could have left me then. Men have never been judged for sex like women have. But he didn't." She reached across Cam then and took Charles's hand, squeezing it in her own. "He even asked me to marry him, knowing we would never have kids of our own."

Cam glanced between the pair and saw the love in their watery eyes as they exchanged a sad smile. It got quiet for a few moments, and Cam continued to search for something to say, maybe some way to change the subject. He came up empty.

Finally Ida took a shuddering breath and turned her attention back to Cam. "We watched everyone else's kids while their parents worked or when they went out. We ended up with more kids than anyone else because of it." She smiled and flipped through some pages to pictures of the pair holding different babies and children through the years.

"The reason I told you this, Camden—" She turned back to stare into his eyes. "—is to say: We all make mistakes in our life. And we are all embarrassed and want to hide them. But sometimes, there is nothing to do for it but to hold your head high and own up to your actions. Sometimes things work out despite it all."

She smiled and closed the photo album, then leaned forward to slide it back onto the lower shelf of the coffee table. When she sat back on the couch again, she patted Cam's hand before pushing herself to her feet.

"Well, now, anyone ready for cobbler and ice cream?" she asked as she headed to the kitchen.

Cam found his mouth hanging open and pulled it closed with a snap. He turned to Charles when the man also patted his hand. Charles's eyes were red-rimmed but clear, and way too knowing. Although, as much as Cam searched, he could find no anger or hatred within them.

What the fuck had just happened?

CAM DROPPED onto his sofa with a heavy sigh. He hadn't gotten any farther into the house than the living room. The evening had drained every bit of energy from him, and yet he had little hope he would be able to sleep that night. Damn those old people! What was wrong with him for letting them get to him? It wasn't like they lived in squalor. They could afford to lose a little money, right? What right did they have to make him feel guilty for it? He should have never gone over there for dinner. It was his own damn fault for being so soft.

With a meow of welcome, Tommasina hopped onto his chest and began kneading. Cam reached up and petted the cat. "You know, I am so fucked," he said, staring up at the ceiling.

CHAPTER 11

JACKSON GOT out of his Mustang and walked across the grass to where the other guys were gathering. He'd gone home after dropping off the Watson kids to change into cutoff sweats and a stretched-out T-shirt. No need to wear anything nicer when they were just going to get sweaty and dirty with red Georgia clay before the end of the touch football game.

When the group already waiting saw Jackson approaching, they whooped and cheered. Jackson had missed the last few games and now was remembering why he enjoyed the scheduled matches so much. He needed to make more of an effort to hang out with his friends, even when he was busy as he had been lately.

"Jackson." Clint Richards made the name come out like a deep dog bark and all the others gave answering barks, clapping Jackson on the back in greeting. "Ready to get your ass beat?" Clint asked and shoved the football into Jackson's chest.

"It won't be by you," Jackson fired back, keeping the ball and turning to the crowd that now circled him. "Have we picked teams?"

"Yeah, we didn't know if you were coming," Clint answered. "We can choose again if you want."

"Nah, just tell me what team I'm on." Jackson wasn't going to make everyone go to all that trouble. He was the one who'd shown up late, after all.

After some arguing among themselves, it was decided that Jackson would be on the skins team, and they all split up to start the game. While some of the guys had let themselves go since their high school days, most still looked good enough for Jackson to enjoy the view. Clint had been Jackson's best friend while in school and also a frequent star in his teenage fantasies, though Jackson had tried his best to never let that show, keeping all his sexual thoughts and actions bottled up, except in private with Grant.

And speak of the devil. "Hey, guys! In need of a cheering section?" Grant called out from the side of the field where he was getting comfortable on the grass with a blanket and water bottle. Ugh. Jackson felt the sudden need to pull his shirt back on.

GRANT STRETCHED his legs out in front of him and leaned back on his arms. He tried to make it every week for this little high school reunion. Not because he didn't see the guys around town already, but because of the beautiful display of skin and man sweat. Too bad there was no tackling. It was better than watching porn and he didn't have to worry about his wife going on a crying jag again if she caught him. Plus, there was the possibility of grabbing some real action from these guys, unlike the porn stars he would never meet in person.

While the majority of these guys were dyed-in-the-wool heterosexuals, that never stopped them from accepting the occasional drunk blowjob, and Grant always tried to make himself available when those opportunities arose. There would be no drunkenness this evening, sadly, but he could still enjoy the view.

Jackson strode out onto the field, his tanned skin sprinkled with golden fur that Grant could still remember licking. It had been a while, though. Jackson had cut him off and good. Not even a drunken blowjob since Grant got married. What a shame. Jackson's body was still in prime condition, and as he bent over, Grant got a fine display of his firm, rounded backside.

Clint took his position on the line across from Jackson. Like night and day, good and evil, the two were beautiful and contrasting young godlings ready to do battle. Where Jackson was golden, Clint was nearly black-headed with fur of the same color in abundance across his muscled chest and firm abdomen. While Clint had on a shirt for this game, Grant was well aware of what hid beneath. In addition to being a regular at the weekly football games, Clint had allowed Grant to help him release some alcohol-fueled frustration in the past.

And Jackson thought Grant couldn't keep a secret. Grant smiled at that. How he'd love to throw his trysts with Clint in Jackson's face, but while Jackson only fumed and grumbled at Grant's supposed lack of tact, Clint would beat him to a pulp if even a whisper of those indiscretions ever got out. And worse, he probably wouldn't let Grant get a hold of that hot schlong again.

There was lots of yelling and running on the field, but Grant paid little attention to the actual game. He clapped at what he thought were appropriate moments, but otherwise, he was only there for the scenery. Most of the time, that kept him busy in his own fantasies with no time for worrying about the score or which team was winning.

Grant pulled out an old church-style fan from his satchel and fluttered it in front of his face. It was still rather hot out, and while he was enjoying the sweat dripping off the men on the field, there was no reason he needed to join the festivities. It was one of the reasons he'd gone into veterinary medicine. He was not made for manual labor of any kind. He also liked a nice lifestyle, and so far, being the town vet, added to his wife's family's money, had provided that for him.

A couple of older teenage girls wandered in the direction of the game. They looked familiar, but honestly, Grant paid little attention to the female population of the town. Except for Regina, his assistant and BFF. Well, and his wife and daughter, but that was only because he had to. As the girls got closer, they clapped at one of the plays, drawing the attention of a few of the guys who were playing. Grant wanted to hiss at the girls and tell them this event was for men only. They were in his territory.

The two paid him no attention, no matter how much he frowned at them. They sat on the other side of the field and cheered at things Grant didn't even notice were worthy of applause. Bill and Pete, who both worked construction over in the new housing developments these days and had kept fine bodies to show for all that sweat and labor, were the first of the group to perk up when the females paid them attention. Soon all the guys were strutting a little bit more, even Jackson, lifting their shirts—those who wore them—to wipe the sweat from their faces and in the process displaying their mostly flat stomachs and defined chests. Okay, maybe Grant could admit that having the girls around was beneficial to him too. But how he wished the men would strut for him, want him to look at their manly physiques.

When the game was winding down, Grant stood and collected his things, then headed for his car in the parking lot. He opened the trunk where he had stored a cooler full of ice, water bottles, and a Ziploc full of hand towels, cooled and ready for the hot and sweaty men to use. *Let's see those girls compete with this!*

A few of the players dawdled to speak to the females, but most of the guys were much more interested in what Grant had to offer for once. *Yeah, if only they'd crowd around me like this when I offer my mouth.*

Jackson and Clint seemed more interested in chatting with each other, rather than paying attention to their loyal fan, but Grant simply watched the pair, licking his lips as they used their towels and water bottles to cool and wipe the sweat from their bodies. Jesus, he could bust a nut just from that alone.

Grant noticed Pete passing his number to one of the girls and considered teasing the guy about jail bait, but decided against it. Pete was one to ignore his hetero status when drunk, and Grant didn't want to endanger any chances he had with the big guy, although he'd rather not share with the skank.

The guys all gave man hugs along with pats to shoulders and asses as they said their good-byes to each other. Grant wished he could be part of that good ol' boys tradition, but he was locked out, either because of his sexuality or perhaps his inability to play football.

CHAPTER 12

CAM PEELED his eyes open as some noise intruded on his sleep. He felt a dead weight on his chest and for a moment couldn't figure out where he was. The noise came again, a banging—the door, it was definitely someone at the door.

"Coming," he croaked. He cleared his throat and tried again. "Coming!" He was louder this time and the banging stopped. He momentarily wondered who would be at his door in the middle of the night.

He lifted a hand, which was numb from hanging down while he slept, and attempted to scrub the sleep from his eyes. He only succeeded in slapping himself in the face. From there, his runaway hand dropped to his chest where it upset the cat lazing atop him. Tommasina squalled her displeasure and jumped down.

Cam tried rolling over and almost fell to the floor, discovering he was on the couch instead of in his bed. Glancing around the room, he also noticed bright light leaking between the curtains. "Oh shit! What time is it?" Cam found his arm still didn't work when he went to push himself up. And one of his feet tingled as he put weight down on it.

Cam ended up hobbling to the door while smacking one of his hands against his hip to get the blood flowing again. When he opened the door, it was to several figures enveloped in bright sunlight. It was like the second coming and probably just as painful. Cam gasped and shaded his crusted eyes.

"Jesus Christ!" he yelped.

"Nope, just Officer Rhodes," the policeman said on a chuckle.

"And Galen!" "And Tony!" "And Luanne!" the kids chimed in.

Cam groaned at all the joy and enthusiasm being tossed around.

Rhodes still had the traces of humor in his voice as he asked, "Hard night?"

"Yeah, big party at the Evanses'." Cam let his sarcasm speak for him. When he peeked out between his fingers, braving the sunlight again, Rhodes had one brow raised in question.

"Nah, just having trouble sleeping is all." Cam looked down to see he still had on the clothes he'd worn the night before.

"Something weighin' on your conscience, Mr. Sanders?" Rhodes asked.

"I had my conscience surgically removed years ago, Officer," Cam replied as he turned away. "Anybody want some breakfast?"

All three kids screamed an affirmative and hurried to the kitchen. Officer Rhodes followed at a more sedate pace, glancing around with enough interest that Cam might've thought he was casing the place had he not known better.

While coffee brewed, Cam made fried egg sandwiches, his specialty, for each of his guests, then went to change into something more suitable to start his day. His head felt as if it was filled with cotton balls and his arm and leg still tingled from having hung off the couch all night long. There didn't seem any use in taking a shower before going out to get greasy in the garage, so he simply pulled on one of the shirts and pants from his work clothes stack, then headed back to the kitchen.

Everyone was where he'd left them around the kitchen table, Rhodes finishing his coffee while the kids sipped at big glasses of milk with Hershey's syrup.

"Okay, kids, I need you all in the front yard again today. Have any of you used a push mower before?"

All three nodded, their attention completely on him. He had to admit they were good kids, and he didn't mind so much having them around.

"I only have two mowers, in the shed beside the house. Y'all can take turns using them until we get all the grass cut in the front and side yards. Understood?"

All three nodded again and chorused, "Yes, sir."

Officer Rhodes stood and made his way to the sink where he placed his cup and turned. "With that, I'm on my way. I'll be back this afternoon. Be good for Mr. Sanders, kids."

Cam had worked through the day with only a few stops to check on the kids and make sandwiches for everyone. His yard crew had the front and side yard of the old house looking like someone actually lived there, and Cam was awfully proud of it. He surveyed the nicely trimmed grass from the back door of the garage while he wiped his hands on a shop rag.

While the kids had worked on the yard, he had been busy trying to fix the hydraulic lift in the second bay of the garage. He was going to have to order a part before it would work again, but at least he'd found the problem and could cross another item off his list of chores to do.

His near-sleepless night had made the day into a long one. Add in the heat of working in the un-air-conditioned garage and a nagging headache behind his eye seemed to be growing by the minute. He sighed and rubbed a spot in the middle of one eyebrow as he remembered he had company coming that evening. But maybe that could release some of his tension, since the animal doc would be a sure hookup.

When the familiar Hog Mountain Police vehicle pulled up in his driveway, Cam walked toward the car, the kids wandering down off the porch where they had all been relaxing with a glass of tea.

"Well, look at what you three accomplished today!" Rhodes exclaimed as he climbed out from behind the wheel. "Looks good." The kids beamed in response, obviously proud of themselves.

"They worked so hard, I'd like to hire them for the rest of the week," Cam said, patting Galen on the back. Cam dug into his pocket and pulled out his wallet. "The way I figure it, that's thirty dollars a day and you'll be working three more days, plus what I owe you today, that makes a hundred twenty dollars." Cam counted out the money while the kids watched with their mouths wide open. "Here you go, Officer Rhodes. That should buy some nice school clothes."

Luanne bounced up and down and squealed as Galen and Tony grinned. Rhodes smiled too and patted Cam on the shoulder.

"Then I better get so we can shop. I'll have 'em here bright and early tomorrow."

Once the police cruiser left, Cam let Tommasina in the house and went to take a hot shower. He considered taking a nap afterward but knew that would just lead to another night where he couldn't sleep. Cam had brought leftovers home from his dinner with Ida and Charles the night before, but they had ended up sitting out all night on the coffee table, so he was stuck with limited choices to eat.

After staring into the refrigerator for several minutes, Cam sighed. With feeding a bunch of kids the last few days, and even Officer Rhodes for breakfast that morning, there was very little left. He was going to have to go shopping soon if he planned to continue feeding a herd of kids for the rest of the week. He put some water on the stove to make some more tea, then considered his choices of fast food in town. There was a pizza place that could deliver, but he'd save that for tomorrow at lunch since it would feed more than just himself. Instead he sat the water off the burner with five tea bags to steep, then grabbed his keys and hurried out the front door.

The Dairy Queen was the quick answer. With a Nerd Blizzard in his cup holder and a double bacon burger and large fries in the bag on the passenger seat, he headed back home to eat before seven o'clock. Cam hoped the food and maybe some aspirin would help clear up the headache still pounding behind his eye.

THE ASPIRIN didn't help and his dinner now sat in his stomach like a lead weight. If it wasn't for the prospect of sex, Cam would definitely call off Grant's house call that evening. Cam popped two antacids and peeked out the drapes to see a little red BMW pull into his dirt driveway. He had no doubt that would be Grant.

When Grant climbed out of his car, Cam was impressed with how well the vet's tight jeans showed off his slender physique. The tight T-shirt could almost be considered a baby-doll style. In Cam's opinion, the good doc looked more like he was going out clubbing than to check on how a cat's pregnancy was coming along.

Cam waited until Grant knocked before approaching and opening the door. "Hey" was his only greeting before he moved aside to let his guest in. Cam wasn't at all sure how this was supposed to go. He'd never had a hookup that was pretending to be something else. Did he need to act like he tripped into Grant, then accidentally bend him over the kitchen table or something?

Grant walked to the center of the living room and stopped, turning around as he took in his surroundings.

"Want a beer or some tea?" Cam offered.

"A beer would be good," Grant answered, wandering over to the television.

Cam headed for the refrigerator and, while he had his head inside, heard Grant ask, "Does this TV even work? I bet you need rabbit ears to pick up a signal."

Cam grumbled instead of answering, tossing the caps in the trash, then headed back into the living room with the beers. He handed one to Grant, who took a sip, then used it to gesture toward the sofa. "Was that your mom's or something? And not one thing hanging on the walls! Did you do the spray paint?"

Cam frowned and headed for the sofa in question, dropping down into the center of it before unzipping his fly and pulling out his cock. He flopped it against his stomach and asked, "Did you come by to critique my décor or suck my dick?"

Grant wasted no time as he set his beer down on the coffee table and then dropped to his knees in front of Cam. Cam smirked with pride at the thought that his decorating skills held no interest for Grant now.

Grant ran his tongue down the length of Cam's cock, and it immediately thickened and firmed in response. "Yeah, that's the only way you need to use that mouth while you're here." Cam lifted his hips and pushed his jeans down farther.

Cam held up his cock in offering, and Grant opened his mouth wide, taking the head in and licking around the edges of the crown. Cam dropped his head to the back of the sofa and stared up at a water stain on the ceiling as Grant began a steady rhythm of saliva-rich sucking and bobbing. Cam reached to thread his fingers through Grant's hair, needing to guide and control the man for maximum pleasure, but grimaced as he met with a hairspray—or maybe gel—stiff helmet, which refused displacement of any kind. He could either grab the entire top layer of hair and use it like a joystick or simply allow Grant to do as he pleased. Cam chose the latter, dropping his hands to the sofa cushions and holding on as Grant went wild on his cock.

It did feel good, though. Cam couldn't deny that. His hips lifted of their own accord, and he began fucking the slobbery lips as Grant moaned and gagged around his dick.

"Take it. Take it all!" Cam yelled and grabbed the back of Grant's head, pulling him down on his cock until Grant's swollen lips met the skin at the base. Grant grunted and gagged, then struggled to get away as Cam shot his load down his throat.

Finally Cam released his grip and flopped back on the sofa in triumph. Grant came up gasping for breath and wiping at his nose and mouth to remove the excess cum that had gurgled out like a slow-flowing volcano eruption.

"Jesus Christ," Grant whispered between ragged gasps. After catching his breath, he asked, "Got a towel around?"

"Paper towels, on the kitchen counter." Cam nodded toward the kitchen but otherwise made no move to help. "I should be ready in a few to fuck if you still want more."

Grant was quiet for a moment, as if considering the proposal, then said, "Okay, I'll check on Tommasina while you recuperate."

Cam hadn't even thought about the cat until that moment and looked over to find the big orange creature perched on the back of the couch, obviously having watched the entire encounter. "What the hell, cat? I didn't come outside watching your ass get laid."

Tommasina stared at Cam a moment longer, then glanced toward the kitchen as Grant came back in, still wiping at the drool on his chin.

"Bring one for me? My balls are dripping." Cam held out his hand, and Grant dropped the wadded paper towel he'd been using into his hand. Cam shrugged and used it to dry off some as Grant headed for Tommasina.

While Grant poked at the cat's belly, Cam drank the rest of his beer and headed to the kitchen for another, stepping out of his jeans to keep from tripping over them. He was tossing the cap away on his new bottle when he realized his headache wasn't bothering him anymore. Yeah, he had seriously needed that and would be even better once he plowed Grant over the back of the couch.

When Cam wandered back into the living room, Grant had taken off his shirt and undone the button on his overly tight jeans. At the sight, Cam stopped and jacked himself until he was hard again, then pulled his own shirt off.

"Oh shit. Look at all those tattoos," Grant groaned out. "You are fuckin' bad-boy hot."

Cam grinned and strutted a bit. He knew he looked good. He wasn't some big muscle-bound weight lifter or anything, but he was tight and well proportioned. It definitely made him feel good to hear someone appreciate it, though.

"You like it? Then get rid of those pants so I can give you some of this."

To give him credit, Grant did try to hurry while removing his jeans, but they were so tight, he ended up having to sit down on the couch and let Cam pull at the hem of each pant leg before they would come off. Cam frowned at the pants as he dropped them on the floor. Why would anyone want to wear something that hard to get in and out of? When he looked back up, Grant was on his knees on the couch, facing the back, with his ass pushed out in readiness.

"Now that's what I'm talkin' about," Cam praised. He walked up behind Grant and ran his hand along the smooth skin of Grant's pale, rounded ass. Grant was a little shorter than Cam and about as slim. Still in nice shape, although honestly, he did have a bit of a muffin top in those tight jeans. But to be fair, Cam wasn't sure he wouldn't in jeans tight enough to move his organs out of place.

While preparing for the evening's festivities, Cam had made sure to shove some lubed condoms in the side table drawer, since he'd had no plans to let Grant upstairs to his bedroom. He was glad to see that Grant didn't seem to have any interest in that either. Having a guy in the bedroom hinted at an intimacy Cam didn't feel with Grant, and he definitely didn't want to give the guy the wrong impression.

Cam grabbed a condom and rolled it down his hard cock, then stepped closer to tease Grant's hole with the lubricated end. "You good with just going in, or do you need prep?" Cam asked, hoping Grant didn't need lots of stretching before the act. That was something else Cam equated with intimacy, and it felt totally wrong with Grant.

"Nah, I keep myself stretched for occasions such as this," Grant answered, and Cam let out a breath he hadn't realized he was holding. That was one good thing about Grant: he understood his place and was accommodating to his sex partners. Cam appreciated that in a fuck.

Cam curled himself over Grant's body and canted his hips forward to push slowly and evenly into Grant's hole. "Oh yeah, nice and easy. You know how to welcome a guy." Cam wrapped his arms around Grant's chest and held him in place as he pulled out, then shoved back in harder.

"Shit! Good!" Grant cried out, and Cam began a steady rhythm. The couch made noises in protest of the rocking and soon Tommasina decided it was time to give up her perch for another that didn't move quite so much. Cam was relieved to see her go, since having the cat as an audience to his fucking was causing severe damage to his mojo.

Cam pounded into Grant until he was sure the couch was going to give under the stress. He wasn't that worried about it since he'd only paid twenty dollars for the thing and this stress relief was worth three twenty-dollar couches at least.

Cam screamed out his orgasm to the stained ceiling with Grant right behind him. He took a minute to get his heart rate back under control, then pulled out of Grant's hole and peeled off the full condom.

He patted Grant on the back and said, "Thanks, buddy. That'll do me." Then Cam padded off, naked, to the kitchen to toss out the condom and get a glass of water. When he came back, Grant was in the downstairs bathroom, if the running water was any indication. He tapped on the door. "Is everything okay?"

When Grant grunted an affirmative, Cam wandered back into the living room and poked at the cum stain on the couch cushion with the wadded paper towel, then dropped it on the coffee table before lying down and covering his eyes with his arm. Shuffling sounds announced Grant's exit from the bathroom and his efforts to dress. Cam didn't move his arm from his eyes or strike up any unneeded conversation as Grant got ready to leave.

It got quiet for a moment and Cam almost peeked, but then Grant said, "So... I guess I'll be getting home. Maybe some other time?"

"Yeah," Cam said. "We can do that again, maybe." He didn't add any more, and after another pause, the door opened and closed. Cam stayed where he was until he heard a car starting, then he climbed off the couch and went about cleaning up the living room and locking up for the night. The doc had known just the right prescription for his sleeplessness, that was for sure! *I'm going to sleep like a baby tonight!*

CHAPTER 13

TRUE TO his prediction, Cam had had no trouble falling asleep. He slept like the dead for most of the night, but something—he wasn't sure what—woke him up at about two in the morning, and after that, he tossed and turned. It was at around four that he finally threw off the covers and shoved himself out of bed, upsetting Tommasina, who left the room with a loud protest.

"Fine! I'll give back the wallet. Okay? Jesus!" Cam screamed at no one and everyone, then stomped into the bathroom and slammed the door. He'd slept in the nude again to enjoy the feel of the soft sheets against his skin, so he had nothing to strip off before stepping into the shower, where he simply stood under the spray and grumbled until the water started to cool.

After drying off, Cam sat on the side of his bed and stared out the window into the night. This was just a onetime thing, right? It wasn't like he was going soft or nothin'. He just wanted to help an old couple out; that was it. He tossed himself back on the bed and closed his eyes, sighing in frustration.

The next time Cam opened his eyes, it was to the pale light of morning and a chorus of birds. With a yawn and a scrub to his eyes, he sat up and checked the time to find it was a little before seven. After stretching, he made his bed and got dressed, then headed downstairs for some coffee.

When Officer Rhodes and the kids knocked on the door, Cam was at the kitchen table with his coffee, the radio set to an Atlanta station that played a mix of alternative and rock.

"Coffee's made. Glasses of chocolate milk are on the counter," Cam said as they filed by.

"Gonna be another hot one today," Rhodes greeted as they all clambered in.

"And I plan on working in here with the AC because of it," Cam declared.

"Won't you lose business if you aren't out at the garage?" Rhodes asked.

Cam shrugged. "Nah. I can put a sign up to come around to the house. Plus, not much business to miss, really." There were only so many cars in the small town and not many others were going to use a mechanic so far off the beaten path. Cam wasn't too worried about it, though. There weren't many bills without a house or car payment, plus he could walk to work.

"And the kids?"

"I want y'all to start on the back today. Just picking up the trash is all right now. But if you get too hot, you come on in. We're gonna order some pizza for lunch."

All three kids perked up at that news. "Like in the movies, where a guy brings it right up to the door?" Tony asked.

Cam and Jackson chuckled. "Just like that," Cam assured.

"Can I answer the door when it comes?" Galen asked.

"No, me!" Tony argued.

The two went back and forth with Luanne trying to calm them down, until Cam assured them that they all three could go to the door and pay when the pizza man came. That got a round of cheers, then all three kids put their glasses in the sink and headed out the back door to start their day.

It got quiet once they were by themselves, and Cam caught Rhodes glancing around as if unsure of himself or what to say.

Rhodes took another sip of his coffee and stood up quickly, almost knocking his chair over and appearing suddenly a bit nervous at being alone with Cam. "I, umm... I better get going too," he said as he placed the mug in the sink.

"Yeah, I got walls to get ready for painting." Cam stood and frowned as he watched Rhodes almost drop his cup into the sink, then fidget toward the front door. *What the hell?*

"You, uh... have a nice day," Rhodes said before turning and hurrying out.

JACKSON SLID behind the steering wheel of his cruiser and sighed. He had just made a fool of himself. He had no doubt about it. He looked up to see Cam staring at him from the front door, a frown still on his face. Yep, a fool.

But as he'd been sitting in the kitchen, a sudden image of Cam and Grant going to town on top of the kitchen table had come to mind. The exact same table where he had been sitting at the moment. Finding himself overwhelmed with disgust… and desire—and what a weird combo that was—he'd known he had to get out of there immediately.

Was it possible they'd had sex last night? What a stupid question! Of course they'd had sex. This was Grant he was talking about. And didn't that do odd things to his innards? For some reason, Jackson felt angry at both of them. And disgusted. And jealous. Only it wasn't so much that he was jealous of Cam. He found he was more jealous of Grant for getting with Cam.

Well, isn't that just fantastic.

IT WAS inching up on noon when he heard the back door open and close. Cam had been busy all morning, prepping the walls and ceiling of the living room for painting. He'd covered all the furniture with a tarp and then used a sealant on all the water spots and spray paint.

Cam turned as he heard footsteps coming through the kitchen and toward him. Galen led the others and had something in his hand. At first Cam thought it was an old muddy rock, but as the boy got closer, it became all too clear what was in Galen's hand.

"Look what we found, Mr. Sanders." Galen opened up the muddy wallet to show all the cards and ID inside, with pictures that left no doubt who the ruined billfold belonged to. "Mrs. Evans lost this last week. And we found it! We're going to give it back to her. Won't she be happy?"

Dammit! Why? Why did they have to find that? Could life get any more irritating? He was pretty sure it couldn't.

Before Cam could even think of what he was doing, he tossed down the brush he'd been using and rushed toward Galen. "Give me that fuckin' wallet!"

As Cam's hand came up to snatch the sodden item from Galen's grasp, a strange thing happened. Galen flinched, his body curling in on itself and his arm lifting to shield his face. Tony and Luanne both gasped, Tony backing away and Luanne stepping forward as if she would jump between the two.

Cam froze and the kids did the same. His gaze flicking between the three children, eyes widening as he read what was clear on their faces. He knew that reaction well, and what caused it. There was suddenly a much deeper connection between himself and these three scraggly kids. With extreme care, Cam withdrew his hand and took a step back.

"Hey, buddy," Cam said as if speaking to a spooked animal. "Giving it back is a great idea, but I was just going to suggest we clean it up some first. Mrs. Evans wouldn't even recognize that nasty thing, right?"

Tony and Luanne seemed to relax, but Galen didn't respond so Cam stepped forward cautiously and placed a gentle hand on Galen's shoulder. "Hey. Sorry for cussing at you, okay? You don't ever need to be scared of me." Cam lifted the hand and patted Galen's arm several times, then took the wallet from his hand. "Come on, let's see what we can do to clean this up, and we have a pizza to order, too."

Cam headed off toward the kitchen, and after a moment, he heard the sound of three sets of feet following him. After putting the wallet on the counter, he searched under the sink for a scrub brush and the dish soap.

He filled the sink with warm water and one squirt of the soap, then pointed over at Luanne. "Pull out all the cards and papers. Everything but the fabric itself, then shove it down in here." He ruffled Galen's hair as he passed him. The boy still seemed a little shaken, and Cam got angry just thinking about why that might be. Except showing anger right then was the worst thing he could do, so he shoved the emotion down to consider later.

Instead, Cam grabbed his phone and waved it at the kids where they were gathered in front of the sink, watching the wallet turn the water brown as Luanne scrubbed away. "What do you like on your pizza?"

All three stared at him with blank expressions. Finally, Tony said, "There are choices?"

Cam chuckled and pulled down a menu from the refrigerator. After pulling out a chair and having a seat at the kitchen table, he read off the usual choices and showed them pictures of the specialty pizzas. After a round of appreciative hums and gurgling stomachs, Cam decided they needed a variety for taste testing.

TOMMASINA HAD followed the kids out the back door after lunch while Cam tossed the wallet in the washer on the gentle cycle, then returned to his work in the living room. The pizza had been good, and the kids had enjoyed eating all the different kinds. It had gotten loud as they'd talked about what they liked and didn't. While Cam wasn't used to kids or even a lot of noise in his house, he decided he kind of liked having these three around.

Before going back out, Luanne had tugged on Cam's sleeve. "Do you think I might be able to take a piece or two home to my brothers and sisters to try?"

Cam planned to consolidate all the leftover pizza and send it home with them. He was pretty sure they had never had pizza from a restaurant before. As Cam sealed over a bright red streak of spray paint, he considered the kids, especially Galen's reaction that morning. He was well aware of what caused a kid to flinch like that. He'd done it for years at any quick movement, and no one had ever stood up for him. He couldn't let that happen to these three. They were good kids and deserved better than that.

About an hour later, the group came back in through the kitchen and Luanne poked her head into the living room. "Mr. Sanders?"

Cam glanced around to see her hair plastered to her head with sweat. The two boys stood behind her in the same condition.

"You think we could get another glass of that Coca-Cola before we go back to working?"

"You drink all you want, kids. And why don't you stay inside for a while? I need a little help in here once you've had your break. Go on now."

As he heard the refrigerator open and glasses filling with ice, Tommasina came strolling into the living room and stopped. She seemed displeased with how everything was covered in tarps. She wrinkled her nose, presumably at the sealant smell, and turned away, strolling off to find some other place to laze away the afternoon.

"Sorry, girl," he apologized to her retreating form.

Cam spent most of the afternoon teaching the kids how to tape off the baseboards and crown molding, when to use a brush and when to use a roller, and even a few minutes on how not to get paint all over their siblings. He'd put each of them in one of his work shirts, which hung down to their knees, so it wasn't such a big deal for their clothes, but he really wanted as much of the paint as possible to go on the walls.

When Rhodes came to pick them up, they were washed and sitting on the front porch, ready to go. Cam waved good-bye as they drove off, taking home two whole pizzas once the consolidation was complete, then closed the door and headed into the kitchen where he pulled the wallet out of the dryer and started putting all the cards and papers back in as neatly as possible.

He needed to do this before he talked himself out of it. He knew he would too. He had already been back and forth on it with himself all afternoon. At one point, he even tried to figure a way he could convince the kids that the billfold wasn't really the one Mrs. Evans had lost.

The wallet wasn't completely clean, and it looked faded where they'd scrubbed at it, but it sure looked a hell of a lot better than it had all dripping with mud. After it was all put together, Cam left it on the counter and headed down the hall to the back bedroom, where he pried the floorboard up and pulled his money jar out. He counted out fifteen hundred dollars and then kept counting.

CHAPTER 14

AS JACKSON drove through town and out toward Ruby Mae's house, the three kids in the back kept the chatter going. He had to chuckle as they went on about how much fun it was to paint and what toppings they had gotten on their pizzas.

"One of them had pineapple on it!" Tony didn't sound at all pleased with that.

"I thought it was good," Luanne chimed in.

Jackson had to admit that Cam was doing well by the kids. Seeing the way he treated them was changing his opinion of the man, that was for sure.

"And guess what else happened today!" Galen cried out. "We found Mrs. Evans's wallet out in the backyard!"

Jackson's gaze shot up to look at the kids in the rearview mirror as they all started talking over each other again.

"Stop!" Jackson said. "One at a time, tell me what happened."

"Well, it was really muddy and all that money she said was in it was gone," Luanne said. "And at first, we thought Mr. Sanders was mad at us, but then he said he just wanted to clean it up some and took it. He said he'd give it back to her."

"Did he now?" Jackson ground his teeth. So much for changing his opinion of the man.

He stayed quiet the rest of the way to drop off the three kids, and after he'd made sure they were in the house, he turned the cruiser back toward Ida and Charles's house.

IDA AND Charles sat side by side on the sofa. Ida handed the faded wallet to Jackson as he dropped into the chair opposite them.

"I heard a knock on the door, and by the time I got there, the wallet was all that was on the front porch. Well, and this note." Charles handed the folded piece of paper to Jackson, who read it to himself.

The Watson kids found this on my property today. They might deserve a reward. They're good kids. Anyway, sorry for what I done.

Camden Sanders

"So he admits to stealing it," Jackson said. "I'll take this as evidence."

"And I disagree," Ida spoke up. "I'm sure he means he's sorry for spilling his tea at dinner. It made quite a mess, didn't it, Charles?"

Charles nodded and smiled at his wife.

"So you are going to let him get away with stealing your money?" Jackson asked, shocked.

"Open it." Ida gestured to the wallet.

Jackson unsnapped the faded fabric purse and opened it to see bills bulging from the compartment behind her driver's license and other cards. He pulled out the stack and started counting.

"There's over three thousand dollars here." Jackson stared at the bills.

Ida nodded. "Yes. I couldn't have earned that in interest if I'd put that money in a bank."

"But Ida," Jackson began.

"Maybe," Charles said in a wheezy voice, "we ought to let"— breath—"him steal your wallet"—breath—"every month." Charles was gasping but smiling, and Ida laughed along with him.

Jackson shook his head. "How do you know he didn't just give it back because he got caught?"

"Because he didn't get caught, Jackson. He could have explained away why it was in his yard. We could have suspected, but we couldn't have ever known for sure. Now here is where we allow him to change."

Jackson wasn't as sure as Ida and Charles. In fact, he was pretty damn pissed that Camden Sanders had taken these people's hard-earned money, and he planned to tell the asshole about it.

CAM SAT in his truck down the block from the Evans residence until Ida had answered her door, and then he drove himself back home and started working in the garage. It was cooler now, and with the bay doors open and the fan on, it was almost pleasant.

He had most of the cabinets cleaned out and washed up. He'd found tools of all kinds and salvaged as many as possible, only trashing the ones that were without any hope of being useful. The part he needed for the lift in the second bay had been ordered and should be in sometime the middle of the next week. He still had a long way to go, but it felt good to make some headway with his list of chores and see his business and house coming together.

He leaned back against the counter with a contented sigh. As much as it might stick in his craw, it also felt right nice to have finally returned that money to Ida and Charles.

Cam heard a car drive up and wandered up to the bay door to find Jackson Rhodes climbing out of his Mustang. "Howdy, Sheriff. You changed clothes to come back here? Is something wrong with your car?"

"I told you I'm not a sheriff," Rhodes said through gritted teeth, coming straight toward Cam at a fair clip with no apparent plans to slow down.

Cam took a step back and then another as Rhodes pushed up into his face, grabbing a handful of Cam's shirt for good measure.

"You stole that wallet."

"I did," Cam said just as aggressively, pushing his face forward until his nose touched Rhodes's.

"How could you steal from a little old lady?" Rhodes growled, still pushing Cam backward.

"I don't know. Sometimes I do things I regret later," Cam said in the same growl, attempting to get a similar hold on Rhodes.

"She might forgive you, but I know you are a slimy, no-good—" Rhodes lost his train of thought as Cam shoved back and the heel of Rhodes's foot caught on the edge of the ramp for the hydraulic lift.

Cam tightened his grip on the neck of Rhodes's T-shirt in an effort to catch him, but that didn't stop the big man from falling back, just added a resounding rip as the material gave way under the strain.

Rhodes landed with a thud and Cam followed him down. The landing pushed Cam's fisted hand up into Rhodes's chin, causing

Rhodes's teeth to clack around his *oomph* when Cam's weight dropped on him.

"You son of a—" Rhodes rolled and put Cam beneath him before Cam could say a word, then drew back his fist and let it fly. Cam only had time to screw his eyes shut before the meaty punch slammed into his jaw.

God, that hurt. It was like being hit by a freight train right in the mouth. He tasted copper and felt light-headed, but he sure as hell wasn't going down so easy. Cam shoved against Rhodes's chest, one hand meeting with bare skin through the rip in his T-shirt. Cam was so shocked by the contact he jerked his hand back.

Rhodes was rearing back for another punch, and Cam knew he had to stop that before it happened. He reached up, took hold of Rhodes's head on each side, just at the ears, and pulled forward with as much force as he could muster, bringing Rhodes in for one mean head-butt.

The move did exactly as intended. Rhodes gasped, dropping his arm and rolling off Cam and onto his back on the cement garage floor. Cam rolled with him, hoping to hold down the insane officer.

"This is police brutality," Cam screamed down at him.

Rhodes groaned. "I came here as a civilian, you asshole." With that, Rhodes bucked up to push Cam off and swung again.

Cam dodged the wild punch, then grabbed Rhodes by the wrists and pushed them back over his head. "I swear to God, I will head-butt you again if you don't stop." From this close proximity, Cam noticed blood coming from Rhodes's bottom lip and a goose egg coming up on his forehead. There were also bulging chest muscles displayed beneath the rip in Rhodes's T-shirt. And wasn't that a sight to see! Cam shook his head and refocused his attention on Rhodes's face.

With very little struggle, Rhodes pulled his hands from Cam's grasp, rolling at the same time to displace Cam's seat of power. As Rhodes bucked beneath him, right before he was sent back to the floor, Cam felt the hardness of an obvious erection grinding against his own. *Interesting.*

Cam tried to struggle out from under Rhodes but was caught by a tight grasp around his throat. Suddenly Cam couldn't breathe and instinct took over. He writhed and kicked and bucked beneath Rhodes until the hand loosened and Rhodes's expression changed from anger to something else entirely. Cam stared up into brown eyes the color of a fine whiskey and felt his heart skip a beat at the intensity he saw there. Then Rhodes's mouth crashed down on top of his own. The kiss was as brutal as the fight and tasted of blood, but Cam couldn't say that was a bad thing as he attempted to catch his breath around the tongue invading his mouth.

Cam pushed his hands up underneath Rhodes's ripped T-shirt, fingertips brushing against a whole lot of hard muscles and silky fur, then took charge of the situation by pushing Rhodes onto his back again.

"Mmm…. Now this is much better," Cam mumbled against Rhodes's lips, pushing up the shirt so Cam could get a better look at Rhodes's chest. He licked over golden brown nipples as Rhodes held on, rolling his head back and forth on the cement floor with a moan of pleasure. Cam sucked each in, one after the other, flicking them with his tongue and playing Rhodes like a violin. Then headed farther south.

Rhodes looked down in what appeared to be shock, but Cam wasn't giving him time to come to his senses. Cam wanted some of the big man, even if he might live to regret it.

Rhodes rubbed over Cam's shorn head, and for a moment, Cam wished his hair was long enough to hold on to. He unfastened Rhodes's pants in a hurry, but had to pause long enough to admire the big, thick cock hidden beneath the white briefs. He'd known Rhodes would wear BVDs. And wasn't that sexy as hell.

"I think that's the prettiest cock I've ever seen," Cam admitted before opening up and taking it as deep as he could. He hummed as he felt the big dick throb against his tongue and above him, Rhodes groaned with need.

Cam started moving, setting up a steady rhythm as he pumped and licked and sucked to his heart's content. Rhodes was making mumbled encouraging sounds, which might have been words but were spoken too softly and interrupted too often by grunts and moans to tell for sure.

Cam caught Rhodes's balls in one hand, then gently tugged and massaged in the same rhythm as the bobbing of his head. Jesus, Rhodes was beautiful, and this might be Cam's only chance to worship at his altar. Rhodes's narrow hips began to pump up in time with Cam's strokes, and it wasn't long before Rhodes tensed.

"Gonna… I can't…."

Cam simply reached around and gripped Rhodes's asscheeks, pulling him in. Rhodes cried out, arched, and then Cam was fighting to gulp down the abundance of cum that flooded his mouth. Once Rhodes pulsed out the last jet of semen, Cam pulled back and sat on his knees, wiping at his chin and grinning like he'd just won the lottery.

"Holy shit, Sheriff, that was fucking hot!"

Rhodes huffed but without any real anger, sitting up. "I'm not a fucking sheriff! And what if someone had come by and saw us?"

"The danger just makes it hotter, don't you think?" Cam raised a brow.

"No. Yes. I mean, people can't know—"

"I know. I get it." Cam stood and reached to help Rhodes up.

Rhodes knocked his hand away and stood by himself, then fastened his pants. "This doesn't change anything. And call me Jackson."

"All right, Jackson. See you tomorrow morning?" Cam asked.

"Yeah, bright and early." Jackson's expression was somewhere between a frown and a smirk. Then he headed out to his car.

Cam wiped blood from the corner of his mouth with the hem of his shirt as he watched Jackson drive off, then pulled down the garage door and closed up shop.

"Wow! Two days in a row, Tommasina," Cam exclaimed to his cat as he hobbled back toward the house. "I'm getting as bad as you."

CHAPTER 15

THE NEXT morning, Jackson groaned as he sat up and smacked the button to turn off his alarm. Everything hurt, and not in that way it usually did after a good workout or game of ball. This felt more like he'd been run over by an 18-wheeler. His head pounded with every step toward the bathroom, and all he could do was stand and stare in the mirror at the mess that was his face.

A big knot stood out above his left brow with bruising surrounding it as well as the eye below. His lower lip was swollen, a stripe of crusted red running across it from where it had split against his teeth. His ass, hips, and shoulders hurt from when he'd landed on the unforgiving concrete, which made it difficult to reach for the knobs of the shower or step over the lip of the tub and into the spray.

After a moment, he managed to extend his arm enough to turn the shower dial to massage, then turned and let it beat down on his shoulders and glutes. He groaned with both pleasure and pain. What had he been thinking? He was acting like some hormonal teenager or something.

Once Jackson had dried off, he popped a few Tylenol, then struggled into his uniform. He hoped this was going to be an easy day, because he wasn't sure he could climb a tree to save a cat or tackle and hold down Michael Peters to keep him from getting hurt during one of his autistic meltdowns.

With a travel mug of coffee and mirrored aviators on, Jackson headed out to the Watson house to pick up the kids. On the way, he called in.

"This is Jackson Rhodes, on duty, over."

"Good morning, Jackson. Over." Brian sounded much more cheerful than Jackson felt.

"Jennifer out again? Over." Jackson asked, starting to worry.

"Her son is giving her heck. She took the rest of the week off to deal with it. Over."

"That's a shame, Brian. I hope things get better for her. Over and out." Jackson replaced the mic and shook his head. Jennifer's teenage son was a handful. He'd already caused Jennifer fines for truancy from school and done a stint with their teen court for fighting and public disturbance. Jackson wasn't sure what the answer was for the boy.

WHEN JACKSON pulled up in front of the Watson house, he honked the horn instead of going to the door. He wasn't trying to be rude, but this was just not the day to risk running into Junior, and he didn't want to explain the bruises to Ruby either.

The kids came running out to the car and Ruby stepped out onto the front porch and waved. She appeared upset about something, but he didn't mull it over much once the three kids had climbed into the backseat. They were quiet and seemed sullen, so he simply shifted the car into reverse and backed out of the driveway with a wave to Ruby.

CAM WAS just stepping out of his truck when Jackson pulled up in his Hog Mountain Police vehicle. When the kids piled out of the backseat, he called to them. "I got groceries. Come help me lug them in."

He grabbed as many bags as he could carry and headed toward the door. "It looks like rain today so I thought we could work on painting some more."

There was a round of mumbles behind him and when he got to the kitchen, he turned to take a look at the motley crew who had followed him in. The three children all looked tired, shoulders bowed and steps sluggish. While he was worried that they might be getting sick, it did his heart good to see the state of Jackson's face. Cam's wasn't a whole lot better and he'd had to put up with some odd looks while paying for his groceries, but he had to admit that Jackson had gotten the worst of it.

"Well, well, what a cheerful bunch this morning. And, Sheriff, you are looking mighty fine, if I do say so myself." Cam grinned, which brought on a wince of pain. His jawbone felt as if it might be cracked. He had bruising along the jawline and the inside of his mouth looked like hamburger. Luckily it only showed as puffiness on the outside.

Jackson frowned at Cam but didn't respond. Probably because of the kids. The fine officer was a bit fidgety if Cam wasn't mistaken. Well, shit. Looked like Jackson Rhodes wasn't good with casual hookups.

Galen had finally noticed the state of both of their faces and stepped closer. "Why y'all so busted up?" he asked. Luanne and Tony abandoned the putting away of groceries to see for themselves.

Cam grinned and looked to Jackson for an explanation, who seemed to stutter over his words before finally coming up with a gem. "We had an accident... playing football."

None of the kids appeared convinced, and Galen humphed his disbelief but turned back to the groceries. "We having cereal this morning, Mr. Sanders?"

"Yeah," Cam answered and turned his attention to the coffeepot he'd started before running to the store. "Pull down the bowls and set the table."

"I got a travel cup in the car," Jackson said with his head down. "I'm gonna get going. Y'all have a good day, ya hear?"

The kids all waved, and Cam joined in before settling himself at the table with the kids and his newly purchased selection of cereal.

THE MORNING passed at a sedate pace. Thunder boomed in the distance, but the rain held off. The dark clouds seemed to fit the dampened moods as they all focused on painting, with little of the chatter that had filled the room the day before.

Cam wondered what had changed with the kids and worked on a way to ask. Right before lunch, Tony reached across Cam for a rag, causing the long sleeve of his shirt to pull up enough for Cam to see the bruises that ringed his wrist. Cam's attention jumped from the injury to Tony's face, but Tony, realizing his mistake, pulled his hand back and turned away. Glancing to Luanne and Galen, Cam noticed they too were being careful not to look his way.

They both had on long sleeves too. In the summer. In Georgia. Why hadn't he noticed? He ground his teeth and set down the paintbrush.

"Time for some lunch. Gonna go clean up. Y'all wash up in the bathroom," Cam said and headed to the kitchen. He cleaned his hands at the sink before pulling out cold fried chicken and biscuits from the grocery deli counter. He had just sat down after pouring tea for everyone when the kids came piling into the kitchen. They sat in silence and began eating.

Cam watched them for a moment before asking, "Gonna tell me where you got those bruises?"

Galen smirked and answered, "Had an accident playing football."

Son of a bitch. Smartass kids. "Okay, look…. Jackson and I got mad and we scuffled, okay? It's the God's honest." He held up his hand as if taking an oath. "I'm sure you and your brothers and sisters do that, right? Now, tell me what happened."

There was lots of glancing and wordless conversation between the kids, but finally Luanne sat up straight and looked Cam in the eye. "Daddy got drunk last night. And he gets mad sometimes when he drinks." She shrugged like it was nothing out of the ordinary and not a thing to do about it.

Cam had to disagree with that. He just needed to figure out what he was going to do. He was finishing his second piece of chicken, deep in thought, when a knock came at the door. Cam opened it to find a familiar face.

"Howdy. There was a note on the garage saying to knock here? I don't know if you remember me. I came by last week with the bicycle?"

Cam nodded and swallowed his last bite of chicken. "Yes, sir. Mr. Barnes, was it?"

"Good memory! I used to have one… I think." They both laughed at the joke. "I got more bikes and wanted you to check the tires and air them up."

"Will do," Cam said. "Let me grab my keys and I'll be right over." Cam closed the door after Mr. Barnes turned back toward the garage. He scooped up his key ring and called into the kitchen. "Got some work at the garage. Clean up your mess and no painting until I get back."

There were mumbles in response. Cam took that as agreement and headed out the door.

Cam was working on the last of the bikes he'd pulled from the back of Mr. Barnes's pickup when he felt Tommasina weave between his legs. Feeling sure he'd left her in the house, he turned to find the kids standing near the garage door, checking out the bikes with expressions very close to awe.

Cam thought he was pretty tough, but the look in those kids' eyes just about did him in. He huffed out a breath and reached down to pet his cat. Casually, he asked, "Y'all know how to ride?"

"We found an old bike down in the woods and we took turns on it 'til Daddy gave it to the pawn shop," Galen said. Cam could hear the resentment in the boy's voice and knew it would only grow deeper if things didn't change.

"Watch them while I go settle up with Mr. Barnes, will ya?" Cam strode off without waiting for an answer. His stomach was simmering with an anger he thought he'd buried with his father.

When Mr. Barnes pulled out of Cam's garage, his pickup was light three bicycles and Cam had promised to repair any further bikes the man collected for free.

Luanne, Galen, and Tony all stood staring between the bikes and Cam, seemingly unsure why they hadn't been taken but afraid to ask.

"They stay here and you only ride them on my property, not in the street. And not 'til you finish your work, you hear?"

While he'd made his speech, each of the kids had begun to bounce, smiles spreading across their faces.

Cam grinned back. "Work is done for today so get busy riding. And be careful, okay?"

"Yes, sir!" they said in unison, each grabbing a set of handlebars and hurrying off.

Cam sighed. He needed a shower and to get dressed before Jackson came back to pick up the kids. He had plans.

Cam could hear the kids outside screaming and laughing as he tied his shoes, perched on the edge of his bed. He'd taken a long shower and now felt a little more human than he had that morning, the hot water washing away many of the lingering aches from the fight.

He headed downstairs and grabbed a handful of apples before going out on the front porch. He sat on the steps and bit into one, enjoying the cool breeze with the smell of rain in it. He could feel the heaviness in the air and knew the storms wouldn't hold off much longer.

When the kids came zooming around the corner of the house, he held up a hand, calling them over. They dropped their bikes on the grass and came to sit with him, each taking an apple and talking over one another with tales of their adventures in the last hour.

It was then that Jackson pulled into the driveway. The kids waved and screamed with excitement as Jackson climbed out from behind the wheel and grinned at the kids. He still had on those stupid sunglasses that made him look even more like an asshole cop than usual, but the man couldn't help looking hot as hell, even with the bruised-up face and swollen lip. The swelling had gone down some over the day, and now it just made him look tough.

"Mr. Sanders got us bikes," Tony called and pointed to them scattered across the lawn.

Jackson took off his glasses, a brow raised to Cam. Cam shrugged. "Mr. Barnes had some extra." Then he turned to the kids. "Go store those in the shed while I talk to Officer Rhodes."

While the kids were obviously disappointed to be done playing, they did as told, wandering off around the corner of the house while pushing their new prized possessions.

"Smart not to send those home with them," Jackson said as he watched the kids' retreating backs.

"I got a favor to ask you, Sheriff," Cam said, changing the subject.

Jackson looked like he was going to correct him but only shook his head and asked, "And what would that be?"

"I want to ride with you to take the kids home." Cam tried to appear as harmless as possible while Jackson considered him.

"Why?" he asked suspiciously.

"I wanted to see where they live, meet their family. Ask if they can keep coming to help me paint. That sort of thing."

Jackson was quiet so long Cam started to wonder if he was going to answer. Finally, he nodded. "Okay. They're dirt poor."

Cam nodded. Obviously it was more than that and Jackson knew it, but Cam needed to get that ride before he pushed the matter.

When the kids came back around the side of the house, Cam stood and came down the steps. "We're ready when you are," he said to Jackson, walking down the driveway toward the cruiser.

Cam got in the passenger seat and the kids climbed in the back. They looked sweaty from playing in long sleeves all day but happier than they had been that morning. He was glad of it.

He turned back to them. "I'm gonna see if you three can keep helping me. Is that okay with you?"

Cam got three squealing affirmatives and grinned at their excitement.

"Is that why you are coming over, Mr. Sanders?" Luanne asked.

"Yeah." Cam nodded. "I figure your mom will want to meet me."

They all seemed confused by Cam's logic but didn't question him. Jackson backed out of the driveway and started toward town. After a few moments in silence, Cam glanced over at Jackson.

"So tell me about their daddy." Cam kept his voice at a level he hoped would avoid the conversation attracting the children's interest.

Jackson cut his gaze over to Cam, then turned his attention back to the road. "Junior's a few years older than me. Got a drinking problem. Not a real nice guy at times. Why?"

"No, I mean…. Okay, if you were on a gladiator show and you had to fight him, would you win?"

Jackson glanced over again, this time as if he were evaluating Cam for the mental ward, but he answered. "Without a doubt."

"Good to know."

"Why? What do you have planned?" Jackson was now alternating his attention between Cam and the road.

Cam smiled. "Do you trust me?"

Both Jackson's eyebrows lifted as high as they could and his voice got loud enough to get the kids' attention. "NO!"

"Then just look at this as a trust-building exercise, okay? I need you to count to a hundred once you first start thinking you need to step in. Got it?"

Jackson was just pulling into the driveway, and as he pushed the car into park, he asked again, "What are you planning?"

The kids all piled out, and Cam opened his door, leaning back in before he closed it behind him. "Just get the kids in the house for me and trust me. They got bruises, Jackson." He closed the door before Jackson could say any more and walked briskly up to the porch where a man was sitting in a rocker with a glass of tea. As he approached, a small woman with a baby on her hip came to the screen door, and four other kids pushed past her to meet up with Tony, Galen, and Luanne.

As Cam reached the first step, Jackson pushed past him, arms out to catch all the kids. "Got a minute, Ruby? I just needed to ask you something inside."

Cam held out his hand for the man, who he assumed must be Junior.

The man looked him up and down and finally pushed himself up from the chair and offered his hand. "Who are you, and what do you want?"

Cam's grin was more a showing of gritted teeth. He took the hand in his own and squeezed until he felt the bones grind, then used it to steer Junior back and against the side of the house, out of view of the screen door.

"Cam Sanders. You these kids' daddy?"

Junior grunted and tried to pull his hand away. Cam pulled him a couple of inches from the wall and then shoved him back against it. "Only polite to answer a man when he introduces himself."

"Yeah. What the fuck do you want?" Junior was still struggling but not hard enough to make any difference.

Cam leaned in closer and whispered, "When I was a little boy, my father liked to drink and beat on me."

"What has that—?"

Cam slammed him against the wall again. "Don't interrupt." Cam looked him dead in the eye. "I never got a chance to get even with him 'cause he died while I was in prison." Cam offered the man a grin that he'd perfected to frighten much larger men.

Junior stopped struggling but called out, "Jackson!"

"Here's what we're gonna do," Cam continued. "The kids are going to keep coming over, and you are going to never touch them again. Or your wife. If I hear a whisper of anything like that happening, I'll come back for another visit. Got it?"

"Officer Rhodes!"

Cam slammed him against the wall again. "I asked you a question."

"Yeah, yeah, I got it," Junior said, and Cam stepped back just as Jackson came out the screen door with Ruby right behind.

Cam gave Ruby a genuine smile and shook her hand while Jackson ignored any complaints that Junior tried to raise. After speaking with Ruby about the kids, Cam waved and smiled to the three.

"See you tomorrow morning," he said and then climbed in the police car with Jackson.

CHAPTER 16

DROPS OF rain hit the windshield as they pulled away from the Watson house. Jackson steered the car to the side of the road and stopped once he'd gotten far enough away, then turned to Cam with a frown on his face.

"What do you think you were doing back there?"

Cam shrugged. "Just having a conversation with the man."

Jackson threw his hands up and let them fall with a thump on the steering wheel. "I can't let you go around threatening violence."

"All I threatened was that I'd come back and visit," Cam responded.

"But the threat of violence was implied," Jackson explained.

"You think that's what Junior got out of what I said?"

"Yes! That's exactly what he got out of that." It was frustrating that he had to explain this to Cam.

"Good. Then my work here is done." Cam grinned and nudged Jackson. "Haven't you ever wanted to punch him in the face?"

Jackson sighed. "Every time I see him. But I'm a policeman. I can't do that."

"And he can't beat his kids either. Someone needs to stand up to him."

"I try. But we have to have evidence and we have to follow the laws. If CPS gets involved, most likely Ruby is going to lose those kids and they are going to get split up into foster homes who knows where. Sometimes right is a complicated thing."

Cam nodded solemnly. "Ain't that the truth. And they got a whole herd of kids too."

Jackson agreed wholeheartedly with that. He pulled back onto the road and they both stewed in their own juices as the rain beat down harder.

Cam pointed out the window as they drove through town. The diner sign was glowing bright in the downpour. "Hey, can we stop and let me order some food to take home?"

Jackson pulled into an open parking space on the street. "Sounds like a good idea. I think I'll get something too."

They ran through the rain, meeting at the door and chuckling as they shook like dogs to get some of the water off themselves. The bell rang as they entered, the air-conditioning making it a little chilly after getting soaked. Heading straight to the register, Cam picked up a menu and looked it over. Jackson shivered and rubbed his arms. He hadn't planned on being soaked to the skin. He had a police-issued rain slicker in the trunk, but he probably would have gotten even wetter just trying to get to it.

The waitress came by and smiled. She reached under the counter and handed each of them a clean hand towel as she spoke. "Hey, guys. Have a seat and wait this out. I'll bring you a cup of coffee while you decide."

Jackson raised a brow and looked at Cam questioningly as he ran the towel across his still-dripping hair.

Cam shrugged and headed for a booth, holding his menu and patting his face with the towel. "Probably drown the food trying to get it home right now."

Jackson had to agree with that. He slid into the booth across from Cam and pulled a menu from the holder on the table. He about had it memorized, but it gave him something to focus on that wasn't Camden Sanders, and that was a good thing. The man was far too handsome with those glowing ice blue eyes and chiseled features. Not to mention the way his wet clothes clung to his body.

Jackson shook his head and huffed out a breath. He had no business even thinking such thoughts. It would lead to nothing but trouble.

The waitress appeared at that moment, sliding a cup of coffee in front of each of them and placing a cream pitcher between them. "Y'all know what you want?"

"Does the meatloaf come with gravy?" Cam asked.

"It's a special red gravy, real flavorful," she answered, leaning against the table with her pen and pad ready.

"Yeah, that sounds good. I want that and mashed potatoes and lima beans. Can you make it a double serving of meatloaf? And sweet tea too."

She nodded and turned to Jackson. "What can I get you? Gonna have the regular, Jackson?"

"Is it chicken and dressing night?" Jackson looked up over the menu. He knew it was. He wasn't sure what was with him right then, but he felt odd sitting out in public with Cam, like everyone would know they had done something together.

"Yes, sir." She grinned and winked.

"Then that's what I'll have. With green beans and cream corn. And I'll take a sweet tea too." He had no excuse for the menu anymore, so he put it back in the holder and stirred a little cream into his coffee. It felt good just holding the cup between his hands.

With the waitress gone, it got quiet for a moment or two as they each sipped at the coffee. Finally, Cam looked up with a smile. A smile that could ensure the man got away with murder. That thought almost stopped Jackson's heart. What if Cam had killed people? But it didn't take more than a second for Jackson to come to the conclusion that Cam couldn't do something like that. He was still off in his own thoughts when Cam spoke, and brought his attention back to here and now.

"So, Sheriff, I guess you always lived here in Hog Mountain?"

Jackson huffed at the nickname but let it go. "Yeah, born and raised. Not many move to Hog Mountain, mostly away. Unless it's to those new subdivisions, that is."

"But they aren't *really* Hog Mountain, are they?" Cam asked.

"That's according to how you mean. They are within my jurisdiction, but do they represent what I think of as Hog Mountain?" Jackson shrugged. "I don't think so." Most of the town wasn't happy about the new additions to their town. They worried at the changes that would come, but no one was refusing the taxes and extra revenue coming from their new citizens.

Cam turned the cream pitcher in circles, and Jackson couldn't help admiring the callused hands. They weren't big and burly like one would expect from a mechanic. In fact, they were a bit delicate, if you could call a hand covered in tattoos that. Cam's fingers were long and slender. Jackson could imagine them gliding over a piano's keys or playing an intricate piece on the violin or driving him insane with long strokes.

"I guess you don't think I'm Hog Mountain material either, then?" Cam asked.

Jackson opened his mouth to give some quick platitude, some assurance that wasn't thought out or sincere, but stopped himself. There was no easy answer to that question, was there? "I guess that remains to be seen, Mr. Sanders," he finally answered, then leaned in to take a sip of his coffee.

The jingle of bells announced the opening of the door to the diner, but since Jackson had his back to the entrance, he didn't bother looking to see who was coming in. He'd hoped, with the weather the way it was, he wouldn't have a lot of people in the diner to see him having dinner with Cam Sanders. But as he looked up, he found Grant Moore staring down at them, his eyes narrowed.

"Look what the cat dragged in," Grant said loud enough for everyone to hear. Somehow Grant had made it into the diner without getting wet. Of course, Grant never looked like a hair was out of place. It was a little creepy, but still a bit enviable.

Before Jackson could come up with a response, Cam grinned, a smile far different from the one he had used when talking to Jackson. This one was just a little frightening, making a person wonder what kind of thoughts were lurking in that mind of his.

"Grant! What a surprise." Cam's voice was just as loud as Grant's, and the few people in the diner were turning to look. "Thanks for the house call the other night. I sure slept like a baby. How about you?"

Jackson made himself busy adding more cream to coffee that didn't need it. If he could have climbed under the table, he would have.

Grant blanched, turned to see who was listening, then leaned closer to hiss at Cam. "You better watch yourself, Cam Sanders. I know about you."

Cam leaned in too, as if sharing a juicy secret, and stage-whispered, "I know about you too, Grant. And I'm not trying to convince anyone I'm anything other than what I am." Then Cam's smile grew bigger and he pushed himself up from the table. "Come eat with us," he said louder, thumping Grant on the back a little harder than necessary.

Grant shrugged out from under Cam's hold and sneered at both of them before heading toward the back of the diner, not saying another word.

"Well, that was special. What did we see in him? I guess an available hole?" Cam mused.

Jackson turned red and glanced around, then leaned across the table, speaking through clenched teeth, "I know you are used to Atlanta, where anything goes, but this is Hog Mountain. And gossip gets around faster than you can drive 'cross town. Shut down whatever you got going, you hear?"

Cam huffed and deflated a little. "Yeah, I get it. But it sure was fun screwing with Grant."

After a moment, Jackson grinned and chuckled. "Yeah, seeing him the color of paste was a real treat. Not many he can't control."

Cam laughed. "I don't like threats, Jackson. They stick in my craw. But I also don't want to throw you under the bus. You're all right in my opinion. I'll watch myself."

"Thanks," Jackson responded, trying not to blush for God's sake. The waitress came with their food and saved him from further embarrassment. As he dug into his dinner, he caught Grant giving them a nasty look from a table toward the back. If Jackson knew Grant, they hadn't heard the last of this.

THE RAIN had slowed to a drizzle as they drove toward Cam's house, both full and quiet. When Jackson pulled into the driveway as close as he could to the front porch, Cam let out a gasp, sitting up straight.

"Shit!" Cam pushed the door open and jumped out as soon as the car stopped moving.

Jackson quickly assessed the situation, searching for the cause of alarm, but relaxed when he discovered that Cam's upset came from the wet cat sitting beside the door, a look of indignation on her furry face.

Cam shoved the door open and let the cat inside, then leaned back out to wave Jackson in.

Jackson knew it was a bad idea. He should refuse and head for home, but Cam was like a siren or something. As much as he didn't want to like him, he was finding that he did. A little. With a sigh, he popped open his door and climbed out.

Cam was kneeling in the living room with a towel, drying off the old orange tabby that had probably lived outside in all kinds of weather for years. Cam seemed to really like the cat.

Cam looked up and gestured toward the kitchen. "I got some beers if you want one."

Jackson shook his head. "Still in my uniform and I have to drive home. I'm good."

Cam nodded to his sofa. "Wanna watch something? I kinda get one channel, or I could put in a movie."

Jackson laughed as he checked out the old TV and the VCR sitting below it. Did they even release movies on video cassette anymore? "Nah. I really need to get going." Jackson backed toward the door and found Cam following him. "I'll see you in the morning." Jackson hoped that was enough talking and he could escape, but Cam grabbed his arm and pushed him against the wall beside the door.

Once close, Cam smiled, and Jackson was a little spellbound. Cam continued to move in, slow but steady, finally pressing himself full-body to Jackson and leaning in for a gentle kiss. "Relax, Sheriff. Just a little stress relief, right?"

Jackson nodded dumbly and was about to go in for another kiss when his cell phone went off in his pocket, causing him to jump and pull away, not stopping until he had crossed the entire living room like the person calling knew what he was doing or something. *Dammit!*

Jackson ran a hand through his hair and answered the phone. "Jackson here."

"Jackson, it's Daddy. The Highway Patrol is calling for aid from the department. There's been a bad accident out on the interstate, just south of our exit. I'm calling in off-duty officers to go help. You up for it?"

He knew his dad was asking if he was sober. That would be about the only reason he would get out of it, and the only reason Jackson would even consider not going. "Yeah, Dad. I can head that way right now unless they need equipment from the station."

"James is taking the halogen lamps and extra flares. It's bad from what I hear, Jackson, and the rain is supposed to last all night. Dress warm and be careful, son."

"Yes, sir. Love you, Daddy." Jackson hung up and looked up to find Cam listening.

"Is there a problem?" Cam asked.

"A big wreck on the interstate. I got to go," Jackson answered, already working through what he might need for the evening.

"Hold on." Cam rushed off up the stairs and Jackson frowned, confused.

"I really have—" Jackson was saying when thumping footsteps came back down the stairs.

Cam handed a couple of thermal undershirts over to Jackson. "I figure everything on top has to be regulation uniform, but this might help underneath. To keep you warm, I mean. And here." He headed toward the kitchen and came back with a few energy bars and some bottled water.

"Thanks, Cam." Jackson took the offerings. Thunder rumbled as he turned toward the door, the rain beating harder against the tin roof. It was going to be a long night, and Jackson wasn't looking forward to it.

As Jackson stepped out on the porch, Cam said, "Be safe, Sheriff."

Jackson smiled, then ran out into the rain.

CHAPTER 17

CAM YAWNED as he sat on the side of the bed. The morning was pale and gloomy, with a drizzle still falling after a night of heavy thunderstorms. He stood with a long stretch, then scratched his belly and headed for the shower and the start of his day.

As he made coffee and got down bowls for cereal, he considered what he would do with the kids all day. They would be disappointed they wouldn't get to ride their bikes, and it was probably too moist in the old house to paint. Maybe he could take them to a movie.

As he watched the rain out the kitchen window over the sink, he remembered that Jackson had been out in the storms the night before. That had to have sucked. *People need to be more considerate and have their accidents in the light of day.* Cam chuckled at his absurdity.

When he heard a car's tires on the gravel drive, Cam headed for the front door and threw it open. He wondered if Jackson had been home at all or if he was coming straight from whatever scene he'd been working. The kids piled out and ran for the porch, but Cam stood frozen in confusion as a police officer that was obviously not Jackson Rhodes climbed out from behind the wheel and walked toward him.

Cam glanced at the kids, who smiled as they clambered up the stairs. "Officer Rhodes had to work all night," Luanne offered as she wiped her feet.

Okay, that made sense. Cam released a breath he hadn't known he was holding and offered his hand to the policeman now stepping onto his porch. "How's it going? Cam Sanders."

The man shook his hand. "Leland Simmons. I brought them over." He gestured to the door of the house, indicating the three who were no longer in sight. "But I don't think I'll make it back by to take 'em home. You gonna be able to handle it?"

"Yeah, no problem," Cam replied. "So Jackson got the day off for his trouble, then?"

Leland frowned and looked down at his highly shined shoes. "Uh... I guess you haven't been listening to the news or anything?"

Cam felt some body part wedge itself into his throat so tightly he couldn't swallow, and he was sure he was going to choke. And yet he stood there without showing any sign of distress, just staring until Leland continued.

"They got the injured from the wreck cleared by midnight, but had the scene to work and all the cars to tow, road to sweep of debris, you know?" Leland ticked all the duties on his fingers as he leaned back against the post of the porch railing, but only for the moment it took him to realize the pillar was unstable and would likely dump him out into the muddy yard if he continued.

Cam needed a seat anyway, so he waved the officer to one of the rockers and they both took a load off. Cam waited for him to continue.

"Anyway, some driver fell asleep at the wheel and crashed his tractor trailer into the mess. It was bad. I don't know all the details, but there are a few didn't make it, including the trucker, I hear. Jackson is at Vernon Wiggins Medical Center off Highway 365 and it sounds like he ain't gonna be transporting kids for a while. You may have to find another way of getting them here, you know?"

"Yeah, yeah, I will," Cam replied. Right. Jackson Rhodes was just a policeman that ferried kids back and forth to his house, right? "Thanks for bringing them over."

Leland stood. Cam followed suit and shook his hand again, then the man was gone, running across the lawn to his car. Cam watched as the police car backed out of the drive, then stared at the drizzle tapping against the leaves on the bushes in front of his dilapidated old house.

It was one of the mysteries of life as far as Cam was concerned. How could people like Jackson, the Evanses, and the kids in his house suffer, while people like Harold seemed bulletproof and unstoppable? It was so unfair. But then, he had learned that life was unfair. Cam felt bad for all the times he'd given Jackson a hard time. He imagined Jackson lying in a hospital bed, hooked up to a dozen different machines, and his stomach turned.

He was still deep in thought when he heard a soft voice behind him. "Mr. Sanders?" Luanne said. "We already ate. You want us to start painting or something?"

Cam shook off his melancholy and turned toward her. "Nah. It's too wet to be painting. You guys up for a road trip?" Cam wasn't at all sure what he was doing, but he knew he needed to do something. "Officer Rhodes got hurt last night, and I thought we'd go visit him at the hospital."

Luanne seemed shocked at the news, but she nodded quickly. "Okay. I never been to the hospital. Is he okay?"

Cam smiled at Luanne, although he didn't much feel like it. "Yeah, that officer said he was good. Let's get ready to go."

THE HOSPITAL was nicer than Cam had expected. Of course, his only recent experiences with hospitals were in prison, and those were about as dated as they came. The kids seemed just as interested in their surroundings, and were quiet like they were kinda scared of the big building. Cam had to admit the place was a little intimidating, especially when their footsteps echoed down the hallway as they approached a lady sitting behind a sign that read Information.

They paused in front of the desk with a bank of elevators beyond and found out that Jackson was in a room on the third floor. When they stepped into the elevator, Tony rushed to push the button that would take them to the right floor. In the enclosed space, the kids seemed more animated and obviously excited at this adventure. Cam smiled to see them having fun, even if this wasn't such a happy occasion.

Signs outside the elevator pointed them in the right direction, but Cam slowed as he saw men in uniform standing around outside several of the rooms. It wasn't like he was doing anything wrong by being there, but he couldn't simply erase all the old fears. He knew from experience that sometimes cops didn't need a reason to fuck with someone. He wrapped his arms around the kids' shoulders and guided them quickly past the officers and to the nurses' desk farther down.

A harried-looking woman with a tag reading "Sandy" stood behind the counter, her attention on a file she was writing in. She glanced up at Cam, then down to the kids before holding up a finger for them to wait. She continued to scribble a moment before closing the file a little harder than was needed and taking a breath.

"May I help you?" she asked, the words sounding weary.

Cam gave her one of his best smiles and she seemed to perk a little, even smiling back. "Sandy, I brought these kids to visit Jackson Rhodes. They just want to see he's okay and all." He left out that he also wanted to see that the officer was alive and well. Cam knew he was leading the nurse to believe the kids were somehow related to Jackson and that was fine by him. Anything he needed to do to get them in.

Sandy took a moment, seeming to consider the request, then nodded. "His parents have been in with him, but I think they went to get some coffee. If you don't stay long, I think it will be just fine." She came out from behind the desk and headed for one of the rooms closest to the station. She walked as if she were in a race and planned on winning, causing Cam and the kids to rush to keep up.

But as she pushed the door open to allow them entry, Cam's steps slowed then came to a halt. The kids stopped too and turned back in question.

"I…." Cam felt a bit panicked. "Is he… okay? For the kids to see, I mean?"

Sandy nodded. "He's even awake. Well, kinda." She laughed and walked farther into the room and beyond Cam's line of sight, but he could hear her say "Mr. Rhodes? You up for some visitors?"

Cam heard a grunt that he could readily recognize as Jackson's, so he stepped closer to get a look. The kids followed him into the room, and Cam smiled when he got a gander of Jackson all laid up in the bed, his eyes a little unfocused from the pain meds and his right arm in a big white cast.

Jackson gave what might have been a smile in return. He appeared a little embarrassed at his predicament but was trying his best to find the humor, at least the part of him that was aware enough.

"What happened, Sheriff? Wild Bart catch you with your pants down?"

Jackson snorted, and the kids piled a little closer, wanting to hear the story too.

"Truck hit a car and it hit me." Jackson's words were more than a little slurred, and Cam turned to the nurse, who was checking some machine, to make sure that was okay.

She nodded and mouthed, "Pain meds." Then she left them to visit.

"So you broke your arm?" Cam figured that wasn't really cause to be laid up with all these monitors hooked to him, but what did he know?

Jackson's eyes popped open as if he'd almost fallen asleep, and he grinned like a lush on a bender. "Spleen was busted. Said I almost died or something. Broke some ribs and popped a lung." His eyes started to close again, and then with one eye cocked funny, suddenly Jackson said, "Hey, kids! What are you doing here?"

Cam rolled his eyes at how loopy Jackson was. While the kids talked, Cam sat down in one of the chairs in the room and took a deep breath. *Wow!* While it sounded like Jackson had really been hurt, it appeared he was going to be okay. Cam discovered that meant a lot more to him than he thought it would.

"Is that pee?" Tony exclaimed, pointing at the catheter bag hanging off the side of the bed. The other kids turned in fascination and released a chorus of "Oh gross!" while Jackson snort-laughed.

Cam pushed himself out of the chair to tell the kids it was time to leave and stop embarrassing the hell out of Jackson, maybe give him a chance to rest, when the door to the room opened and a man and woman entered. From looks alone, Cam could tell the two were Jackson's parents, and he felt weird being caught in the room with their son, even though he hadn't snuck in or anything and he had all his clothes on.

Mr. Rhodes paused when he saw the visitors, then grinned at the kids. Jackson noticed his parents and said, "Mom, Dad, this is Camden Sanders. He brought these guys up to see me."

Cam found himself the center of attention and gave his best smile. "Mr. and Mrs. Rhodes, it's a pleasure to meet you."

"Nice to meet you too, son. You can call me Walter. Everyone else does. And my wife is Pamela, but some call her Pam." Mr. Rhodes clapped Cam on the shoulder, then turned back to his own son. "Everything okay in here?"

Mrs. Rhodes smiled and nodded at Cam but was obviously more concerned with Jackson. "How you feeling, darlin'? Need anything?"

"'M good, Momma," Jackson said, never opening his eyes. "Yeah, just fine." His lips curled into a close-lipped smile to rival that of a seriously tanked stoner.

"We're gonna head out," Cam announced, waving to the kids. Then he turned back to Jackson and his parents. "Think it would be okay if I dropped by again?" Cam wasn't sure why he asked, what he thought he could do for the man that his own family couldn't, but it was already out there and he couldn't much unsay it.

"Actually, Mr. Sanders," Walter started.

"Don't you dare, Walter," Pamela spoke over him. "We've discussed this. The trip is cancelled."

Cam wasn't sure what either of them was talking about. Jackson seemed to be trying to pry his eyes open to get in on the conversation, but for all Cam knew, he was going to interject something about manatees just being overweight mermaids or how weird the word *sandwich* sounded if you said it over and over.

"Dad. Dad. Dad, dad, daddaddaddadmom," Jackson repeated until it was just one word, then he seemed to forget what he wanted to say and went silent.

Cam glanced between Walter and Pamela, wondering how rude it would be to just walk out and never look back. How had asking if he could visit their son started some family thing?

Jackson appeared to be asleep, so no help was coming from that direction.

"Okay, well, like I said, we're—" But Cam was interrupted before he could finish.

"Go," Jackson said without opening his eyes, startling everyone. At first, Cam thought he was talking to him, like he didn't want him there or was warning him to run for his life. Then he continued, sort of. "Don't cancel, Momma. Cam can take care of me."

What? Take care of him? What did that even entail, and why did he have to be the one to do it?

Pamela smiled at Cam like he'd been the one to offer. "That's nice of you, but I'm not leaving my son like this."

"I.... What?" Cam was at a loss.

"Pam is the scheduled speaker at a Baptist women's conference. It's a big honor." Walter nodded and it was obvious he was proud of his wife. "It's not 'til Thursday morning, but she has decided to cancel." It was also obvious that Walter didn't agree with his wife's decision.

It wasn't like Jackson was going to be much trouble, all laid up in the hospital. "Well, I can come visit him every day if you need me to."

Walter patted his back. "That's good of you. But the doctor plans on him being released by then."

"Stop talking about me like I'm not here. I'm taking care of Jackson and that is that." Pamela was frowning at Cam like he was the one arguing with her.

Released? Oh boy. He didn't know anything about taking care of someone, especially someone who was injured, and all he needed was a cop in the house. Even if it was Jackson Rhodes, all laid up and helpless….

"Yeah, I think that would be best," Cam agreed, like he had some say in it.

"We can help," Luanne interjected, then turned to Jackson's parents. "We go to Mr. Sanders's house to do yard work."

"And paint!" Tony added.

"And paint…," Jackson said, eyes still closed. "Cam's gonna take care of me, Momma." Why did he keep saying things like that?

Pamela smiled and patted Jackson's hand. "We'll discuss this later, honey."

Cam nodded, although he knew she wasn't talking to him. "Sure enough. We're gonna get." He waved the kids out and herded them down the hall and past the policemen gathered around one of the other doors. What the hell was Jackson doing volunteering him for this shit? At least his mom had more sense than to put him in charge of a sick person's care. It was a wonder Cam could even take care of himself. And here he was responsible for three kids too. Speaking of which, he needed to entertain them for the afternoon. It occurred to him then, that prospect wasn't as bad as he would have thought in the past.

CHAPTER 18

SATURDAY MORNING, Cam found himself at loose ends. He didn't have children coming over or any real plans for the day so he took his time getting started for a change. With a fresh cup of coffee in hand, he and Tommasina went out to the front porch for a bit. The afternoon before, he'd taken the kids to a movie after they left the hospital. Cam had enjoyed seeing their faces light up with excitement as the theater had darkened and the movie began. They'd each had their laps full of snacks and sat totally enraptured for the entire show. He smiled as he thought about them now. It was hard to believe how much he had grown to like the kids in just a week. Enough to miss having them around on a quiet Saturday morning. He rocked and enjoyed the cool breeze until his coffee was gone, but soon enough his thoughts got to firing on Harold and what might be happening in Atlanta. That was a topic he needed to keep his mind away from, so he pulled himself up from the chair and headed back inside.

He spent the rest of the morning cleaning the house. He changed the sheets on his bed, did laundry, swept and vacuumed, and deep cleaned both the bathroom and the kitchen. Although the work was hard, it was also mindless, leaving him fighting to keep his thoughts away from things he had no business thinking of. Around noon, he decided to run get some lunch and then spend the afternoon working out in the garage. For some reason, the house seemed too quiet and he needed to get out.

Cam was already halfway through his sub sandwich when he parked his truck in front of the garage and climbed out. A blue Ford Taurus was parked in front of one of the bays, and Dotty Calhoun stood in the open driver's door waiting for him.

"I had about decided you weren't working today, young man," Dotty said with a smile.

Cam smiled back and wrapped the rest of his sandwich up for later. "Sorry about that, ma'am. What can I do for you?"

Dotty stepped to the back of her car and patted the trunk. "I need your expertise. There is an odd rattling noise when I drive and I'm scared it's something serious. Can you take a look?"

Cam nodded and held out his hand. "Let me take it for a short drive so I can hear what it's doing." Once he had her keys in hand, he headed for the door to his waiting room and unlocked it. "You can wait in here. Turn on the AC if it gets too stuffy, all right?"

She paused once inside the room and turned back to Cam, a worried expression on her face. "If it costs more than a couple hundred to fix, I may have to wait 'til next month to get it done. I don't like to dip into my savings if I can help it."

Cam gave her a reassuring smile. "Let's don't get worried just yet. Let me see what we're dealing with first, okay?"

Cam climbed in the car and backed it out into the road, then drove off. The car smelled like a little old lady, with a pine-scented air freshener and remnants of some flowery perfume. There was a travel pack of Kleenex in the cup holder and the radio tuned to some conservative talk station. Her purse still sat on the passenger seat, even unzipped. Dotty was everything Cam looked for in a victim. She was trusting and had already told him how much she was willing to spend in repairs. Well, unless he wanted to let her pay the balance the following month or convince her it was important enough to pull from her savings. Normally, his mind would be spinning with the possibilities of the scam, but he found himself feeling a bit nauseated at the mere thought of putting a fast one over on Dotty. In fact, he was hoping that he'd find the cause of her problems to be a cheap and easy fix.

"I'm getting soft," he said to himself as he pulled back into the garage parking lot. He unlocked the garage bay door and pushed it up, then turned as Dotty stepped out of the waiting room and looked at him expectantly.

"Let me get it up on the lift and I'll tell you what I think," he said before getting back in the car and pulling it into the bay.

Once he'd gotten underneath the car and poked around for a minute, he turned to Dotty, who still stood close by, as if she was waiting for a doctor to tell her what was wrong with one of her kids.

A few weeks ago, he would have made this visit into a moneymaker, and he silently questioned himself one last time if that wasn't what he wanted to do now. Instead, he waved Dotty over and pointed up at the underside of her car.

"See this right here? It's the heat shield that wraps around your muffler. And this screw right here? It's loose. Which is causing it to be able to do this." He moved the shield with his hand, re-creating the clanking sound Dotty had been hearing.

"So how do we fix it?" Dotty asked, still not seeing how simple the repair was going to be.

Cam sighed at the easy scam he was giving up and reached behind him for a wrench. "Well," he said, all professional-like. "We take this and twist this bolt right here. And then—" He attempted to move the heat shield again, but it didn't budge. "Fixed."

Dotty's mouth dropped open as she stared at Cam. Finally, she asked, "That's it?"

He nodded. "That's it. Now, if it starts rattling again, we might need to replace the bolt, but it's nothing urgent and still won't take but a minute to do." He guided her out from under the car and then lowered it back to the garage floor.

She still seemed in shock, but after Cam had backed her car out, she asked, "How much do I owe you?"

Cam chuckled. "To turn a screw? That's on the house."

"Oh no! You are not in business to give your services away for free. No matter how simple, I would never have been able to fix that problem without you. Now how much do I owe you?" Dotty had wagged her finger at him through her little speech, and Cam was grinning when she was done.

"All right. How 'bout another of your pies? That seems like a fair price."

That put a smile on Dotty's face, and she offered her hand to shake on the deal. "I'll plan on doing some baking this week, unless you are in some hurry."

"No hurry, ma'am. Just when you have time." Cam shook her hand and then watched as she climbed in the car and backed out. He waved as she drove off, then went and fetched the remainder of his sandwich.

Leaning against the front quarter panel of his truck, he leisurely ate the rest, bewildered at his inability to run his usual con.

"HELLO?"

It was after dark when Cam asked to be connected with Jackson Rhodes's room, but he'd expected Jackson's parents to answer, not the man himself. Jackson sounded less like a junkie than he had the day before, which made Cam consider hanging up for a second. What was he doing? It wasn't like he and Jackson were friends or anything.

"Hello?"

"Oh, hey," Cam finally said. "I, uh…." He got stuck there and went silent again.

"Cam?" Jackson asked. "Is that you?"

"Yeah, I just, you know, wanted to…." What? What did he want to do?

"Thanks for bringing the kids by yesterday. Mom said you were here. I don't remember much of anything that happened, but…." He chuckled and Cam found himself smiling.

"You were pretty fucked up there, Sheriff. I was wondering if that truck didn't hit you in the head or something."

Jackson laughed harder, then groaned and got quiet. "Shit. Don't make me laugh," he grumbled, but then chuckled again, although a bit more carefully. "Sorry if I said anything crazy while you were here."

"No problem. I'm thinking I might could blackmail you with some of it, though." Cam grinned. "So how you feeling?"

"Better. I'm still pretty loaded on pain meds, though. I'm sure I wouldn't be half this good if I weren't." Jackson got quiet, and Cam searched for something to say, but then Jackson sighed and added, "The state patrol officer who was standing right next to me…. He died this afternoon. I, uh…." Again with the silence.

Cam grunted and struggled for a response.

"Do you ever think about dying, Cam?"

Whoa. Hadn't this conversation taken a turn for the morbid real quick? "Yeah. Not looking forward to it."

"That guy was thirty-two. He had a kid and a wife." Jackson's voice cracked, and it took a minute before he continued. "I just…. Why was it him and not me?"

And now they were on to philosophy, not his strong suit. Cam scratched his head and frowned. "Why does anything happen, Jackson? I know you believe in a God and all that. But do you think he sticks his fingers in everything that happens down here? Maybe it's all just a game of chance and we can't control anything, you know? So we do the best we can and hope it's good enough." He shrugged. "I'm sure you'd get better answers from someone else. I just wanted to check in on you, you know?"

"Yeah. Sorry for going all weepy. This is screwing with my mind."

"No, I get it. I wish I could give you answers, but obviously I got no clues, right?"

"Actually, what you said made a lot of sense. I think I just need more sleep and things will even out some."

"Yeah. You get some sleep and I'll check in with you later, okay?"

"Night, Cam."

"Night, Sheriff."

CHAPTER 19

SUNDAY MORNING was another quiet one, and Cam found himself looking forward to having the kids back the next day. He sat on the porch again with his coffee, and once it was done, he had no idea what to do with himself. It was unlike him to need constant interaction, and it wasn't like he didn't have tons to do around the house, but he was feeling itchy that morning for some reason.

He went back inside, poured another cup of coffee, and grabbed his cell phone on the way back out. Cam stared at it a good long time before finally dialing his mother's number and putting the phone to his ear.

When he heard his mother's voice on the other end, he said, "Hey, Mom, just checking in."

"Hey, baby," she responded, and then he heard the click of her lighter and pictured her lighting her first cigarette of the day, or maybe her tenth for all he knew. On an exhale that he could imagine producing a halo of smoke around her head, she asked, "Everything okay?"

He nodded. "Yeah, pretty good. I like it here. It's... different, you know?"

"Mmm, that's good, but what you gonna do about the people calling here for you? One man came by. He looked mad that I didn't know anything. Maybe you shouldn't have left your car here."

"What did he look like? And what did you tell him?" Cam leaned forward and put his elbows on his knees. Maybe he shouldn't have called his mom. He'd be better not knowing this shit, right?

"He was crazy-looking, Cam. And one of his eyes was all wrong, like it didn't work or something. I told him I didn't know where you were and he said I better find out."

Cam's heart was pounding. His mother hadn't been the best in the world, but he hadn't meant to leave her in this kind of situation, and he was pretty sure Harold would have no problem whatsoever messing up his mom.

"Listen, Mom. You been wanting to go visit Aunt Mary, right? Why don't you pack up and go up there for a visit? It'd be a good time, you know?"

"You think he'd do something to me, Cam?"

Cam let that hang in the air a moment as he thought about all the things Harold had done. Finally, he answered simply. "Yeah."

"I don't have the money to go on a trip. What am I going to do?" His mom sounded hysterical.

"Mom, calm down. Pack a bag. I'll go wire some money to the Western Union at the grocery store, okay? You go today, okay? Don't wait."

"Okay. Today. Send enough to get me cigarettes and maybe take Mary and her husband out to eat while I'm there."

Cam sighed. At least his mother was worried about the important things, right? He rolled his eyes. "Sure, Mom. Go pack. Love you."

He hung up and sat for a moment. *Shit.* Harold wasn't going to give up, was he?

Well, this gave him something to do for the next hour, at least. He headed for the back room to dig out his money jar.

AFTER WIRING money at the grocery store, Cam decided to go ahead and pick up a few things he needed and a whole bunch he didn't but couldn't resist. He was toting his bags out the sliding doors of the store when he ran into Grant.

The vet was accompanied by his wife and kids, all dressed in their Sunday go-to-meetin' clothes. Cam had to admit that Grant looked mighty fine in his suit, but the nasty smirk on his face and the fake wife at his side ruined the effect for Cam.

"Well, if it isn't our local tomcat," Grant sneered. His wife and kids kept walking, obviously trained by now that they weren't needed in Grant's conversations.

Cam leaned in. "I was sure that was your title. Anyway, I got more important things to do than listen to your shit." Cam started around Grant, but Grant grabbed his arm and stopped him.

"I hear your cop is in the hospital." Grant gave him a knowing smirk.

"He ain't *my* cop," Cam stressed, looking down at the hand on his bicep.

"He won't come out of the closet for you."

Cam smirked. "I ain't looking to go steady. With you or anyone else. Get your hands off me and keep your nose out of my business." Cam shrugged Grant's hand off and headed for his truck before the man could say any more, but he could feel Grant glaring at his back as he went.

CAM SPENT the rest of the morning and most of the afternoon painting and worrying about Harold and what the asshole was doing, might do, could do. Cam finished one of the downstairs bedrooms and most of the hall before he finally gave up for the day. His stomach was wavering between hunger and nausea, and he figured he better eat something before it decided to eat itself.

He pulled out the rotisserie chicken he'd bought at the grocery store along with a few sides he'd gotten at the deli counter and fixed himself a plate. Tommasina appeared and began weaving through his legs while he prepared his meal, causing Cam to chuckle.

"All right, all right," Cam told her and placed a saucer of chicken on the floor. "You are one spoiled cat, you know it?"

Tommasina was too busy eating to answer, but Cam didn't really expect one. He took his own plate to the table and dug in, wondering if his mom had made it to his aunt's house already. He would have to call her in the next day or so just to be sure.

After he was done eating and his dishes were washed and drying, he went and grabbed his cell phone again, then headed out on the porch. This had somehow become the place he went to make phone calls. He had to admit, he liked rocking and being on a call gave him an excuse to sit still and do it.

When he'd dialed the number, he listened to the ringing before a female voice answered. He remained quiet until he heard some shuffling and her say, "I'm alone, goddammit."

"Sorry, Detra. I just…. Listen, you sure you don't wanna come…?"

"Shut up! No. He knows I talked to you. I don't know how. Things are bad, Cam. Go away. Don't make this for nothing. Have a good life and forget all about us, okay?" And then she hung up.

Cam sat as the sky darkened into night, just staring off into the distance and feeling angry and helpless to do a damn thing about it.

CHAPTER 20

CAM REFUSED to admit that he was using the kids as an excuse to go see Jackson again. He'd headed straight for the hospital once he picked them up on Monday morning. But he needed to keep busy, keep his mind off everything, and the kids were all worried about Jackson. So it worked out for everyone.

The hospital was fairly quiet, and Cam figured it probably wasn't their rush time for visitors or for accidents and such. He herded the kids down the hall and nodded to the nurse when she waved them on into Jackson's room.

Jackson looked up from his tray of breakfast and smiled as they entered, and Cam was surprised to see he wasn't alone. Jackson's father stood beside the bed, dressed in his police chief's uniform.

Cam shook the older man's hand and said, "I hope it's okay if we stopped by."

"I was just leaving," Walter responded. He patted his son on the knee and said, "I'll see you tonight, son."

"Dad," Jackson said before his father could go. "Mom doesn't need to keep spending the night, and both of you need some sleep. Go on home tonight and y'all spend a night resting, okay? I got nurses here to watch out for me, right?"

Walter paused, then nodded. "You're right, son. Now if I can just convince your mother."

They huffed out a laugh, both obviously understanding what a task that would be, then Walter patted the kids on the head and left for work.

Jackson greeted the kids, then turned his attention back to his breakfast. "Y'all eaten?" he asked, sounding as if he felt bad about eating in front of them.

"Yeah, no problem," Cam answered.

"We got Hardee's," Tony exclaimed.

Cam grinned when Jackson looked over at him and said, "You sure are treating these kids good. Thank you for that."

Cam nodded and sat down in the chair beside the bed. "Feeling okay?"

"Better," Jackson replied as Luanne and Galen started checking out the machines positioned around the hospital bed.

Tony went to the window and looked out at the cars driving by. "You can see a long way from up here," he said to no one in particular.

Cam and Jackson watched him for a moment before turning back to each other, neither seeming to know what to say.

"You, uh… said the other day that you, uh… might need me to take care of you when you got out…."

Jackson looked surprised. "I did?"

Cam was regretting bringing it up, but pushed on. "Yeah, uh…. You were pretty wasted at the time. I just… you know… the kids got all excited and wanted to help. And, uh… well, I finished painting the downstairs bedroom, so if you need to…. Well, you know… we could help." *Shit!* That had been like pulling teeth, and he wasn't even sure what the hell he was doing.

The kids all turned toward Jackson from what they had been doing, puppy-dog eyes turned up to eleven. "Pleeeeeeease, Officer Rhodes?" Luanne begged for all three.

Jackson sat for a moment, staring at his breakfast, then started to chuckle followed by a groan as he held his ribs for a minute before continuing. "You know, I could use an excuse to get away from a bunch of women eager to baby me to death, and my mother heads the pack. You mean it?" He gave Cam an examining look.

Cam laughed and nodded. "Yeah. We can save you from that fate."

Jackson sighed and nodded. "Okay. Let me talk to my mom and I'll get back to you. They are talking about maybe releasing me tomorrow. You up for that?"

"Sure. I got nothing better on my calendar." Cam grinned. "But remember, I haven't ever been a nurse before."

WHEN THEY returned to the house, Cam got them all busy setting up the downstairs bedroom for their soon-to-be patient. He changed out the sheets and moved things around to make it easier to get Jackson in and out of the room, then opened the window to let in some fresh air.

Over lunch, Cam explained their jobs. "Now while you need to make sure he has what he needs, you also have to remember the guy needs his rest, right? So no driving him crazy. You might have to go out and ride your bikes for a while."

They didn't seem too upset by that suggestion, so Cam figured they were going to do all right.

"Now once y'all are through eating, let's go run some errands." He stood and took his plate to the sink, the sound of scraping chairs announcing the kids were right behind him.

At the dollar store, Cam picked out some plastic drinking cups with lids and straws for Jackson to keep beside his bed, and a big bottle of pain reliever, some bandages and ointments, a few cheap towels to go in the downstairs bath, and a lap tray. He also stocked up on board games and decks of cards, much to the kids' delight, and some cheap VHS tapes from the bargain bin since he didn't have cable and didn't plan on getting it any time soon.

Next, they hit the grocery store and picked up cans of soup and anything else Cam could think of to feed someone sick. They headed home with the bed of the truck just about full, and found Jackson's mother waiting for them on the front porch when they pulled into the driveway.

She stood from where she had been sitting in one of the rocking chairs, but stayed on the porch while he instructed the kids on how to unload the truck and where to put away their purchases. Once he was done, he met her on the porch and had a seat with her.

"Ma'am," he greeted.

She nodded, but her gaze followed the kids as they tromped up the stairs and into the house with their load of goodies. Once they were inside, she turned to Cam. "Why are you taking care of those kids?"

Cam was taken back for a moment, then answered, "Well, I needed some help around—"

"No, I mean why?"

Cam's eyes widened. "Look, Mrs. Rhodes. I want what's right for those kids, and I'm better than that man they call Daddy. Although,

I don't see how I could be much worse. You can ask them if you want. I would never—"

"There's no need for that," she assured him, smiling now. "I just needed to be sure."

He nodded. "And I'm glad you did, ma'am. They deserve someone watching out for them."

She looked at her hands in her lap for a moment, then back at Cam. "And why do you want to take care of Jackson when he gets out of the hospital?"

Oh boy. Now that one was going to be harder to answer. "Well… the kids wanted to help and I got room and…."

"And you think you can take care of him better than his own mother? A man you hardly know?"

"Ma'am… look, I'm from Atlanta and I guess you know I been to prison a time or two. And there ain't no such thing as being neighborly there. Not really, not where I was from, anyway. But since I moved here, well, everyone has been real nice. To be honest, I didn't like it much to begin with, but it's kinda growin' on me and I wouldn't mind doing my part. If you don't mind, that is. And you're right. I don't know much about taking care of someone, so if you think I can't do it, I'll understand."

Pamela studied him for a moment before finally nodding. "No, I think you'll do just fine. But don't think I won't be over here checking on him regularly."

"Of course, ma'am."

"And I'll warn you now. Your house is going to be Grand Central Station with all the visitors he'll be getting." *Oh wonderful!*

"Yes, ma'am." Cam figured there was no arguing so why even try.

Pamela stood and looked over Cam's front yard. "I can tell you've been working on the place. It was a mess when you bought it."

"It still is, but it's coming around. The kids have helped a lot." He smiled, proud of his house and the kids who had helped him.

She patted his shoulder. "You are a lot different than I thought you would be. A pleasant surprise." With that, she stepped past him and down the stairs. "They are releasing Jackson tomorrow around noon. No need to come to the hospital, though. His daddy and I will bring him here and pick up his prescriptions." She paused and then turned with narrowed eyes. "Will there be a problem with his pain meds?"

He knew what she was asking and simply smiled. "No, ma'am. Never cared for drugs."

She nodded and turned away, continuing on to her car. When she had the car door open, she said, "Jackson wants me to go to my conference on Wednesday. I'll wait to make that decision until I'm sure things are settled."

Cam nodded and she slid into the car and drove away without a wave. "Wow. Talk about a mother lion," he mumbled as he headed inside.

CHAPTER 21

EXCITED SCREAMS from the children were Cam's first clue that Jackson was there. While the kids had been outside riding their bikes, Cam had meant to be making sure things were all in order before their patient arrived, but instead had spent an inordinate amount of time staring out the kitchen window with his cell phone in hand, thinking about his mother and Detra. His mother had yet to call to let him know she had safely reached her sister's house, and he'd heard no more from Detra either. Cam knew he needed to call his mother but couldn't seem to make his fingers dial the number.

When the noise grew louder with the opening of the door, Cam turned away from the window and left his phone on the kitchen counter. He would deal with that later.

"Mr. Sanders? Where do you want us to put Jackson?" The voice came from Pamela, and Cam hurried his steps. The kids were already showing Jackson's parents to the front bedroom by the time he stepped out of the kitchen.

Cam followed behind and stood in the doorway. He smiled at Jackson as his parents got him situated in the bed. "Let me know if that's not comfortable. I slept on it before I got my new bed, but we all prefer different."

Jackson looked weary just from the ride and seemed relieved to be able to lie down. He was dressed in a baggy T-shirt and old ratty sweats that looked a size too big but also comfy as hell. Pamela pulled out a large pillow and exchanged it with the one already on the bed, then fluffed it for her son.

"I brought a few of his things from home to make it more comfortable for him." Pamela, who was dressed in a smart-looking pantsuit and low heels, unloaded a stack of magazines and placed them on the floor by the side table, then began instruction on the medicines

Cam would need to be sure Jackson took during his recovery. There were symptoms to be on the lookout for, reasons to call 911, a list of contacts in case Jackson needed something, and a few suggestions on foods Jackson either liked or didn't.

Cam nodded through it all, trying his best to look like a responsible adult, although he felt more like a kid being left without a babysitter for the first time.

Walter, in his uniform, stood off to the side, seemingly used to leaving these things to his wife. He appeared to be ready to go, but also prepared to stay for quite a bit while his wife finished whatever she was doing. The kids were busy showing Jackson all the things they'd gotten at the dollar store for him, in particular the large stack of board games in the corner.

Jackson smiled dutifully, but was obviously wearing pretty thin and needed quiet. Before Cam could interrupt and corral the kids, Pamela caught on and did it for him. Jackson was given his pain meds, then everyone was shooed from the room and the door closed for good measure.

"You cannot let those kids keep him from getting the rest he needs," Pamela began after turning to Cam.

Walter looked like he might be thinking of stepping in but decided against it, so Cam assured her. "No problem, ma'am. They have jobs and bikes to ride."

"Don't think twice about calling if you find you can't handle this," she said.

Cam nodded. "You'll be the first to know."

Pamela stared for a moment more, taking stock one last time, then turned and surveyed the bit of the house she could see. Tommasina was curled on one of the couch cushions and appeared to have slept through all the commotion.

"As I said before, you will have guests coming to check in on Jackson. Don't feel bad about telling them he's resting or doesn't need visitors, but they'll still want to come in and visit. It's just the way it is here." She turned back to Cam. "You should probably keep coffee made, have a pitcher of iced tea ready. Maybe lock the cat away in another room. Do you want me to stay for a while?"

Cam's first instinct was to say no to the offer. He honestly didn't need Pamela supervising him as he let Jackson sleep, but then he reconsidered. While Pamela came off as bossy, Cam was pretty good at reading people, and he could see the hope in her eyes that he might ask her to stay for a while. This was her son after all, and she had almost lost him.

"Actually, ma'am, it would be right nice if you would. Just to show me how it's done before leaving me on my own."

The smile he got from Jackson's mother was payment enough. She nodded. "All right." She glanced around again, appearing to consider her options. "Let me ride with Walter back to the house and I'll come back in my car so he can get back to work. You'll be fine until then?"

"Yes, ma'am. I'll start the coffee."

She nodded again, seemingly pleased, and headed for the door.

Walter leaned over and shook Cam's hand. "Smart move, boy." He grinned and followed his wife out of the house.

Cam stared over at Tommasina, who lifted her head as Walter and Pamela left. "Looks like you'll have to sleep on my bed for the rest of the afternoon."

THE REMAINDER of the day went by in a blur of visitors, each bearing a casserole dish, a Crock-Pot, or a dessert of some sort. Pamela was the consummate hostess, holding court while Cam poured coffee and glasses of tea for their guests. A few of the younger women, presumably former classmates of Jackson, were allowed in to visit for a few minutes, but mostly Pamela kept everyone away from her mending son.

The women who did get to see him seemed to hover around him like bees to a flower, all too eager to claim his nectar for their own. Cam was unimpressed and wished Pamela would run them off as quickly as she had the kids when they'd been eager to have Jackson's attention. But Pamela seemed very proud of how many women obviously wanted her son and made no beef about showing it.

When Cam left to take the kids home for the day, Jenny Miller was just coming out of Jackson's room but had accepted an offer for a glass of tea. Cam frowned as he slid into the truck and got it started. That woman was like a dog with a bone. He could tell. She seemed to have it in her mind that if she was unrelenting enough, she could somehow convince Jackson Rhodes that he loved her. He could only imagine how annoying that would be.

Cam wasn't usually a social person, and although he had done very little to entertain the guests who had come by that day, he felt like he'd run a marathon just having them wandering in and out of his house. There was now enough food in his kitchen to feed an army for an extended siege, and he had heard and forgotten enough names to fill his lifetime quota. If he was this worn-out, he could only imagine how Jackson felt. He hoped this would not continue, because at some point, his graciousness was going to run out, and it was going to be sooner rather than later.

Upon returning to the house, he was pleased to see that Jenny Miller's car was gone. He walked in to find Pamela relaxing on the couch, looking far more drained than she had while surrounded by people.

"That should be the last of them," she said wearily. "They do mean well. They all want to help and don't really think of how much work they put on an already-stressed family. But then again, gossip will know who all didn't come by or make something, and who brought store-bought too." She smiled at Cam. "Is it like that in Atlanta or just here?"

He shrugged. "It might be in places. I never saw anything like this. Are you okay? Can I fix you a bite to eat?"

She seemed to shake off her lethargy and stood. "I'm fine. It shouldn't be as bad tomorrow. Maybe a visitor or two. I told Jenny not to come by tomorrow, but I wouldn't bet money on her staying away. You can call me if she's a bother. As much as I wish Jackson would settle down, he doesn't seem to cotton much to the girls around here." She shrugged and headed toward the kitchen with her tea glass.

"I tried to keep things washed up as they were used. If you don't mind, I'm going to take one of these casseroles home for dinner. Talking is more tiring than manual labor."

Cam couldn't have agreed more. "Take all you want, ma'am. I think we have enough."

She smiled and peeked under the aluminum foil on a few. "Throw these here in the freezer. They'll do fine. And the rest in the refrigerator. I'll bring some containers tomorrow so we can wash these Crock-Pots and dishes before Wednesday night service. I can drop them by the church before we head out tomorrow evening."

She must have seen Cam's eyes widen when she mentioned coming over the next day, so she went on to assure him. "I won't be staying tomorrow. I'll come by and check on my boy and bring you the containers. Maybe do a rack of dishes if you need it done. I can also run off Jenny if she is hanging around. But then I'll leave you to it."

Cam grinned and nodded. "Yes, ma'am."

After picking out a casserole to take home with her, she said good-bye to Jackson, then headed to the door, collecting her things along the way. "Call me if you need anything," she said over her shoulder before closing the door behind her.

Cam sighed in relief and hurried upstairs to let Tommasina out, then slumped into one of the kitchen chairs once he came back down.

After a few minutes, just as Cam was considering getting up and putting things away, maybe even figuring out what to have for dinner, he heard Jackson calling from the bedroom.

Cam hurried to the door and peeked in. "Hey, man. Getting hungry?"

Jackson shrugged. "A little. Mostly I need a change of scenery. Think I could come out in the living room for a while?"

"Yeah, of course. No one here but us. I can fix you a plate to eat in there." Cam stepped to the side of the bed but just stood, not sure where to touch or grab in order to help Jackson up.

Jackson slowly pushed his feet off the bed and turned to sit. He puffed like he'd just climbed a mountain or something. Cam grabbed the meds on the dresser and went through them until he found Jackson's in-between pain pills, the one he could take when he needed something between doses of his heavy-duty medicine.

"Here, take a couple of these and then we'll get you up and moving."

Jackson swallowed down the pills, then looked up at Cam. "Let me hold on to you, not the other way around. There's no good place on my torso to grab, with ribs and spleen and bruises."

"You only got one good arm, though," Cam argued.

"It still works pretty good, even if it is my left." Jackson flexed to demonstrate, then reached out and grabbed Cam's forearm. Cam tensed his arm to give Jackson something firm to use for support.

The trip to the living room was slow and full of grunts and moans from Jackson. He walked a lot like Charles Evans, including the huffing and puffing, and Cam worried that maybe Jackson was doing more than he should. He had a momentary panic at the thought of Jackson's mother going full-out gangster on his ass if anything happened to her son.

Once he'd successfully gotten Jackson settled on the couch and propped his feet up, Cam relaxed a bit.

"We have enough food to end world hunger, so what do you feel like eating? There's casseroles and roasts and soups. Anything sound good?"

Jackson thought for a moment. "Is one of them pork roast?"

Cam nodded. "I think so. With veggies all around."

"That sounds good. In a bowl, with lots of the juice. Almost like stew." Jackson laid his head back and closed his eyes.

Cam patted his knee and headed for the kitchen. "You got it." He put the pork roast in the microwave and then started finding spots in the refrigerator and freezer for the rest of the food. He poured iced tea for each of them and even went ahead and cut pieces of pie. He grabbed the lap tray he'd bought and loaded it up once the roast was hot, then took their meals into the living room.

Jackson pulled his feet up to give Cam room at the other end of the couch and they settled in to eat their dinner. It only took a few bites for Cam to realize all that visiting had been worth it if the rest of the food tasted this good.

They were both quiet until their initial hunger was sated. Then, while poking at a potato, Cam asked, "So that girl, Jenny... I think she kinda...."

"Yeah, I know. In school, she was an easy choice for a date when I needed one. I never thought much about it, but I guess she expected we were going somewhere." Jackson winced when he shrugged. "I've tried to distance myself in the past years, but she isn't taking no for an answer."

SNAKES AMONG SWEET FLOWERS 141

Cam watched Jackson pick at his food. "You really think it would all fall apart if they knew?"

"What?" Jackson said it like he was frightened someone could possibly hear. "Yes! I mean they know that gays exist, but not here."

"But... Grant. Are you telling me no one knows about him?" Cam just couldn't believe it.

"No! Well, I mean... no." Jackson appeared to be working it out in his head and finally looked up at Cam. "They never talk about it, and as long as he doesn't either, I guess that makes it okay. I guess. I think it would have to be shoved in their faces for people here to believe it was real. Because it's something that happens other places."

Cam nodded and grinned. "So it's the worst-kept secret ever."

Jackson huffed out a laugh. "Yeah."

Cam dug into his pie and took a big bite. After a moment, he ventured on. "I don't know this town like you do. Probably never will. And I'm not trying to push you to do anything you don't want, but seems like an awful lot of people around here think the world of you. Just look at the crowds coming by here today."

Jackson nodded. "That's why I can't ever let anyone know. It would be bad, Cam. Real bad."

Cam let it drop. After all, he was still learning something new every day about living in a small town, but it seemed to him it was far easier to hate someone you didn't know than someone that was the town golden boy, no matter what the cause.

CHAPTER 22

AFTER THE dishes were done, Cam stepped to the kitchen doorway to find Jackson staring off into space with Tommasina now comfortably settled on his lap. Although Jackson's attention appeared to be elsewhere, he was busy sliding his hand down her back.

"More tea?" Cam offered.

Jackson seemed to shake off whatever he was lost in the blue thinking about and smiled. "Yeah. That sounds good."

Cam went back into the kitchen, and as he was grabbing the tea pitcher from the refrigerator, he heard Jackson call out to him. "What do you do for fun around here?"

Cam chuckled. "Not much, Sheriff. That TV…."

"Yeah, I don't see it picking up cable or anything."

"Nah. Got it hooked up to a VCR player, though, if you want to see a movie. Other than that…." Cam came into the living room carrying the glass of tea and a beer for himself. "We could call Grant."

Jackson's eyes widened and he quickly said, "No!"

Cam had to set the glass down, he laughed so hard. "I was kidding," he finally got out. "Just kidding. I don't want that man around either."

Jackson chuckled too and reached for his drink. "He's nothing but trouble, Cam."

Cam nodded. "I seen that for myself." After looking around the room, he continued. "Usually I go out on the front porch and listen to the crickets at night. I could get you out there in one of the rockers if you want."

Jackson scrunched up his nose. "And I'm the country bumpkin? I don't ever remember going outside just to listen to the bugs. Are you sure you're from Atlanta?"

Cam laughed again, then shrugged. "Maybe it's just new and special to me still. You had it all your life and don't know what you really got here. I didn't even know places like this existed, you know?"

Jackson nodded and tried to reposition himself. "Yeah. I guess that makes sense. I don't think I can handle sitting in a wooden rocker, though. Maybe we could open the window and let the night in to us?"

Cam grinned. "Yeah, I can do that. Hold on, Sheriff." He pushed open the two main windows in the living room so that the breeze came in through the screen, leaving the curtains open wide, then took the cushion off the back of the couch on his end and tapped Jackson on the shoulder. "Lean forward."

Jackson looked up to him quizzically as he did. "Where are you gonna sit?"

Cam grinned. "You're the patient. Let me worry about me, okay?" Cam made sure Jackson was comfortable, straightening his legs and even draping a blanket across him, which caused the cat to abandon her spot and stalk off toward the kitchen. Cam then settled on the floor at Jackson's hip with his back to the sofa.

"You can sit up here," Jackson said.

"I can sit over in that chair too," Cam responded. "But here I can use the coffee table and we can talk. Okay?"

"Yeah, okay." Jackson reached over and took Cam's beer from his hands and turned it up, taking a deep swig.

"Your mom said no alcohol while taking your meds." Cam frowned.

"One drink of a beer ain't gonna kill me."

"Probably not," Cam conceded, but he took his beer back to be sure Jackson made no further indulgences. For several minutes, there was quiet between them, a companionable silence. Cam picked at the label on his bottle while Jackson stared out the window into the darkness.

"I usually keep the TV or music on all the time," Jackson said after a while.

"I got a clock radio upstairs if you want me to get it," Cam offered. "I bring it down sometimes." He drew his legs up to let Jackson know he would get up if needed.

"Nah, maybe tomorrow. I kinda like this. I was just saying."

Cam nodded. "Yeah, I always kept some noise going too. But since I've been out here, I've grown to like the quiet. It feels good."

"What made you move out here?" Jackson asked, turning to look at Cam.

Oh boy, and wasn't that the subject Cam wanted to chat about. He dropped his head and stared at the bottle in his lap, silent for long enough that Jackson obviously knew he'd asked the wrong question.

"You don't have to tell me. I was just...." Jackson shrugged and turned back to the window.

"It's okay, Sheriff. I just like pretending all that never happened as much as possible." Cam sighed and looked over at Jackson. "I got in with a bad crowd. No, that sounds wrong. Like I'm blaming someone for things I did. I was *part* of a bad crowd, that's what it was. But not all of them were really bad, or maybe it was just that some were more bad than others. Anyway, sometimes making a change means wiping the whole slate clean and beginning all over again. I couldn't change there, and it had to happen or I wasn't going to be around much longer. So here I am." That was sharing, right? And all the sharing he wanted to do.

Jackson seemed to be searching Cam's face for something, then nodded and looked away. "You got any family?"

Cam's heart raced as he remembered he still hadn't called his mother. He really needed to do that in the morning. "Yeah. My mom is still around. We aren't close like your family, though. Your parents really care about you."

Jackson smiled at that. "I'm pretty lucky. I get annoyed at Momma sometimes, but I wouldn't have her any other way, I guess."

Cam could just picture how Pamela would react if Walter had ever smacked Jackson around. It would have been a very different scene from what had happened in his own family, that was for sure. It made Cam smile.

"What?" Jackson asked.

Cam glanced over. "Just imagining your mom if little Jackson had ever been mistreated."

Jackson threw his head back and gave a full belly laugh that was quickly cut off, turning into a groan as he wrapped his left arm around his ribs. "Shit," he murmured.

"Sorry," Cam said, climbing to his knees but not sure what to do to help.

"Don't do that," Jackson admonished as he slowly relaxed back into the pillows. With a huff, he finally said, "Momma *is* a bit protective."

"You think?" Cam laughed.

Jackson started to laugh again but bit his lip instead and held his ribs.

"I think it's about time for your meds. I'll go get them." Cam climbed to his feet and hurried to Jackson's room. He should have given Jackson his pills a half hour before. This was going to take some getting used to. He came back with a handful of bottles, reading labels along the way. "I think it's time for your antibiotic too, but it says to take with food." Cam glanced up at Jackson for advice.

"Got a piece of bread or something?" Jackson asked.

"How about a dinner roll? We got plenty of those."

Jackson nodded and took the bottles from Cam. "I'll get the pills out, you get the roll."

Cam headed back off toward the kitchen, where there were now several packs of dinner rolls thanks to the ladies who had visited, as if they were a necessity to a meal or something. Cam couldn't remember ever having dinner rolls at a meal that wasn't either Thanksgiving or Christmas. Unless it was at a restaurant. He grabbed a couple of the rolls and resealed the package, then popped one in his mouth as he grabbed another beer and made his way back to the living room.

From the doorway, he made to throw the roll, making sure Jackson saw it was coming so he wouldn't flinch. Once Jackson's hands were raised, Cam easily tossed the roll right into them, and Jackson grinned.

"Good throw. You play ball?" Jackson took a bite of the roll, then swallowed down the pills with some tea.

"Just for fun in the yard." Cam shrugged.

"We should play some time when I get better. Some of the guys have a game once a week."

Cam grunted and nodded as he sat back down on the floor. "Yeah. That could be fun." Cam opened the bottle and took a swig, and then Jackson swiped it from him again. "Hey! Your mom'll kill me!"

Jackson shrugged and took a drink. "Sure you done worse."

Cam smirked but took back his bottle. "Maybe."

"Them tattoos hurt?" Jackson asked before taking another bite of his roll.

Cam looked down at his arms and shrugged. "A little. It's not that bad."

"Why'd you get them?"

Cam ran his fingers along the blue rose, then up his arm. "To remind me of things. Some, anyway. You got any?"

"No. Sometimes I think about it, but it seems…." Jackson canted his head as if searching for the right word.

"Out of character?" Cam tried.

"Yeah, I guess. Like me trying to be something I'm not."

Cam nodded and smiled. "Kinda hard to shake that golden-boy image, Sheriff."

Jackson frowned and let his head drop back on the pillow, eyes closing. The meds appeared to be working some. He was relaxing, maybe the beer helping them along. "Why do you call me that?"

Cam chuckled. "Because that's what you seem like to me. Like the good guy in those old westerns, running the bad guys off and saving the town."

"Are you one of the town folk or one of the bad guys, Cam?"

Cam scratched his head and glanced over at Jackson, who still had his eyes closed. "Good question there, Sheriff. I guess we'll have to watch the rest of the movie to find out, huh?"

Jackson nodded and hummed, still not opening his eyes.

"Starting to drift off on me?"

"A little." Jackson smiled like a drunk on a bender.

Cam snorted out a laugh. "Yeah, I need to get you back to bed. Come on."

CHAPTER 23

THE NEXT morning, Cam came down the stairs with his clock radio in hand. He set it up on the kitchen counter and tuned in to an Atlanta station while coffee was brewing. He liked music but hadn't listened to the radio more than occasionally since getting out of prison unless he was in the car. While inside, the radio had been his faithful companion, keeping him out of trouble and making the time go by faster. It was a nice change now, though, and he found himself singing along as he pulled out a breakfast casserole and shoved it in the oven to heat up.

Cam's cell phone rang just as he was pouring a cup of coffee. He answered the call and took it and the mug out to the porch so he could hear, Tommasina coming along and settling on the stairs.

"Hello?"

"Cam?"

"Mom. Is everything okay?"

"That's what I want to know. I'm at Mary and Doug's, but I keep getting calls asking for you. Did you give anyone my number?"

Cam's heart began pounding and he leaned forward, his elbows on his knees and his head cradled in his hands. "No, I ain't given anyone your number. What are they saying? Man or woman?"

"It changes. Sometimes it's a man and sometimes it's a woman. They sound mad, Cam. They asked where I was, like they know I'm not at home."

"Shit."

"What is it, Cam? This is scaring me." Her voice quivered.

"Cut your phone off, okay, Mom? Don't answer and don't go home. I'm sorry, okay? I'm really sorry."

"How will I know you're okay if I cut off my phone?" she asked.

"I always land on my feet. Isn't that what you always said? Don't worry about me. Just stay safe."

"Okay. You too," she responded, sounding uncertain.

"Bye, Mom." He hung up and slumped over even farther. Cam looked up when he heard the screen door open. Jackson was standing there, a bit unstable but looking better than he had the day before. For a moment, Cam wondered if he had been overheard, but Jackson showed no sign of it.

"Good morning." Cam even managed a smile as he stood and grabbed his coffee off the railing, slipping his phone into his pocket.

"Hey. Is everything okay? You look upset." Jackson held on to the doorframe and looked a little worried.

"It will be once this coffee gets working. Want to sit out here to drink yours or in the kitchen?"

"The kitchen is good." Jackson started to turn, but then canted his head, eyes narrowing. "You sure you're not upset about something?"

"Yeah, just…. Mom called and we don't have the good relationship you got with yours, you know?"

"Oh." That seemed to satisfy Jackson, and he patted Cam on the shoulder, then headed for the kitchen.

Cam followed, trying to get his head in the game, even though what he really needed was to find a quiet place to beat his head against the wall for about an hour. "We got breakfast casserole in the oven. You hungry?"

"Yeah, and then I need to take my medicine, I guess." Jackson sat in one of the kitchen chairs and watched as Cam poured coffee and pulled out plates.

Cam had just sat down with their coffee when there was a clamor from the living room and a voice called out, "Knock knock!" A moment later, the three kids and Jackson's father entered the kitchen. "I figured I'd save you a trip over to pick them up. The cat came in with us. I hope that's okay."

"Thank you, sir. And Tommasina has made herself at home, so she's welcome," Cam said as he stood. He was certainly more grateful than Walter would ever know for the distraction. "Coffee? I got some breakfast casserole heating too."

Walter patted Jackson on the shoulder and sat down beside him at the table. The kids went about making themselves glasses of chocolate milk, already treating the house like it was home, to Walter's amusement.

"Sure, I'll have something before I go," Walter answered, then turned to Jackson. "Feeling any better?"

Cam turned down the radio but left it on, then pulled down a few more plates and began serving up the meal, trying to act like everything was okay.

"Yeah, I'm good. Did Mom decide to go to the conference?" Even while Jackson was talking to his dad, Cam could feel him glancing repeatedly in his direction, probably still sensing his upset.

Cam passed each of the kids a plate and told them to go sit at the coffee table, then served Walter before reseating himself. He wasn't really hungry, what with worry over his mom and what this all meant for him, but he shoveled in food to keep from having to join the conversation. He wasn't in the mood for small talk about the weather and plans.

While Cam wasn't a violent man, the thought of going after Harold and taking him out of the picture entered his mind. It might be the only way to get rid of the threat, but even if the man did deserve anything that happened to him, Cam wasn't willing to be the one to give it to him or spend the rest of his life in prison because of it. Cam fidgeted and chewed his thumbnail, staring off into space until Jackson reached across the table and thumped his arm.

"Hey! Dad's talking to you."

"Oh, sorry." Cam turned to Walter, who was giving him an appraising once-over. "I, uh…. My brain isn't firing on all its cylinders yet."

Walter laughed and nodded. "I was just asking if you're still okay with watching Jackson if we head up to Chattanooga overnight. I don't want to leave you in a bind, but Pam is supposed to speak at that conference in the morning."

Cam waved off his concern. "No problem at all. I figure in a day or two, I can put Jackson to work painting." Cam grinned, and Walter chuckled.

Jackson huffed. "Be better than laying around all day."

"The boy never liked sitting still," Walter quipped, nudging Jackson gently. "I think your momma is gonna stop by later. I got to get going." He downed the rest of his coffee and then took his plate and cup to the sink. "You boys have a nice day, you hear?"

"Bye, Daddy," Jackson said, giving a one-armed hug before his dad turned to go.

Walter spoke with each of the kids in the living room before the screen door closed, announcing his departure.

Cam was feeling off-kilter and needed to get this all straight in his head. He grabbed the plates and took them to the sink, then started washing them to have something to do with his hands.

What was Harold capable of? That's what Cam needed to determine. As he scrubbed, then dried, he decided that although Harold was violent and vindictive, Cam really didn't think he'd be able to find his mother, especially if she kept her cell cut off and stayed out of town. But she couldn't stay away forever. At some point, his mom would need to go back home, and what then?

Plus, if Harold couldn't find him through his mother, what would the asshole do next? Detra had said Harold knew they had talked. How much did he know? Did he know Detra helped him to leave? He couldn't possibly know that or he'd have gone nuts on her. Wouldn't he?

And wait! His mom had said a woman had called too. That had to be Cally. Detra wouldn't be looking for him. And if Cally was helping Harold look for him, then what did that mean for Detra? Cally and Detra had once been close friends until Harold had twisted their relationship. Before Cam had left for Hog Mountain, the two had been competing for Harold's attention, with Cally being the more insidious and undermining. When Harold was paying attention to one, the other was miserable, and he switched back and forth to watch them both squirm, obviously enjoying the power immensely.

"Hey."

Cam blinked and found that he had been staring out the window over the sink, lost in thought with the dishes long done. He turned to Jackson and could see the concern in his expression.

"I sent the kids out to play for a while," Jackson said. "Mind if I get comfortable on the couch?"

"No, of course not. Did you take your pills? Let me get them and a glass of tea for you." Cam needed to be doing something and out from under Jackson's examining gaze.

"Nah, I'm moving. Let me get it. I'll call if I need you." Jackson seemed to know Cam wanted some time to think.

Cam nodded. "Thanks, man. I'm gonna go out to the garage for a bit, but I'll have my phone if you need me, or send one of the kids. And um… I hate to break it to you, but they expect you to play those board games with them."

Jackson laughed, but kept it light and held his arms to his side as if to stabilize his ribs. "I figured. And I'm a pro at those kinda games, so bring it on."

Cam smiled as Jackson hobbled off toward his bedroom. Cam grabbed his boots and went out to the porch to put them on. He needed to putter and think for a while.

ABOUT LUNCHTIME, Cam trudged back across the lawn toward the house. The morning had been nothing but frustrating. With his mind only half on what he was doing, he'd ended up with several bumps and bruises. Plus he hadn't really come up with any resolution for his problem, other than calling Detra again. But she'd hung up on him last time, so he wasn't sure how much good that was going to do him either.

He kicked off his boots and left them sitting outside the front door, then called the kids in as they rounded the house on their bikes. "Let's fix some lunch."

"I already got one of the casseroles heated up on the stove," Jackson said from his spot on the couch. He had the cat snuggled up with him, her tail swishing as he petted her. It wasn't until then that Cam noticed the mouthwatering scent coming from the kitchen.

Cam turned toward Jackson, surprised. "You ate without us?"

"Nope, I was waiting for y'all to come in so we could eat together."

Cam smiled at that, and Jackson returned it.

As Cam headed into the kitchen, Jackson got up and followed more slowly. "Jenny stopped by and spent some time and then Momma dropped in too."

Cam didn't like that; for some reason, it got his goat that Jenny had been there hanging out with Jackson while he'd been smashing his fingers in the garage. He ground his teeth, imagining her feminine giggle as she placed her hand on Jackson's leg and patted, her limpid eyes casting some spell over her victim.

Unaware of Cam's overactive imagination, Jackson continued as he took a seat at the kitchen table. "Momma packed up some of the food and told me to tell you she filled up your freezer." Jackson laughed. "I think she likes you, Cam. She and Daddy are going up to the conference later this afternoon, and she told Jenny to let me have some peace for a while. I was kinda surprised about that."

Cam found himself inordinately pleased to hear that. He dismissed his thoughts of Jenny, humming as he made plates and served up their meal.

After lunch, they spent the afternoon playing board games. The kids decided Sorry was their favorite, but Cam wasn't so sure he agreed. Even though they'd all laughed and had a good time, he was ready when it was time to take them home for the day. Jackson seemed relieved too. He looked tired and went to take a nap when Cam headed out the door with the children.

CHAPTER 24

THE HOUSE was quiet when Cam walked back in. It was odd how quickly he'd grown accustomed to living alone. This was his first real experience with it, what with having lived on someone's couch or in an overcrowded prison most of his adult life. Having the kids over or Jackson staying didn't bother him, but he was finding that having time to himself had quickly become quite important to him.

Cam plopped down on the sofa and sighed. He didn't expect to hear anything from Jackson for another hour or so, which made time for propping his feet up and relaxing. Dinner wouldn't take more than popping it in the microwave, and there were still a few beers in the fridge. He had to say, having everyone in town cook for him wasn't half bad.

The next thing Cam knew, he was hearing the pop of the bedroom door opening. The noise surprised Tommasina, who had at some point settled in his lap, and sent her running for the stairs. His eyes opened, and he found himself slumped down on the sofa, his feet propped on the coffee table. How long had he slept? He glanced over to the hall as Jackson hobbled into view. While he was still obviously hurting, he was getting around much better than he had the day before. Jackson seemed to be in prime health and was bouncing back a lot faster than Cam would have thought.

"Hey, Sheriff. Have a good nap?" Cam greeted, sitting up and stretching.

"It hit the spot. How about yours?" Jackson grinned and headed over to join Cam on the couch.

Cam shrugged. "I think you and your lazy ways are rubbing off on me."

Jackson's eyes widened as he sat. "Lazy? I'll have you know it takes a hell of a lot of energy to put up with an afternoon of playing Sorry."

Cam chuckled. "That's probably what did me in too. I think I've played my fill for a year or so."

Jackson nodded in agreement. "The kids sure enjoyed it, though."

"Yeah, they did." Cam picked at a spot on his jeans and they grew quiet for a bit. Finally Cam looked over at Jackson. "You hungry?"

Jackson shook his head. "Not really, but I guess I should eat so I can take my pills."

Cam nodded but made no move to get up.

"You been acting like something's wrong all day, Cam. What's bothering you?" Jackson asked.

"I just...." How was he supposed to tell Jackson—a policeman, for God's sake—what was going on? Cam still had no idea what to do about it, if there was even anything he *could* do. He'd gotten himself into this mess and it looked like there was no way out. There didn't seem to be any use in pulling Jackson into all of it, anyway. "My mom brings up lots of old shit. Things I don't want to think about, you know?"

Jackson nodded, but it was obvious he really didn't know. How could he? He had a nice family who all loved each other and treated each other the way they were supposed to. Cam could tell Jackson didn't want to drop it, but Cam sure did, so he pulled himself up off the couch and headed toward the kitchen.

"Want me to turn on some music?"

"Okay, that sounds good," Jackson said, staying where he was. "Got any plans for tonight? You know, you don't have to stay with me twenty-four seven."

Cam poked his head out of the kitchen and grinned. "You trying to get rid of me, Sheriff?"

"Nah, just don't want you feeling tied down because I'm here."

Cam went back to microwaving their dinner. "I'm not big on nightlife. Is that what you like? Going to clubs?"

"I've been to some in Athens and Atlanta." Cam could hear the indifference in Jackson's voice. "Not really my style, but it used to be the only way to meet people, you know?"

"Yeah, I know. Grindr was a big surprise when I got out of jail this last time. You used it?"

"A few times, but I'm scared to have the app on my phone or tablet."

"What else you gonna do, though? A man's gotta get some sometime, right?" Cam said as he carried two plates out and set them on the coffee table. Each had a large serving of some creamy noodle and chicken stuff with broccoli. It smelled good, and Cam had added a roll and some salad to the meal to round it out some.

Jackson seemed to have found his appetite when he smelled the food, because he dug right in. He nodded to Cam's question and, after swallowing a bite, said, "It's hard making sure no one ever knows."

Cam took a bite too and then asked, "Have you ever thought about finding a position on another police force, like in some other state where you could be yourself?"

Jackson sighed. "I've thought about it. But I can't help feeling this is where I belong."

Cam could understand. Even without having much to keep him tied to Atlanta, he found it hard to leave. And when he did go, he had only gone as far as Hog Mountain. He could only imagine how hard it would be to leave with as many ties as Jackson had to his home.

Cam decided it was time to change the subject. "Want to watch a movie tonight? I don't have a lot of VHS tapes, but I have a few."

Jackson shrugged. "Maybe. I kinda liked sitting with the windows open and just talking, if that's okay with you."

Cam nodded. "Yeah, that's fine with me."

While Cam washed dishes, Jackson took his pills and even opened the windows on a sky that was just starting to darken.

Cam returned to the living room waving a pack of cards he kept in one of the kitchen drawers. "Ever play gin?"

Jackson laughed. "Are you a card shark too, Camden Sanders?"

"While I'll admit I have an excellent poker face, I don't have the skill to be successful at cards, even after all my years playing with my bunkmate in the hoosegow." Cam dropped onto the couch and offered the cards to Jackson.

Jackson took the cards but didn't open them. "Did you really play in jail?"

Cam nodded. "It passed the time and kept me out of trouble. I guess you've never been in any trouble, huh, Sheriff?"

Jackson offered a somewhat embarrassed grin. "After the final game of our senior year season, me and a couple of friends on the team went out to celebrate. Clint and Wiley got into a fight outside a bar, where we had used fake IDs to get in. We all ended up charged with public intoxication and underage drinking. My dad, being a chief of police in a neighboring city, was able to get the charges dropped." Jackson grinned again and looked down at his lap. "That's the only time I've seen the inside of a jail, and it wasn't fun. Daddy was furious too."

Cam shook his head. Since Jackson was an officer of the law, he logically had to understand that prison was far worse than that little cell in a small-town police station, but Cam was pretty sure that Jackson really had no idea. And that was good. It was just odd that Jackson seemed completely safe from the threat of doing time, like he had some kind of invisible bubble wrap around him that wouldn't allow anything to ever even threaten his perfect existence, while on the other hand, Cam seemed to have a big rope tied around his middle, ready at any moment to jerk him right back into the hell that was prison life. Like he could just blink too fast and someone would decide he wasn't good enough to be mingling with the general population.

Cam examined the grease stains etched into his fingers and thought that maybe prison had left some stain on him too that other people could see when they met him. He was pretty sure his days of enjoying this normal life were numbered and depended on when Harold caught up with him. That would knock down his house of cards and he'd feel the first tug of that rope around his waist.

"Hey. I lost you again."

Cam looked up to find Jackson staring back with a concerned expression.

"You okay? Did I say something wrong? You look awful sad."

Cam felt a strange inability to answer. His attention was drawn to Jackson's eyes. How odd that they were the color of good whiskey, lighter than most people with brown eyes, but they went well with his complexion and blond hair. He really was a good-looking guy, and seemed to honestly care about whether Cam was sad right then. Weird that Cam had made friends with a cop of all people. How had he ever let that happen? But Jackson wasn't like most cops that Cam had encountered. He seemed to honestly want what was best for people and his community. Jackson really was one of the good guys.

For a moment, Cam wasn't sure where to put his hands as he leaned forward. Jackson was still pretty beat up and the last thing Cam wanted was to make it any worse. Cam just knew he needed to do this, wanted to do this while he had the chance. His hands finally decided on Jackson's cheeks, the sheriff's eyes widening as Cam leaned even closer. And then their lips met and Jackson lifted his arms; the one covered in a cast simply rested against Cam's side, while the other tightened at Cam's ribs, pulling him closer.

Cam usually wasn't big on kissing. Get in and get out was his regular modus operandi. But Jackson's lips looked so delicious, so ripe for kissing, and Cam couldn't help himself as he nibbled and licked across them. He felt the need to apologize, but he didn't know what for. It was an odd sensation, which he had to mentally shove away. Since Jackson wasn't complaining, Cam decided to keep his apologies to himself, instead gently helping Jackson to lie back on the couch.

When Cam pulled away slightly, they were both breathing hard. An attractive blush radiated from Jackson's skin and Cam needed to see more of it. He fumbled with Jackson's shirt, considering how to remove it without hurting the man, until Jackson finally took the hem and pulled it up and over his head, only grunting a few times as parts stretched and moved that weren't quite ready to.

At seeing Jackson's sculpted chest, even covered with the bruises and scratches, Cam let out a groan that had nothing to do with pain. Carefully placing his hands to either side of Jackson's chest, Cam lowered himself until he could lick and suck at the broad expanse, avoiding any spot that looked too tender. The golden dusting of hair was as soft as silk against Cam's lips as he trailed to a hard nipple, where he set in like a starving man offered a steak dinner. Cam had never spent any extended amount of time on exploring another man's body—not to say he'd never enjoyed nipple play or touching, but it was usually with the urgent expectation of something more, not a lingering enjoyment of the act itself. For the moment, Cam was happy right where he was. He wanted to memorize Jackson

Rhodes from head to toe so he could take the image with him if things turned bad.

Jackson's good hand found the hem of Cam's shirt and began pulling it until Cam sat up and removed the garment, tossing it over with Jackson's. He grinned as he watched Jackson visually traversing Cam's physical landscape and the veneer of tattoos that covered most of his body. Jackson seemed spellbound by what he saw, and Cam rose, popping open the button of his pants and letting them drop so he could step out of them. More tattoos were revealed, running down his legs and even across the tops of his feet. There were spiderwebs, guns, and skulls, but there were also colorful flowers and birds along with intricately scrolled sayings and vines. They all had a special meaning to Cam, and together became a rather cryptic telling of his life story. Although he was sure Jackson wouldn't know the symbolism behind most of the tattoos, it felt more intimate to display them than it did his naked body.

Cam turned his back to Jackson and stood for a moment, showing the additional ink there, including a huge snake with a fanged skull that appeared to be wrapped around his spine and readying to strike his neck. In stylized letters among the throngs of blooming vines to each side were the words "Snakes among sweet flowers do creep." It was the story of his life up until that point. Those he counted as friends and family had done the worst to him.

When Cam turned around, Jackson's attention was no longer on his tattoos, but instead on his thickening cock and the heavy set of balls beneath. Cam smirked with pride at the look of obvious hunger on Jackson's face. Cam could relate and was eager to get another look at Jackson's equipment. He knelt next to the couch and was reaching for the waistband of Jackson's sweatpants when there was suddenly a bright light coming through the living room window.

Cam frowned. It wasn't fully night yet, but dark enough that he could tell the source had to be headlights as a car pulled into his driveway. Jackson was frozen beside him, looking to Cam for instruction. It couldn't be Jackson's parents; they were out of town for the evening. And it was far too late for any of the townsfolk to come for a visit.

When the light was extinguished and a car door could be heard opening, Cam stood and made his way to the front window to look out.

"You're naked," Jackson said unnecessarily.

"It's Grant," Cam responded. Shuffling sounds came from behind him as Jackson sat up.

"What does he want?" Jackson asked, and Cam figured he really didn't expect him to answer.

Instead, Cam stepped away from the window and toward the door. "He has something in his hands."

"Cam! Don't you want to get dr—"

Cam pulled the door open enough to see and be seen, then pushed open the screen. "Grant, to what do we owe this pleasure?"

"Don't let him in," Jackson hissed.

Grant's eyes widened and roamed up and down before finally settling on Cam's face, a grin firmly in place. "I... I brought my wife's famous three-layer coconut cake." He handed over the offering to Cam, who accepted it.

"Thanks, that was real nice." Cam made no move to allow Grant to enter. He raised a brow when Grant still stood there.

"Is Jackson in? I wanted to visit."

"He's not taking visitors this evening," Cam said. "But I'll let him know you stopped by."

Cam started to close the door, but Grant threw out his hand and stopped it. "Please, Cam. I'll do whatever you two want. We can have some fun."

Cam canted his head to the side, as if considering, then wrinkled his nose a little. "Nah. We're good. See you later." He pushed at the door again, and Grant shoved his foot in the way this time.

"Anything you want," Grant offered again.

"No," Cam said firmly.

Grant's face transformed as his pleading expression became a hateful sneer. "You'll be sorry, Camden Sanders. I'll—"

But Cam's expression transformed too. He put on his I'll-cut-you face and leaned closer, speaking low. "Don't even think about it."

Grant pulled back, and Cam closed the door in his face. Through the door, Grant yelled, "Fuck you! Fuck both of you," then stomped down the steps and out toward his car.

"We got cake," Cam announced, turning back to Jackson and displaying it like he was Vanna White.

Jackson chuckled and slowly lay back on the couch again. "I can't believe you did that."

"Why? It's not like he doesn't already know about both of us. And I'm not scared of him."

Jackson shook his head. "You were just so...."

"Honest?" Cam filled in.

"Yeah, I guess." Jackson chuckled again, and Cam set the cake on the coffee table.

"Now, where were we?" Cam went to his knees beside the couch again and took hold of Jackson's sweatpants. "Let's get these off of you."

Jackson huffed a bit as he lifted his hips but helped as much as he could while Cam pulled the pants down and off.

"Damn, Sheriff. You put a beer can to shame." Cam ran a hand up Jackson's thigh and then wrapped it around his cock, giving it a few good pumps before lowering himself to wrap his lips around the head.

Jackson made some unintelligible sound, one hand landing on the back of Cam's head, nails scratching for purchase against his scalp. Cam's lips stretched around the girth of Jackson's cock as it completely hardened within his mouth. He hummed out his pleasure and felt Jackson thrust upward in response.

Cam reached down and scooped Jackson's balls into his grip, rolling them as he took the cock as far as he could into his mouth.

Jackson gasped and then murmured, "Wait. Wait." He struggled to sit up, and Cam pulled back.

"What? Are you hurting?"

"Just to get you in my mouth. Let's take this to the bedroom so I can reciprocate." Jackson sat up and Cam helped him to his feet. Together, they made their way into the bedroom Jackson was using, and Cam fell over on the bed while Jackson sat gingerly and then lay back.

Cam turned himself so that they faced in opposite directions on the bed, then focused his attention back on Jackson's cock and balls. Jackson's hands were soon on Cam's penis and guiding him into Jackson's warm mouth. From there, coherent thought ceased, and grunts, groans, and slurps filled the air as they both fought for their pleasure and that of each other.

Jackson shot first, his cum thick and salty on Cam's tongue, which he savored before swallowing. Once he had licked Jackson clean, he laid his head back, breathing hard with his eyes closed, as Jackson finished him off. Jackson knew how to put that mouth to its best use, and Cam soon released his own load down Jackson's throat.

The room grew quiet except for their panting breaths, until finally Jackson spoke in a rough voice. "Come up here."

Cam pushed himself up and turned around, lying on his back beside Jackson, then looked questioningly into Jackson's eyes. Jackson smiled, laid his casted arm across Cam's abdomen, and closed his eyes, relaxing. Cam watched his face as Jackson dropped off to sleep. He'd never slept next to a man before. At least, not in a romantic way. It was odd, but Cam had to admit it was nice. Cam turned his head and looked up at the ceiling. *Yeah, this is nice.* That was the last thought he had before he too dropped off to sleep.

CHAPTER 25

CAM REALIZED he was not in his bed when he woke. He lay with his eyes closed, trying to remember his location and why he could hear another person breathing beside him. His heart slowed some as memories of the previous evening replayed, and he took a deep breath in relief. For a moment, he'd thought he was back in prison, that his release and everything about Hog Mountain had been a dream.

But right behind the relief came distress as he also remembered the conversation with his mother. Cam opened his eyes and stared up at the ceiling with a sigh. *Shit.* He glanced over to see Jackson was still asleep. He looked good, still golden-boy fresh, even first thing in the morning. If only some of that ability to save the world could solve Cam's problems... but Cam was pretty sure there was no helping him.

Cam sat on the side of the bed, leaned over, elbows on knees, and rubbed his face in his hands. What was he going to do? Wasn't that the question of the day, of the century, of his life.

"Morning" came a sexy murmur from behind him.

Cam jerked his head up and dropped his hands, glancing behind him. Jackson was all sleep-softened and still appeared sated and happy from their activities the night before. It looked good on him.

"Hey," Cam replied.

Jackson's smile dropped. "You regretting what we did or something?"

Cam shook his head. "Nah, just...."

"Your mom?"

"Yeah, I can hang on to a worry worse than a dog to a bone." Cam started to stand, but Jackson grabbed his wrist.

"Tell me about it. Please?"

Cam grimaced and searched for a good reason not to.

"Do you not trust me, Cam?"

Well, shit. After a moment, Cam nodded. "Okay, but we gotta have coffee." He stood and headed for the kitchen. He made a detour and grabbed his jeans from the living room, carrying them with him and pulling them on once the coffee was percolating. He filled the cat's bowls as he considered what he would tell Jackson. He could tell some of the story without going into all of it. Jackson didn't need to know every detail of his life, and it was better for everyone if he didn't.

Cam flipped on the radio but cut it down so they could talk comfortably over it. He was just pouring both of them a cup when Jackson shuffled in. He had bottles of meds in his hands, reminding Cam that he needed to heat up some breakfast so Jackson could take his pain pills. Once he'd nuked two servings of the breakfast casserole, he set it all out on the table and took a seat. He wasn't looking forward to this conversation, but he might as well get it over with.

Jackson took a few bites of the food, then washed his pills down with a sip of coffee. Once that was done, he turned to Cam.

Cam sighed and fiddled with the handle of his cup, trying to figure out where to start. Finally he said, "I've run scams for years with a few others. There was no changing as long as I hung out with them. And, well, I lived with them too. I had to get away. But one guy, he can be controlling…." And wasn't that an understatement. "I just took off and he's been lookin' for me ever since. He's bugging my mom and I'm just worried about it."

Jackson frowned as he listened, obviously concerned, but Cam knew he wasn't fooled. Jackson was too smart not to realize that there was more to the story, but Cam wasn't spilling any more than he had to.

"Anyway, that's the story." Cam stood and headed back toward the coffeepot. This was definitely a multiple-cup morning. Jackson's cell sounded, and Cam collected breakfast plates to wash, offering some privacy as Jackson answered.

Cam could tell it was Jackson's father on the phone and wondered if Pamela had given her talk yet. Cam's attention turned inward, and he stared out the window over the sink as he went back over the things he had just told Jackson.

The radio's volume seemed to get louder as the station turned from music to the top-of-the-hour news. Cam huffed and reached to turn it down, but froze as he heard:

"And in local news: A mutilated body found Monday in a remote area of Candler Park has been identified. The deceased is thirty-three-year-old Detra Lynn Willis of DeKalb County. No official cause of death has been released, although William Grey of the DeKalb County Police Department has confirmed that the body was not in one piece when discovered."

Cam couldn't remember when he fell to his knees, but it must have alerted Jackson to the news report because not only was Jackson now holding on to Cam's shoulder, he was also asking his father to contact the DeKalb Police Department for additional information about the death of Detra Lynn Willis.

When Jackson hung up with his father, he said, "Cam, there is no way I can lift you off the floor, so if you don't help me, you may have to stay down there 'til Daddy gets here."

Cam's brain didn't seem connected because even after he gave his body the order to get up, he continued to kneel on the tile floor.

"Okay, listen," Jackson said. "Can you crawl to the couch?"

Cam brushed his hand across his face and found it covered in tears. Detra....

THE NEXT time Cam was aware of what was going on around him, Walter had his hands hooked under Cam's arms and was lifting and dragging him toward the living room. Jackson walked alongside, concern written all over his face.

"I think you need to tell Daddy what's going on, Cam. All of it. Okay?"

Cam tried to answer, although he had no idea what he was attempting to say and never would since it came out as an unintelligible mumble. Walter heaved him up onto the couch and Cam collapsed there, staring up at Jackson in a state of panic.

Harold had killed Detra. Cam was sure of it. And he was pretty sure he knew why. Which led to the prospect that Detra had spilled what she knew about Cam before she'd died. Which then led to the possibility that Harold knew where Cam was... and might have known since Monday or even earlier. Cam was numb.

The couch sunk in to Cam's left, and he glanced over to see Walter's patient but expectant face. "Son, I need you to tell me what's going on and what you know about Detra Willis. A couple of DeKalb County officers are coming out to talk to you this afternoon and we need to be ready for them."

Fuck! He was so going back to prison. But wasn't that where he belonged? Maybe he just needed to accept it and quit fighting the inevitable.

He nodded and swallowed painfully. "What do you want to know?"

"All of it," Jackson said, sitting on the arm of the sofa right next to Cam and patting him on the shoulder. "Tell him all of it."

Cam nodded again, and Jackson held a glass of iced tea to his lips, tipping it so Cam could drink. Cam took a long draw off the refreshing beverage and felt tears burn in his eyes as he thought about losing all he had built for himself in the small town.

"We were a gang of criminals," Cam started. "Our last job was on a temporary warehouse unit used by Tinneman & Sons." The company was a well-known high-end electronics store that carried all the latest gadgets for the wealthy of Atlanta's Northside.

"I heard about that. The huge take at Christmas?"

Cam nodded. "We had a guy on the inside at the warehouse where the company rented temporary space for their extra inventory through the holidays. He knew when Tinneman was moving product in and out, so we were able to hit when it was at its fullest. Anyway, he let us in, made sure we wouldn't be detected, and we cleaned the place out. I was already wanting to get away from all that, but after our guy came to us the next day, freaking about the police questioning him, we all had a fight."

"We who?" Walter asked.

"Harold Livsey, he's the one that I mostly was arguing with. Detra was there too, but she always stayed quiet, just went along with whatever. And Cally, she was always around, but she would go along with Harold no matter what. We hired any other help, so it was just us. Anyway, it was me that argued. Because Harold decided we needed to get rid of the guy who helped us, before he cracked and told the police anything. He wanted to kill him."

"There was a guard found dead after the robbery," Walter said. "Some of the electronics were found in his house, and it was ruled as a suicide." He stared at Cam. "Are you saying it wasn't?"

"It wasn't no suicide, but I left before it happened, so I didn't see nothing."

"Go on, then, tell the rest," Walter said.

"Well, Detra talked to me. She knew I didn't want to kill that guard, and she told me to take the money that—"

"Son," Walter interrupted. "This is an investigation into that woman's murder, not your past crimes. Let's stick to the facts, hear me? So you left and came to Hog Mountain? And now he's looking for you?"

Cam felt stunned for a moment, then nodded. "Yeah, right, okay." He went on about the phone calls to Detra and how she feared Harold knew she'd been involved in Cam's disappearance but she still wouldn't leave. He told about all the calls to his mom's cell and how she had left town because of it.

When Cam finished, the room was silent for a long while, and then Walter asked, "Now what do you want to do?"

Cam looked up in confusion. "I guess I don't have much of a choice, sir. Looks like I'm going back to prison."

Walter chewed the inside of his mouth and thought for a moment. "You know, I get the impression you want to do the right thing. Let's meet with the officers coming by and see if we can work something out."

Cam nodded and chanced a glance over at Jackson, who now looked a lot more like a cop than the guy he'd slept with the night before.

CHAPTER 26

JACKSON AND his father packed up all Jackson's things and moved him home. It had been decided that with everything going on, including the police questioning Cam, it would be better, as an officer of the law, to distance himself from the situation. Jackson had made no arguments, and the deed had been done. The two came back at lunchtime, both in their uniforms, although Jackson was still officially out on injury leave.

Walter laid a picture of Harold on the kitchen table in front of Cam. "Is this an accurate representation of the man who you think killed Detra?"

Cam winced, then nodded. "Yeah, that's him." The milky deadness of Harold's right eye gave Cam the creeps even more than it used to.

"My officers are going to circulate this around town, make everyone aware that he might be dangerous."

Cam nodded more vigorously. "I don't want anyone getting hurt because of me. I should probably go back and give him his money."

Walter and Jackson both shook their heads. "Just hold still, son," Walter said. "We'll figure this out." He turned away and pulled out his phone, giving instructions to his officers to go ahead with using the photo of Harold Livsey.

While Walter was on the phone, Cam turned his attention to Jackson, who kept his gaze lowered as if completely mesmerized by the kitchen table.

"Sheriff?" Cam tried.

Jackson glanced up but only for a second, then spoke to the table. "Just give me a little bit to process all this, okay?"

Cam nodded and turned to look out the back window. "Yeah, I get it."

Most of the afternoon was filled with DeKalb County cops grilling Cam for details on both the robbery of the electronics warehouse, the possible murder of the warehouse security guard, and the possible motives and suspects for the death of Detra. Walter and Jackson stayed close by, taking their own notes and making comments. The interview seemed to be coming to an end when Walter received a call that had him waving for the other policeman to stay where they were.

"Can you bring her by? All right, see you soon." Walter hung up and addressed those waiting to be filled in. "We have a confirmed sighting of Harold Livsey in Hog Mountain."

"What?" Jackson and Cam yelled at the same time. Cam continued, standing and fidgeting. "Where? Where is he?" He needed to do something. He couldn't allow Harold to be roaming around Hog Mountain. It was like having a fox loose in a henhouse.

"Cam?" Walter said, waiting until Cam gave him his complete attention. "Sit down. You'll know when we know, but you aren't going off half-cocked, hear me?"

Cam nodded and sat again, but his knee bounced and he picked at a small irregularity in the fabric of the couch. Jackson paced and seemed as nervous as Cam. *But what can Jackson do?* Cam wondered. He was injured and had a cast on his gun arm. He was just another sitting duck for Harold. Cam couldn't let him get hurt either.

About five minutes later, a car pulled up in front of the house, car doors closed, and voices could be heard approaching the front door. When the door opened, Cam felt his heart drop all the way to his toes at the sight of Ida Evans. She had seen Harold? If he had hurt her....

It was then that the fog of sadness, which had settled in Cam's mind at Detra's death, burned off. Cam's eyes narrowed with anger, and he knew, come hell or high water, he was taking Harold down before the man did any more damage to Cam or anyone else he knew.

Ida was seated, eyes wide at all the uniforms, but she gave Cam a reassuring smile and patted his leg. "It's gonna be okay, honey."

"You say you saw Harold Livsey?" one of the DeKalb officers asked.

"If you mean that man from the picture with the dead eye, I talked to him. He said he was a friend of Cam's."

"Ma'am, he's no friend of mine," Cam corrected.

"He was really nice. The eye was a little scary at first, but a person can't help things like that."

"Can you tell us about the meeting?" the officer asked, obviously trying to get the conversation back on track.

"Well, I was at the cleaners and I told them my name so they could get Charles's suit. I get it cleaned once a month whether it needs it or not. And then that man, Harold you said, he stepped up and asked if I was the Ida that Camden Sanders had been talking about. Now that was right nice to hear, and I said I could be, since I knew Camden. He said he was a friend from out of town, hadn't seen him in a while, but had heard all about Hog Mountain from someone who stayed in contact with Cam. He asked me not to mention meeting him, said he wanted to surprise Cam with a visit."

Cam ground his teeth, his hands squeezing into fists.

"And you saw him today?" Walter asked.

"Oh my, no. It's been days ago."

The attention of everyone in the room flew to Ida as she opened her purse and flipped through some papers. "Hmmm. What day did I go to the cleaners? Oh, here it is." She held up the receipt, then pulled it close as she squinted to read. "That was... Monday. Monday afternoon, just after lunch. I remember because Charles and I ate at the diner, then picked up his suit on the way home for our nap."

Monday. Detra's body had been found Monday morning. Cam had called her Sunday evening. Harold had been in Hog Mountain on Monday. It was already Thursday. Why hadn't he come for Cam yet? Harold had to know where he was. What game was Harold playing?

As Ida was preparing to leave with a Hog Mountain policeman who had been waiting to carry her back home, she paused. "Wait."

Everyone immediately stopped and turned to her.

"He said he heard you had three kids now. I laughed and told him they weren't yours, that you were just watching them and helping them out. I told him how good you were with them, how much you cared about them." She must have seen the worry on Cam's face, maybe on the others', because she paled and asked, "That was a mistake, wasn't it?"

"We don't know, Ida. We'll check it all out. Don't you worry about it," Walter consoled her, patting her back and guiding her to the door. "You call if you think of anything else he said or asked."

She waved at Cam, looking worried, and he worked up the strength to smile back. "Thank you, ma'am, for letting us know."

Ida took Walter's arm and pulled him out the door with her. Cam could hear voices outside but was unable to make out any of the words.

When Walter walked back in, he immediately pegged Cam with his gaze. "What is this man capable of?"

"Anything, sir. I wouldn't put anything past him. We got to get out to those kids." Cam again came to his feet, but so did all the officers in the room, and Cam quickly sat back down, knowing from experience that going up against cops would get him nowhere.

Walter pulled out his phone and turned away from the group. He was about to dial when it rang with an incoming call. "This is Walter Rhodes," he answered. A frown grew deeper as he listened. "When?" He nodded. "Was Junior there? … Okay, thanks. Listen can you run by and just check on the Watson family?" He closed the phone and turned back to those assembled in Cam's living room. "It seems our Mr. Livsey has made two visits to the Dairy Queen in town. On Monday and again on Wednesday. He's looking for Junior, who is back to work by the way, but he missed him both times."

"Shit. What is he doing?" Cam said, mostly to himself. Cam felt a nudge at his arm and was surprised when he looked down and found Tommasina braving all the company for some petting. Cam ran a hand over her coat and sighed. Everything was going to shit, and he had to stop Harold from hurting anyone in Hog Mountain.

Again the DeKalb officers were collecting their things to leave. Cam watched them as he considered what he should do and what Harold's plan might be. He glanced over and caught Jackson watching him. Cam gave a hesitant smile, then leaned forward.

"Sheriff, what do you think your father is planning to do about this? I feel like I need to get to Harold."

Jackson frowned. "You worried we might arrest him?"

"I'm worried he might kill someone before you do." Cam frowned harder. "What the fuck? You know me better than anyone around here. I'll be the first to admit I'm not a big sharer, but fuck, Sheriff, you think I'm not worried about all this? He's already killed Detra." Cam's voice cracked. "She was my best friend. I can't let him do that kind of damage to Hog Mountain. Not when I can stop this."

Jackson looked down at his hands and then stepped closer to Cam. "Look, after Daddy leaves, I'll call and we can talk, okay?"

Cam nodded, realizing Jackson was scared his dad would see something between them that would give Jackson away. Was there even anything to see anymore? Cam wasn't sure. And that was all Harold's fault too. No, he guessed it really wasn't. Cam had made his bed, hadn't he? And now he needed to lie in it. Whatever that meant.

Walter walked the other officers out to their cars, leaving Cam alone with Jackson. Cam watched him, wondering if he would jump at the chance or if Cam would have to initiate any talking.

It took a moment, but finally Jackson said, "I really will come back over, Cam." He left it at that.

Walter came back through the door and, in an all-business voice, said, "So that's all worked out. You testify and things will go well for you. They're getting it worked out with the DA."

"But we have to stop him first. Before he hurts someone." Cam was about to go insane with the need for action. "Shouldn't we be out looking for him?"

"Cam?" Walter said. "*We* are out looking for him. I have my entire force out. You need to let us do our job."

Cam scrubbed his head and then his face. "Sir, no offense, but I need to stop him. He is showing me that he can hurt people. If simply talking to them doesn't get me moving, then he's going to up his game." Cam froze, his gaze jumping to Jackson. Jackson was the one person who he cared about that Harold hadn't made a move for. Was the fact that he was a policeman keeping Harold away? Cam doubted it.

"What?" Jackson and Walter asked at the same time.

"He's going to do something to Jackson," Cam stated. He didn't know what, but Harold was going to try to hurt him. And the fact that he was a cop would only make it sweeter for Harold.

"Like what? Why do you say that?" Walter asked, seeming to take the issue seriously.

"Because he wants to destroy my new life."

"And why Jackson?" Walter appeared clueless, and was about to ask more when his phone rang again.

Cam was getting to hate the sound of that phone. It always meant trouble.

It ended up being Jackson's mother on the line. Cam could tell by the one side of the conversation going on. It was indeed trouble, although it seemed to be something personal and Pamela needed Walter to come home to talk about it.

Walter appeared to be in a big hurry once he was off the phone. "Your mother is in one of her tizzies and she won't tell me what is wrong until I get there. Do you need a ride, Jackson?"

Jackson nodded and got up to go, but he cut his eyes over to Cam before following his father out the door, Cam guessed to let him know he hadn't forgotten his promise.

Cam stood at the front window and watched them go, then sank down on the couch and waited. It seemed so lonely to think of having no one in the house all evening. And the children wouldn't be by the next day, either. Things were just starting to go right. Was he going to let Harold ruin this for him?

About twenty minutes later, as Cam was feeling himself start to doze, his cell rang. "Yeah?"

"Cam, I can't come by tonight." It was Jackson, and he sounded upset.

"But you promised. Is everything okay?"

"Cam, there's a rumor all over town. Mom's been called by most of the ladies at church. They say we're sleeping together." Jackson let out a muffled sob. "I told Momma and Daddy the truth, but…."

"Oh, Sheriff. I never meant for this to happen."

"I know. I just… I need to handle this, okay?"

"Was it Grant?"

"I think so," Jackson said quietly.

"Are we okay?" Cam asked.

"I… I-I don't know."

Cam nodded. "Okay. Night."

Cam threw the phone onto the coffee table and sighed. The thought was just crossing his mind about how quiet the house was when a familiar voice came from the darkened kitchen.

"Having problems, Cam?"

He would recognize that smooth, deep voice anywhere.

CHAPTER 27

CAM SAT up straight, immediately on full alert. "Goddamn you, Harold. What the fuck are you playing at?"

Harold stepped out of the shadows of the kitchen, a sinister smile on his lips. "You don't know, Cam? Well, let me tell you, then. I'm teaching you a lesson. Your place is with me, and I can destroy anything else you try to build, especially with my money. You got it?"

"Yeah, I got it. Now leave these people alone, Harold. Just take me back to Atlanta and let's be done with all this shit."

Harold laughed. "You'd like that, wouldn't you? But I'm not done here. You will regret this for the rest of your life. And these people will *hate* you."

Cam stood, his hands curling into fists, and stalked toward Harold. "Don't you dare do anything to the people of this town, you hear me?"

"Or what, Cam? What will you do to me, hmm? You know, Detra said 'don't you dare do anything bad to Cam.' Do you think that threat did a thing to save her, to save you?"

Cam released a feral scream as he dived at Harold, arms outstretched. Harold fell backward, hit the kitchen table, then they both went to the tile floor where they scuffled and rolled. Cam landed a few punches, but so did Harold before holding Cam down with a large hand around his neck and stopping the fight.

Cam gagged and kicked out at Harold, but Harold simply punched him—hard—in the gut. With a groan, Cam attempted to curl in on himself, but Harold prevented the move by bracing his knee over Cam's thighs, then continued to punch into Cam's abdomen, over and over.

Until Cam lay still.

WHEN CAM stirred again, he was still on the floor, but Harold was no longer over him, and Tommasina was nudging at his hand in search of pets. With a groan, he rolled and tried to get up, every movement shooting pain through his body. Cam glanced around the dark room, on guard for another attack from Harold, but was surprised when it didn't come.

He hobbled to the wall and flipped on the light. After wincing and shielding his eyes until they grew accustomed to the brightness, he was able to see that the back door stood wide open and there was no sign of Harold anywhere. Just to be sure, Cam closed and locked the door, then searched the entire house, including inside closets and under beds, but he was alone except for Tommasina, who followed him curiously. For a moment, he felt relief at that conclusion, but then began worrying about where he might be.

"Shit," Cam mumbled and pulled out his cell phone. It was two in the morning. Could Harold be out in the town somewhere? Cam couldn't take the risk.

He pushed his finger across the screen, then tapped a few times before lifting the phone to his ear. It took a few rings before he heard "Hello?" Jackson's voice was rough from sleep and sexy as hell. Just the sound made Cam's heart leap and then plummet as he considered that things with Jackson might never be fixed.

"Hey, Sheriff."

"Cam…. It's late."

"No, listen. He was here. I know you're not happy with me, but I need to tell someone. He was here."

"What?" Jackson sounded much more awake. "Harold was there? Where is he now?"

"I don't know. He beat me good and left me on the floor in the kitchen. I think I've been out for a while."

"Cam! Are you okay? Do you need me to call an ambulance?" The concern in Jackson's voice gave Cam a warm feeling, and his lip quirked up on one side in as much of a smile as his face was giving at the moment.

"Nah, Sheriff. I'm pretty tough. But he's planning on hurting people here. He pretty much said it. I don't think I can just sit here and wait for it to happen." Cam's mind was spinning with the faces of all the people he'd met in the small town, even those he'd only seen but hadn't had a chance to get to know. "They don't deserve to get hurt for my mistakes."

"I'm calling Daddy. You sit tight, okay?" Jackson hung up, and Cam waited.

Cam went into the bathroom and rinsed his face off with cool water, then lifted his shirt to have a look at his severely bruised chest and abdomen. He winced just from the movement and wondered if he didn't need to be seen by a doctor, but he really didn't have the time. It was more important to stop Harold. That needed to be his top priority.

His phone rang, and Cam grabbed it up from the counter where he'd laid it down. "Yeah?"

"Your favorite kids are all sound asleep, Cam. Just thought I'd let you know."

"You son of a bitch!" Cam yelled, but the line went dead. He pulled back his fist and almost punched the wall, but was able to pull up short. He needed to store all this anger up and let it out on Harold.

The phone rang again as Cam fumed. "WHAT?"

"Cam?" It was Jackson.

Cam huffed out a breath and told Jackson, "He's at the Watsons' house. He just called and said the kids were all sleeping sound." Cam's voice cracked as he said it.

"Fuck. Listen, a cruiser is coming by to pick you up."

"No need. I'm on my way to those kids." He hung up before Jackson could try to talk him out of it and headed for his truck. As he cranked the engine, his cell rang again, and he answered while backing out of the drive. "Yeah?"

"Cam, we'll meet you there. Don't go in loud, okay?" Jackson asked.

"He already knows I'll come," Cam responded. "He knows he's baiting me."

"But he doesn't know we're coming too, right?"

Cam huffed. Jackson might have a point. "Okay, yeah. So what's the plan? Maybe I should go in loud and draw his attention." He drove through the darkened town, everything closed for the night, and wondered where else Harold had gone, what other houses had he broken in to in the last couple of days while Cam didn't even know he was in town. The thought made him grind his teeth.

There was muffled talking as Jackson conferred with someone— Cam guessed it was Walter—then Jackson said into the phone, "Okay, you go in loud, right up to the door. Maybe even honk the horn like you are trying to warn them. We'll park down the road and come in quiet. We're calling more backup, so let us handle any takedown, you hear?"

"Yeah, okay, I got it. See you there." Like Cam was going to stand back and not take any chance he had to take out Harold. He sped up, an image haunting him of Harold standing over those innocent kids as they slept.

CHAPTER 28

As Cam turned into the Watsons' driveway, he laid on the horn, one nonstop blast until he skidded to a halt at the base of the stairs leading to the porch. He left his headlights on, aimed right at the front door, and jumped out, screaming for someone to open up as he stomped to the front door.

Cam only had to knock once before a very annoyed Junior Watson jerked the door open. It was a surprise to see Junior sober and that was obvious even just woken from a dead sleep. Cam tried to push by him, but Junior wasn't giving an inch.

"Have you been drinking, Cam?" Junior asked.

Cam would have taken the time to joke at the irony of that question, but he needed to check on the kids. "Junior, there's a man up in the room with your kids. Go check and ask me how I know once we're sure they're fine."

Junior frowned and appeared to be ready to argue but then glanced back at the stairs, concern written on his face. He nodded and hurried off, Cam and Ruby following in his wake. Cam hadn't gone into the house in all the times he'd been by, and he glanced around now, taking in the stark but spotless appearance of the ancient home.

The stairs squeaked, and Cam couldn't help but think that if Harold was waiting for him, he sure knew they were coming. On the second floor, Junior threw open the first door on a narrow hallway and stepped inside. Cam pushed in behind him and waited for his eyes to adjust to the gloom.

There were four single beds crammed in the room, all with lumpy shapes snuggled in the covers. Junior pulled back the covers to check each one, and Ruby stepped around Cam to help, then she hurried across the hall and did the same in the girls' room.

Cam stepped to the window and stared out. The screen had been cut and pulled back, either a way in or way out, maybe both.

Junior looked over Cam's shoulder at the window and then to Cam. "You want to tell me what this is about?"

Cam nodded and left the room. As they started down the stairs, Jackson came in the front door, weapon drawn but held awkwardly in his left hand.

"The kids' rooms look clear," Cam told him.

"We still need to check the rest of the house," Walter said, coming in behind Jackson. "Why don't y'all wait outside until we do."

Ruby looked back up the stairs, obviously worried over any threat to her kids.

"Just leave them sleeping." Walter patted her shoulder as he passed, and she nodded and did as she was told, wringing her hands.

Once on the front lawn, Cam could make out other policemen searching through the yard and surrounding areas.

Junior turned to Cam and said, "Well?" He was dressed in an old ripped T-shirt that he might have worn to bed, a pair of jeans that looked to be hurriedly pulled on, and he wasn't wearing shoes, but Junior looked clear-headed and honest-to-god worried about his family. It was refreshing to see.

Cam set about explaining the situation to Junior, and as he did, Ruby placed a hand over her mouth and began crying. Junior wrapped an arm around her but kept his attention on Cam.

"This the same man who keeps asking for me up at the Dairy Queen?" Junior asked.

Cam nodded. "I would imagine it is. Milky eye, about six feet, mustache and beard."

Junior nodded back. "Sounds like the guy. So he's after you?"

"He's out to hurt me, Junior. And he knows I care for the people of this town, especially those kids."

Junior frowned and looked over his shoulder at the bedroom windows where his kids slept.

"I'm sorry," Cam said.

"You can't help what other people do, Cam," Junior said. "You can only control your own actions."

It sounded like something from a twelve-step program, and Cam wondered if Junior wasn't going to one. He hoped it worked if he was. He remembered Jackson saying that Junior fell off the wagon every so often. While that wasn't good, it also meant that he tried to be on the wagon at times too. It was more than he could say for his own dad.

When a group of officers formed near the house, around Walter and Jackson, Cam walked closer to hear what was being said. Walter ordered a few to check farther down the street, focusing on any place Harold might could hunker down, and take care to check any windows and doors on neighboring houses. Walter made it clear they didn't want to leave and find out Harold was in a nearby home, holding the family hostage, but that they also didn't want to wake everyone up if there was no cause at the moment.

When the officers dispersed, leaving Walter and Jackson as control central, Cam stepped closer. Now that the adrenaline of the moment had stopped, his aches and pains were coming on, and Cam could tell the same was true for Jackson, who stood with his shoulders tense and cradling his right arm.

"You okay, Sheriff?" Cam asked quietly. He wasn't sure what Walter had saved up to say to him and didn't want the older man to think he was about to have some gay episode with his son right there in the middle of the Watsons' yard.

Jackson nodded, but Cam wasn't buying it. He glanced at Walter to find him also watching Jackson with concern.

"How about you, Cam? You said Harold got you."

Cam ground his teeth at the reminder. The son of a bitch. Cam raised his shirt and looked down at the mottled bruises on his abdomen.

"Damn!" Walter exclaimed. "You need to be seen for that."

Cam shrugged and dropped his shirt. "Had worse. I just want to find the son of a bitch."

"We all do, son," Walter agreed. When Cam glanced over at him, Walter gave him a soft smile that Cam hadn't expected. If things were so bad, shouldn't Walter be ready to finish him off? Because no matter what Jackson decided to do, Cam wasn't going to go back in the closet. He wasn't going to get a bullhorn out, but if someone asked, he wasn't going to lie. It wasn't some moral thing. Cam had lied more than his fair share in his life, but well, there was a lot Cam wanted to fix about himself. Being gay wasn't one of them.

Cam sighed and looked around the yard, pausing to watch Junior comforting Ruby as she cried over the threat to her children.

"Like night and day, isn't it?" Walter asked, gesturing toward the two. "He's a good enough boy most of the time. Just a mean drunk."

They both watched the couple for a moment, and then Walter turned to Jackson. "I put an APB out on Livsey. I'm sure DeKalb has too. Can you think of anything else we need to do here?"

Jackson looked like he was about to fall over. Cam wanted to stand closer and shore the guy up, but knew that would not be welcomed. So instead, Cam kept an eye on him, ready to step in and catch him if needed.

"I—we could have the patrols swing by more often," Jackson offered.

Walter was nodding when Cam's cell buzzed in his pocket. He frowned and looked down at the offending technology. That would be a text and he didn't get texts, not since he had moved anyway. He dug the phone out and pushed a few buttons. The text had come from an e-mail address, hlivsey@gmail.com, and said:

The cops? Really, Cammy boy?

Cam felt the sudden urge to vomit. He held his stomach and leaned over, knowing that if he heaved, it would hurt like hell. A big warm hand slid across his shoulders, and Walter reached to take the phone from his hands. After a moment, he heard both men swear.

Another moment and the phone buzzed again. Cam stood and read over Walter's shoulder.

Ready to go home now? No? Maybe I should play somewhere else then.

The phone buzzed again, and they were looking at a picture. The small photo was dark and it was unclear what they were looking at until Walter reached and enlarged the image. It was of a face. Most of it covered with a plastic oxygen mask, eyes closed in sleep. Charles Evans. Harold had to have been standing over the older man as he took it.

Cam sobbed. Harold was in the Evanses' house. And then he ran.

CHAPTER 29

THE EVANS house was dark and quiet when Cam pulled up in front. He didn't honk the horn or make any noise. If Harold hadn't woken them up, then it would be best if they slept on. He had the unpleasant image of Charles waking to find Harold looming over him and having a heart attack from the shock.

A police cruiser pulled up behind him and Walter and Jackson got out. Cam joined them in front of the house and they all stared at the silent residence, unsure of how to proceed. Walter finally stepped forward, turning on his flashlight and aiming it at the ground, then headed around the side of the house where the bedrooms were located. Jackson pulled his gun and went in the opposite direction. Cam followed after Jackson, sensing a need to protect the wounded man.

They met up with Walter at the back of the house, where he was examining the sliced screen of an open window. "I don't think he's still in there, but I reckon we need to be sure," Walter commented softly.

"Who's there?" came Ida's voice from inside the room. "I've got a gun and I know how to use it."

"It's Walter, Ida. Don't shoot. Is anyone in there with you?"

"Well, of course, there is. Charles is here. What are you doing at his bedroom window?" She pulled back the curtain, still holding a shotgun that looked too big for her to even lift, much less fire. After squinting out at the three standing on the other side of the window, she put the gun down. "You boys planning on climbing in, or should I go open the front door?" Charles stood behind her, his hair standing on end from where he had pulled off the oxygen mask he'd worn for sleep.

"I'm not sure I want you walking through the house to open the front door," Walter responded. "Mind if I climb through and check the house first?"

Ida's eyes grew large, and she reached over and grabbed the shotgun again. "Come on through." She kept hold of the curtain as Walter pulled himself into the house.

"Meet you in the front, boys," he said and turned away.

Jackson and Cam hurried back to the front door and waited for what seemed way too long before it was finally pulled open by Ida. "Come on in. I want to know what is going on, and it looks like you all could use some coffee."

While Ida made coffee, Walter called a paramedic from the local fire department to come by, to everyone's protest. "If nothing else, I want a record of the damage done by this man. Charles, this is stressful. Let them look you over. Cam, you too. He got you good. And, son, you aren't even cleared to be working. I need to be sure you're okay."

Walter wasn't accepting arguments, so instead, they took their coffee and went to sit in the living room and wait for the paramedic. Cam tried to explain what was going on during that time, apologizing profusely for the trouble he had caused.

"This isn't your fault," Ida reassured him, patting his shoulder. "You did the right thing, getting away from someone like that."

While the paramedic crew checked everyone out, Cam noticed that Jackson looked worse and worse for wear. "Hey, Sheriff. About time to call it a night?"

Jackson looked up, dark circles under his eyes, and simply nodded.

"Take him home, Cam. I'll stay here and hit the hardware store when it opens for a new screen," Walter said. Then he walked the paramedics to the door. They'd decided everyone was okay for the time being, but left a list of symptoms for each to watch for.

Cam nodded, surprised that Walter would suggest it. "Come on," he encouraged, offering his hand to help Jackson up. "Time to hit the hay." Cam wondered how long it had been since Jackson took his pain meds and decided to make a point to be sure he did once Cam got him home.

Jackson looked as if he was going to refuse the help to stand but then thought better of it and accepted Cam's hand. He grunted and groaned as he stood, and Cam had to hold back a few of his own as his stomach muscles contracted when he pulled.

After saying their good-byes, Cam helped Jackson out to his truck and into the passenger seat. He was sure Jackson was going to collapse at any moment, but as they drove through town, Jackson surprised him by pointing to the diner, which looked to already be open for the morning.

"Let's stop. I need to eat something before I take my pills."

Cam nodded and pulled into a parking place. He could definitely eat. It had been way too long since he'd put even a bite into his mouth, and he was sure it was the same for Jackson. When they got out of the car, Cam took a minute to scan the parking lot and area for Harold, but he had a feeling Harold was going to go silent for a while. At least, he hoped so.

Jackson entered ahead of him, but Cam didn't miss the way all eyes came up and everyone in the restaurant stopped what they were doing. The only noise that didn't stop was the jukebox in the corner.

"Looks like we are the talk of the town, Sheriff," Cam whispered to the back of his head.

"Yup," Jackson answered over his shoulder, then slid onto a stool at the counter. "I think maybe we should order to go. We can eat over at my place if you don't mind."

Cam nodded, then noticed the waitress who had overheard Jackson's proposition, her eyes wide and mouth hanging open.

He turned all his attention to her, a grin spreading across his face. "Good morning, Susan. We need a to-go order. For refuelin', if you know what I mean."

"Cam...."

"It's okay, Sheriff. I'll be civil," Cam reassured him. "I'll take a sausage biscuit and another biscuit plain with lots of jellies."

Jackson nodded. "Same for me. Thank you, Susan." He seemed completely drained, and hung his head.

"Y'all need some coffee while you wait?" Susan asked after she put the order in.

Cam was looking around the restaurant, making sure all the people staring at him knew he'd noticed them. "I'll have a water."

Jackson didn't look up, but answered, "Yeah, water is good."

"So you sure it was Grant?" Cam asked.

"Pretty sure, after what you said to him that night."

"One way to find out," Cam said.

"What do you mean?"

Susan came back and slid two waters in front of them and was about to move on down the counter, but Cam reached out and took hold of her wrist.

"Hey, Susan. Who told you?"

Jackson finally found the energy to lift his head and stared at Cam in disbelief.

"I don't know what—"

"Oh come on, Susan. Don't be coy. Who told you about"—Cam waved his hand back and forth between himself and Jackson—"us."

Susan's mouth opened, but nothing came out as she seemed to try to work out how to answer. "Well, I—" she finally got out.

"Yeah?" Cam encouraged.

"It was Regina, okay?" She sounded a little mad that Cam had asked.

Cam turned to Jackson. "Regina?"

"Grant's assistant," Jackson filled in.

Cam turned back to Susan. "She told all these people?" Cam pointed to the others in the restaurant.

"Well, I think that's more been by word of mouth." Susan gave that *duh* look.

"Ah! The old Christian way." Cam nodded.

"Cam…," Jackson said warningly.

"Well, I think what you guys are doing is against the Bible, right?" Susan sounded very unsure of her conviction.

Cam shrugged. "I think it says you shouldn't gossip too. So we're both up shit creek, Susan."

"Oh." About that time, the bell dinged for an order up and Susan hurried off. She seemed happy to have a reason to get away.

"So you think Grant told Regina to tell people about us?" Cam asked.

Jackson shrugged. "Does it really matter, Cam?"

Cam considered that for a moment. "Yeah, it does."

Susan appeared in front of them again with a plastic bag full of their breakfast. She sat a ticket down in front of them, and Cam scooped it up.

"I got it, Sheriff." Cam doled out the total due and a nice-sized tip on top of it, then slapped it down on the counter and grabbed the bag.

Susan seemed pleased and smiled to show it as she collected the money. "Thanks, guys, come back any time."

Cam waved as they headed out the door. "You can count on it."

CHAPTER 30

ONCE THEY were back in the truck, Cam floored the gas and got them both out of there. It pissed him off that people were making his life their business and especially that they had upset Jackson so much because of it.

With a few mumbled instructions from Jackson, Cam pulled up in front of Jackson's small home. It wasn't as big as what Cam lived in, but it was nice, clean, and looked like it was built in the last millennium. Cam bet everything in the house was organized and nothing was out of place. The sheriff had that kind of vibe about him. Jackson had his life compartmentalized completely. There were no items or people that crossed over in the highly restricted sectors of Jackson's life. *But then there's me*, Cam thought. Cam had to admit he kinda fit in more than one of Jackson's boxes. Huh....

After putting the truck in park, Cam turned to Jackson. "Still want me to come in? I can take mine home with me if you would rather be alone."

Jackson looked down at his lap and took a moment before answering. "Come in and eat with me. I still feel a little strung out by all this. I was hoping you could tell me what's going on."

Cam shut off the engine. "Yeah, okay. I don't really know either, but we can eat together, maybe make sense of it all." They both climbed out and headed for the door.

Cam felt guilty for taking this time, like he should be out beating the bushes for Harold, but as worn to the bone as both of them were, Cam wasn't sure what they would do once they found him. Maybe collapse on top of him and smother the asshole to death? The fucker was playing with him, Cam knew that, but he was also playing with the innocent lives of the people who lived in Hog Mountain. Maybe it was time for Cam to give up and go back to Atlanta with Harold. It could put an end to all this. Cam was about to make the suggestion to Jackson when he noticed he'd become surprisingly alert. Cam froze as Jackson drew his gun and pulled them both against the side of the house.

"The screen on the farthest window is cut," Jackson whispered.

The other intrusions had upset Cam, made his blood boil, but Cam was tired and he knew Jackson was in even worse shape. "Goddammit!" Cam yelled and pushed away from the wall. "You stupid son of a bitch! You want me? Here I am, you one-eyed asshole!"

Jackson's eyes widened, and he tried to pull Cam back against the side of the house, but Cam shrugged away and marched up to the front door, where he began yanking on the knob once he realized he couldn't go in.

"Let me in, you motherfucker!" Beyond the pounding blood in his ears, Cam made out the squawk of Jackson's radio and knew he was calling it in. But Cam felt crazed, wanted to pull Harold apart piece by piece. He was still screaming, most likely incoherently, and tugging at the door when a uniformed man pushed him aside and used Jackson's key to open the door.

Jackson pulled Cam out of the way as other policemen entered the house. They both stood silent as they waited for the house to be searched, shoulder to shoulder and breathing hard. Cam had used the last of his strength in his rail against the door. He had no doubt he and Jackson were on the verge of falling over right where they stood.

Walter walked up, frowning, as one of the officers stepped out onto the front porch. "Sir, I think you need to see this." Walter walked up the stairs to the porch and Cam and Jackson followed him. Inside, the house was ransacked, but the officer led them all to the back bedroom, which appeared to be the one used by Jackson.

Walter stopped in the doorway, blocking Cam and Jackson from entering, but from over his shoulder, it was still obvious that the room had been trashed and covered in what appeared to be blood. Cam pushed his head past the doorframe to read what had been scrawled on the walls.

DIE FAG PIG!

Cam's heart pounded at the thought. Could Harold be planning to kill Jackson? Cam couldn't let that happen. He couldn't let Harold kill anyone. This had to stop. Cam pulled out the cell and found the text message from Harold, then started typing.

"What are you doing, Cam?" Jackson asked.

"I'm ending this," Cam answered.

"It's not blood," one of the officers told Walter. "It's paint."

Walter took a step into the room. "Ida Evans said some of her painting supplies were gone from the garage."

"Cam...," Jackson said. "What are you doing?"

Just as Cam hit Send, Jackson pulled the phone from his hands and read. Cam had sent:

I'm ready to go home, Harold. Let's go.

"No!" Jackson yelled. "No. You aren't going with him!"

Walter turned around and glanced between the two of them, then grabbed the phone and read the text. While he still held the phone, it announced an incoming answer.

I already decided to take one of these kids instead.

Cam swore under his breath. He was pretty sure Harold was baiting him, but how could he not take the message seriously?

Walter pulled his own phone from his pocket and tapped at the screen. When he put the phone to his ear, he said, "Junior, this is Walter. We have reason to believe our suspect may be on his way or already at your location. We are sending officers. You need to get your family somewhere safe."

Walter hung up and called for the officers, telling them all where they were headed. Cam and Jackson both hurried to accompany them. They climbed into Cam's truck and Cam took off ahead of all the police cars, determined to get to Harold first.

Cam no longer felt the lethargy he had only minutes ago. Adrenaline was now pushing him to his limits. His hands tightened on the steering wheel, a deep need to strangle Harold bubbling up inside of him, causing his fingers to turn white with the pressure he was exerting.

Beside him, Jackson was quiet, his jaw set firmly as he stared out the window. The back of the truck slid as they turned onto the dirt road leading to Junior and Ruby Mae's house, but Cam didn't slow down. He had to make sure that Harold didn't hurt anyone. He had to stop this once and for all. Harold was capable of just about

anything. The asshole had proved that when he killed Detra. Detra....
And didn't thinking of her just make him that much angrier.

Cam slammed on the brakes as he pulled up in front of the
house, then jumped out of the truck and ran toward where Junior and
Ruby were trying to get their mess of kids into the old beat-up station
wagon they owned.

"I'm getting them out of here," Junior said as he scooped up the
toddler and turned to put him in his car seat.

Cam nodded and looked over the car at the older kids, who
were opening the back gate to climb in. Cam tried to offer a smile
of reassurance but wasn't sure he was able to pull it off. The kids all
looked scared to death, and he couldn't blame them. Cam hated that
any of his shit had blown back on them.

Over Galen's shoulder, Cam saw a movement and was immediately
on guard. Harold stepped from behind a bush, reaching out to wrap his
arm around Galen's neck and pull him against his body.

"No!" Cam yelled and started to run. He sensed Junior running
beside him and put on more steam. He needed to get to Harold before
the other man did. Ruby surprised everyone by sideswiping Harold,
bowling him over so that Galen was released as both Ruby and Harold
fell to the ground.

Cam skidded to a halt and Jackson stopped beside him, but
Junior ran right past them as Ruby scrambled to her knees and then
grabbed Galen to pull him farther away from Harold. Behind them,
all the children were screaming, and Cam could hear the thud of more
feet as all the police officers made the scene. Cam scooted Ruby and
Galen behind him and motioned Ruby and the kids to get in the car
and lock the doors.

Junior dove for Harold, taking him on one-on-one, and Cam
was unsure what to do that wouldn't make the situation worse than
it was. The two men rolled across the front yard, stirring up dust as
they kicked and punched. The officers continued to step closer to the
pair, and Cam and Jackson took cues from them, becoming part of the
circle that was cutting off any escape for Harold.

When the fighting slowed, it was because Harold had gotten
the upper hand and held Junior with an arm around the man's throat.
Harold stared straight into Cam's eyes as he reached up and grabbed

Junior by the chin and jerked the man's head to the side; the loud, sickening crack as Junior's neck snapped was simultaneous with the man going limp in Harold's arms.

Without conscious thought, Cam reached over and pulled Jackson's firearm out of his hand, then raised it and fired. The bullet stayed true, hitting Harold right between the eyes and sending his body backward until both Harold and Junior lay still, one slumped across the other on the ground.

There was silence after that. Or maybe it was just the shock setting in, since Cam could see mouths moving, and what must have been an anguished cry from Ruby as she threw herself on top of Junior. There were crowds of people moving around Cam, hands on him. And then... he didn't know anything more.

CHAPTER 31

CAM REMEMBERED leaving the scene and being transported to the hospital. He remembered being checked out in the Emergency Room no matter how many times he said he was fine. He remembered the questions from cops in all different uniforms, and he remembered shooting Harold Livsey after the man killed Junior Watson, although all of it seemed to have happened in a deep fog with muffled sound and strange light. In fact, that one horror-filled event was now playing on repeat in his brain and Cam wondered if he'd ever get it to stop.

The doctors hadn't admitted him, although they had discussed it. It seemed that in addition to being black and blue, Cam was suffering from shock, and the doctors were worried about allowing him to leave on his own. But with handcuffs holding him to the bed, Cam didn't think they needed to worry much about him going anywhere but to jail.

The policeman who'd placed the handcuffs on him had said Cam was considered in police custody for the time being, and Cam knew what that meant. He would be on his way back to prison as soon as the doctors decided he was well enough. And didn't he deserve it. He'd brought nothing but problems to this quiet little town.

Cam closed his eyes and thought about his farmhouse and garage, his big soft bed with the open window right next to it that let in the sun each morning. He thought about Tommasina and how much he'd loved scritching behind her ear when she sat in his lap, and about his kitchen where he could make food the way he liked and eat anytime he wanted. About eating a slice of Dotty's pie and a big glass of milk as she gabbed and made him feel almost normal. He thought about eating dinner with Ida and Charles, about fixing bicycles for kids that lived in a group home. He thought about shopping at the grocery store and getting everything he wanted, about sitting on the porch with a big glass of tea, watching the kids ride their bikes, laughing with them as they painted, and Officer Jackson Rhodes climbing out of his patrol car, all broad shoulders and slender hips, his uniform pressed to perfection. He thought about taking Jackson in the house and stripping that uniform off, and about what that muscled golden body had looked like, felt like.

Cam brushed tears from his eyes, then opened them to find Walter Rhodes walking into the room. Cam coughed and sat up a bit more. No use getting all emotional now; not like it was going to change anything.

Walter grabbed a chair and pulled it up beside the bed. "The doctors say you still seem to be out of it, son. You gonna be all right?"

Cam nodded. "Yeah. I'm good." What good was it to tell him otherwise? Cam stared at his lap, not really feeling like having a visitor at the moment.

"We're gonna release you from custody for the moment. We may need to ask some more questions, but right now, the shooting is being ruled as justified. You'll need to stay in town until the entire investigation is completed, okay?"

Cam looked up to be sure Walter wasn't kidding. "I'm free?"

Walter nodded. "Looks that way. You gotta stick around for now, though."

Cam nodded. "Yeah, no problem."

"Since your trouble is out of the way, you thinking of leavin' here? After the investigation is over, I mean," Walter asked, and Cam got the feeling it was more suggestion than curiosity.

"In a hurry to get me gone?" Cam was surprised at how much it hurt, but he was sure the whole town felt the same way.

Walter cocked his head to the side and gave a little shrug. "This town isn't used to having someone gay around. It might be easier on everyone."

Cam's eyes widened. He'd expected Walter to want him gone because he was a criminal, because of what had happened with Harold, but because he was gay? That just beat everything.

"Just 'cuz you didn't know about it, doesn't mean this town has never had a gay person in it. I know you like to think you're in control of everything here, and I guess you might have the power to push your son back in the closet, but ignoring something doesn't make it not so." Cam huffed. "And yeah, I guess once this is all over, I'll head on down the road."

Walter looked sad and Cam couldn't figure out why since the man had gotten his way. Cam frowned but stayed silent as Walter got up and left the room.

JACKSON STEPPED out of a curtained-off exam area where he had been given fluids and his wounds had been checked. After finally being released, he was anxious to see how Cam was doing. He still felt like hammered shit, but lying on that hard-as-a-rock hospital gurney sure wasn't making him better. That torture device must be a way to gauge how bad off patients were. If they were well enough to complain about the bed, they were well enough to go home.

As he got closer to his parents, he heard his father say, "I told him, Pam, but I think—"

"Shhh. Here comes Jackson," his mother hissed.

Jackson frowned. "What's going on?"

"We're just eager to get you home where you belong," his mother assured, taking hold of Jackson's arm and attempting to steer him toward the exit.

Jackson dug his heels in and turned to his father, who looked guilty and a little disgusted with himself. "Dad? Want to tell me what's going on?"

"Son, listen to your mother. She only wants what's best for you."

"Oookay. Well, I'm going to check on Cam before I leave. I'll be fine, Momma." Jackson patted her hand and then pried it from his arm, already waving down a nurse to ask where they had placed Camden Sanders.

When he pushed back the curtain, Jackson wasn't prepared for what he found. Over the past weeks, Cam had become larger than life to Jackson, a force of nature. The man never seemed to be frightened of any situation, but just jumped in, ready to do whatever needed doing. At that moment, though, Cam looked small and scared. One hand was cuffed to the bed rail, shoulders slumped, and his eyes were red like he had just been crying. The IV in his arm looked so large, and even his bright tattoos appeared pale under the fluorescent lighting.

"Hey," Jackson said, his voice just above a whisper, afraid he might startle Cam.

"Hey," Cam answered, sounding strangled.

Jackson pulled the chair closer and sat, taking Cam's hand. "I thought they released you from custody."

"They did. I'm just waiting for the officer to come collect his cuffs. Are you okay?" Cam squeezed Jackson's hand and then pulled away.

"Good enough to go home. You?" Jackson was a little worried at how Cam was acting. Must be the shock.

"Yeah, I think they're done with me." Cam nodded.

"You can come home with me to my parents' house, then. Mom said she'd take care of us for a while."

"Nah." Cam looked stricken. "I think I just want to go home, you know?"

"Yeah, I get it. I'll go there with you, then. We can watch one of those movies you got and we have plenty of food in the freezer, right? Plus Tommasina is probably anxious to see you. And I like listening to the evening sounds. It's peaceful."

Cam frowned. "You want to come over?"

"Yeah. And I need to talk about stuff. I figure you do too." Jackson really did need to talk about how he was going to handle everyone knowing he was gay. Cam seemed like the best choice to talk to. Plus, he liked hanging out with him, and Cam gave the impression he might need watching right then. Jackson didn't think he could leave Cam alone at the moment. It felt too wrong.

"I don't think your dad is going to like it if you come over."

"My dad? Did he say something to you?" Jackson turned and frowned at the curtain, as if he could see his parents through it.

About that time, the curtain was pulled back enough for a uniformed officer to step through. "Gonna remove those cuffs, Mr. Sanders, and then I think the nurse said she is ready to release you." The man gave a cursory smile to Jackson and then unlocked the cuffs and took them with him as he left.

Jackson helped Cam to get his pants on, and after a nurse removed his IV, Cam pulled the stained T-shirt over his head. Cam still looked fragile, like the last twenty-four hours had crushed his soul, at least a little bit. While Cam tied the laces on his boots, Jackson stepped out into the hall to talk to his parents.

Jackson's parents were still standing together against a wall and turned as Jackson appeared. "Are you ready to go home, honey?" his mother asked.

"I'm not going home with y'all. I'm heading to Cam's house."

"What? Jackson, you need to be with your family right now," his mother argued, but the look on his father's face told Jackson a lot.

"I don't know what was said to Cam, but it hurt him... bad. He needs someone right now." Jackson looked between the two of them. "Tell me what you said to him."

Jackson's mother pursed her lips and cut her eyes over at Walter, but Walter sighed. "Son, I asked him if he was leaving now that no one was after him."

"And well he should," Jackson's mother added. "Look at the trouble he's brought here."

Jackson ground his teeth and looked back at his father, who nodded and continued. "I suggested it might be best if he did."

Jackson shrugged off his mother's touch when she reached for his arm. "Neither of us have a car."

"I'll give you a ride," Jackson's father offered and reached in his pocket for his keys.

"Walter...," Pamela started, but both men turned away.

CHAPTER 32

THE RIDE was awkward. Cam sat in the back where he figured a criminal should be anyway. Mostly there were a lot of quick glances that darted away when someone else caught them looking.

Walter stopped by Jackson's house so he could run in and get his meds. The police officers had finished collecting data from the scene, but until it was cleaned, Jackson would have to make other arrangements. While Jackson was inside, Cam and Walter had a competition to see who could be the quietest. Since Walter cleared his throat once, Cam was pretty sure he'd won but didn't rub it in.

Jackson came back to the car with a duffel bag, which surprised and pleased Cam. He hadn't been sure how long Jackson planned to stay with him instead of going to his parents. Walter didn't seem to notice the bag as Jackson piled back into the front seat. But instead of putting his police vehicle in gear, Walter sat for a moment, then huffed and turned in the seat so that he could see both Cam and Jackson.

"Listen, here's the truth of it." Walter scrubbed his face with his hand. In that moment, he looked far older than his age.

Jackson appeared ready to interrupt his father, but Walter was not to be stopped.

"I'm sorry. I shouldn't have asked you to leave to save my son this misery."

"Wait. You asked him to leave because of me? Because he's gay?" Sometimes Jackson was a little slow on the uptake.

"Yeah, and I'm sorry for it. In the last days, your momma has been treated like a pariah by her women's group because of the rumor going around." Walter held up his hand when Jackson and Cam both opened their mouths. "She came to me crying. Not for herself, but because she couldn't let you make a decision that would cause this kind of treatment for yourself for the rest of your life. People are acting like you got some disease or something." Walter sniffed and scrubbed his face again. "I don't want that either, son."

Walter turned farther around in the seat and stared at Cam. "Is that what it's like? Every day?"

Cam was confused. "I don't know—"

Walter talked right over him. "Are you treated like you're a leper just because you're gay?"

"What?" Cam was incredulous. "Do you know what year this is?"

"Daddy." Jackson reached over and touched his father's arm. "You taught me to fight my own battles. Right? Let me fight this one, okay?"

Walter nodded and looked over the seat again at Cam. "I really am sorry."

"It's gonna be okay." Cam hoped he was right.

WHEN CAM stepped in his front door, Tommasina came running to greet him, meowing and rubbing up against his legs. He knelt down and scrubbed her head, then looked around at his home and smiled. The ramshackle old house was really important to him and so was his pet.

"Come on, girl. Let's get you and those babies some food." Cam stood and headed for the kitchen where he filled her bowls. "You hungry, Sheriff?"

"Nah. Mostly I'm just worn-out. You?" Jackson stood in the doorway to the kitchen, filling the space nicely. Tired or not, the man looked good in Cam's house.

"Yeah, just tired." Cam pushed Jackson back so he could pass, then took his hand and grinned. It felt weird but right. He'd never held hands with a man before. Cam would have thought it was too mushy before that minute. But this was different, right? "Come on," Cam encouraged as he pulled Jackson toward the stairs that led to his bedroom. And this was another first. Cam had always imagined this decision as a hard one, one that took a bunch of deliberation, but in reality, it had been easy. It just felt right.

They clomped up the stairs and Cam paused at the top, eager for Jackson's reaction.

"Oh wow," Jackson exclaimed. He let go of Cam's hand and walked over to the bed, running his hand over the metalwork of the footboard. "This is beautiful, Cam."

Cam grinned with pride. He almost admitted getting it at a garage sale but then decided against it.

Jackson wandered over to the big open windows and stared out at Cam's overgrown backyard.

"We still haven't really cleared it." Cam felt a need to take up for his inaction, although things had been a little hectic in the past few weeks.

Seeing Jackson in his space kinda made Cam's heart do this extra-beat thing. It made him wonder at his sudden feelings. Was it because of his cry in the hospital? Because he'd felt vulnerable and now he'd opened himself for all these other feelings? Or was it because of the death he'd seen? Did that sort of thing make a man ready to let someone into his private space? Cam wasn't sure. Maybe he'd change back in a day or so and would have to tell Jackson to beat it. Who knew?

"So...," Jackson started as he turned to Cam. "Want to get comfortable and maybe talk about things?"

Cam raised a brow. "And by talk about things, you mean...? Is that some euphemism?"

Jackson chuckled. "Yeah, probably. I mean, I do need to talk, but...."

Cam canted his head toward the bathroom. "A shower first? I'm feeling grungy."

"Who first?" Jackson appeared to be serious.

"Um.... Do you really think I'm going to sit out here while you get naked in my bathroom?" Cam grinned.

Jackson laughed. "Yeah, no, I guess not. I've never showered with anyone before," he admitted while taking off his shirt. "I mean, in gym and after games, but not like this."

"Yeah, not like this," Cam agreed as he began stripping off too. "I don't remember ever being so eager for the showers in prison."

They both chuckled. "I'll need something to cover this," Jackson said, holding up his right arm to display the cast still surrounding it.

Cam nodded and stepped into the bathroom, where he opened the cabinet under the sink and pulled out a roll of small trash bags.

After carefully securing the plastic over Jackson's cast, Cam turned to set the temperature of the water.

Cam was feeling a little nervous but wasn't sure why. He'd always been confident when it came to sex, but this was out of his depth for sure. It didn't help that Jackson seemed fidgety too.

Cam pulled back the shower curtain. "After you, sir. Front or back?"

"Uh. Is this answer more significant than where I stand in the shower?" Jackson teased with his brows raised.

"Nah. Get in." Once they were both under the warm spray, Cam added, "We can switch out, anyway. And *that* was more significant." He grinned at Jackson.

"Agreed." Jackson grinned back.

They both started soaping themselves, but it didn't take long for that to change. Cam watched Jackson run his one big hand over golden skin covered in a light dusting of blond hair, but Cam itched to touch and it seemed the same was true for Jackson.

After running his hands down Jackson's thick chest, Cam lowered to his knees and took Jackson's heavy set of balls into his mouth one after the other, sucking and licking each in turn.

Jackson leaned back against the tile wall, groaning out his desire, his hips pushing forward and his engorged cock bobbing against Cam's cheek.

Once Cam had had his fill of Jackson's heavy balls, he leaned back and gave the thick cock above it the attention it deserved. He sucked and swirled his tongue along the shaft, then up to the head and across the slit. Cam kept Jackson's sac in his hand, massaging as he serviced the sexy man standing in front of him.

Jackson dragged his fingers against Cam's shorn head, not finding any purchase against the barely there black stubble. Cam hummed his pleasure at the feel and redoubled his efforts, swallowing and taking Jackson's cock as deep as he could. The thickness pushed at the walls of his throat, making his own cock swell in excitement. Cam slid his lips along spit-slicked flesh, traced the throbbing vein that ran the length, then delved into the slit at the tip to discover every last drop of precum.

"Fuck. Cam, I'm gonna…." Jackson thudded his head against the tile and arched his back as Cam drank down thick spurts of cum.

Cam reached between his legs and only had to give his cock a few pumps to join Jackson in his release.

The water was already starting to cool, so Cam stood and they both made sure the other was rinsed, then they dried themselves and headed back into the bedroom. Cam pulled back the covers and slid in, then invited Jackson to join him.

Jackson lay down on his back and got comfortable, while Cam was positioned on his side next to him. Jackson put his hands behind his head and turned to look at Cam. "I've never had a boyfriend before. I mean, I thought I did once, but... well, I never had one that anyone knew about."

Cam nodded. "Me neither."

"Is that where this is going?" Jackson asked, a little insecurity seeping into his expression.

"Yeah, I think it is, Sheriff. But that's uncharted territory for me, you know?" Cam definitely didn't want Jackson to think he had all this stuff figured out.

Jackson turned his head to stare at the ceiling. "So I guess that means I'm coming out."

"You okay with that?" Cam asked softly.

Jackson nodded. "It feels right."

Cam agreed and they both grew quiet, lost in their own thoughts.

After a while, Jackson mumbled, "Your bed is real comfortable."

Cam grinned. At some point, they both drifted off to sleep.

CHAPTER 33

RAZOR-SHARP CLAWS dug into his scalp, and Cam swatted them away angrily. Instead of easing up, the pain grew more intense, and suddenly everything hurt as Tommasina used his torso as a scratching pole. Struggling to get free, he moaned in frustration when he realized he couldn't go anywhere. He was stuck in muck, back in the Watsons' front yard with Harold struggling on the ground with Junior. Tommasina squalled and ran away. He knew what came next, but now he had a chance to change the outcome. Cam ran toward the pair, but his feet felt mired. So many people milled around the yard for some reason: the kids zoomed by on their bikes, Ida and Charles tried to stop him for a chat. Cam pulled away while apologizing, stumbling closer to Harold. Cam had to stop him. His heart beat a mile a minute as he pushed by another townsperson who held a casserole and asked him if he was gay. Then the police officers all pulled their guns and aimed them at him. Walter yelled for him to halt, and Cam couldn't make his mouth form the words to tell the man about Harold.

When he kept running instead of obeying their commands, the officers opened fire and Cam felt his body become riddled by bullets, striking him all over until he was only able to drag himself forward just enough to grab at Harold's leg. But when he looked up into Harold's eyes, he knew he was still too late. There was an evil glow of victory from Harold and a sad acquiescence from Junior just before the reverberating crack of each bone in turn. *Pop, pop, pop.*

Cam gasped and jerked awake, sitting straight up in the bed. He groaned with the exertion on bruised and aching muscles. At the answering groan next to him, he turned to find Jackson holding his ribs and struggling to sit, most likely jerking awake due to Cam's sudden movements.

"You okay?" Jackson asked, reaching to rub Cam's back.

Cam was still breathing hard. It felt like he had run miles instead of sleeping in his nice, soft bed. He nodded but couldn't work up the energy to speak. He was still too busy trying to separate what was real from what had been a dream, and felt a thick cloud of misery hanging over his head at the sudden realization brought on by the dream. This was all his fault. Not that he hadn't already known he'd brought this evil to the town, but it seemed more concrete now, more absolute.

Jackson appeared to read Cam's body language well, scooting closer and wrapping an arm around Cam's shoulders. "Hey, it's okay. Let's get up and have something to drink. Sound good?"

"Yeah," Cam managed to get out. He climbed out of the big bed and looked around for his pants.

Jackson lifted his cell and checked the time. "It's six o'clock. Ready for some dinner? I know I'm hungry."

"Yeah," Cam said again. He couldn't seem to get his brain to leave that dream behind, and he kept hearing the bones cracking and seeing the light dimming in Junior's eyes.

From downstairs came the sound of someone tapping on the front door, and Jackson pulled on his jeans. "I'll get it," he said. "You come on down when you're dressed."

Once Jackson had left the room, Cam huffed and slumped on the edge of the bed, scrubbing his face with his hand. "Shit," he mumbled.

JACKSON PULLED open Cam's front door and was surprised to find Dotty Calhoun standing on the front porch with a pie and a bag of groceries in her hand. He glanced down at his bare chest and blushed but then reached out and took her bag with his uncasted hand and stepped back.

"Welcome, Dotty. What brings you by this evening?"

Dotty patted his arm as she stepped into the dark house. "I heard about all that's happened, and I owe Camden a pie. Seemed like a good time to bring one by." As Jackson flicked on lights, she made her way into the kitchen. "I'm glad he has someone here to look after him, turnabout and all that. How is he, Jackson? And how are you?"

Jackson sighed. "Physically, he's fine and I'm feeling good too. But all this has done a number on him, you know?"

Dotty nodded and tsked. "Y'all eaten?" She started pulling containers out of the bag Jackson had set on the table.

"No, ma'am. I was about to heat something up."

"Well, I needed some company, so I brought enough for all of us to eat." Dotty smiled and opened a cabinet to pull down plates. About that time, footsteps could be heard on the stairs. "Come on down, Camden," Dotty called. "I brought you dinner and some of my pie for dessert."

When Cam came around the corner, Jackson soaked him in. The narrow hips barely holding up his baggy jeans, the slender but well-muscled chest and arms, tattoos peeking out from both sleeves and the neck hole of his shirt, bare feet that were long and narrow and also covered with ink. Cam's face looked freshly washed, his blue eyes near glowing in the room, but he looked sad, and that ate at Jackson's heart. It was all he could do not to go to him and offer comfort. Although, how did that even work? What would Dotty think? Should he care? He stood frozen in indecision.

Dotty, on the other hand, was not torn in her compulsions. She headed immediately to Cam and wrapped her arms around his waist. "Bless your heart. Come on and sit down while I fix you a plate. You too, Jackson."

Dotty bustled around like she owned the kitchen, and Jackson and Cam did as told, both silent as she chatted.

"It's a shame what happened to Junior, but none of us know the hour or the day. And you can't blame yourself for what evil wrought. I heard all about it. Of course, you both know how the gossip in this town is. That's a shame too, if you ask me. But I'm just glad you two have each other." She placed a heaping plate in front of each of them, then brought her own plate to the table and took a seat.

Jackson glanced at Cam, who had his brows raised at what she had just said. "You mean you're glad we're gay?" Cam asked.

"Well, now, that's silly. Like saying I'm glad you're left-handed or something, right? Just glad you found someone to love. We all deserve that." She took a bite and chewed, but as soon as she'd swallowed, she continued. "Back when I was just a girl. Well, things were different then. And my brother Lennie—you have never met a sweeter boy. I took care of him a lot while Momma worked. It was a hard time. But Lennie was different. I tried to protect him, I really did. But by the time he was about sixteen, it was obvious, and Daddy wasn't having any of it. He took Lennie out to Milledgeville State Hospital, where he was given shocks to try to fix him." She grew quiet and then sniffed. "I still have dreams about him. They destroyed my sweet boy and he never came back home from that horrible place. I swore I would never let anything like that happen to someone I love."

Cam and Jackson were no longer eating, their forks hanging in midair as they stared at Dotty. Finally, Jackson shook himself and stood, stepping around the table to kneel beside Dotty and rub her back.

She sobbed. "If only he were alive today. He was such a happy boy and this is such a better time."

Jackson patted Dotty's shoulder and looked across the table to Cam, who appeared completely shocked by her admission. "I'm so sorry," Jackson said.

She nodded and seemed to pull herself together, dabbing her eyes with a paper towel. Finally she continued. "So I am not going to let a soul speak ill of you boys, you hear? You deserve happiness like anyone else." With that, she waved Jackson back to his seat. "Eat up, we have pie after this."

DOTTY STAYED for another hour or so after dinner. She seemed happy to have company, and Cam enjoyed her visit. Once she was gone, he and Jackson dropped onto the couch and sighed.

"Wow," Cam said.

"Yeah, that was some good food," Jackson agreed.

"Nah, I mean about her brother. I can't even...." Cam wasn't sure how to finish.

Jackson shook his head, seemingly lost in his own thoughts. After a few minutes, he turned to Cam. "So what happens now?"

Cam shrugged. "I guess we just keep living our lives and see what tomorrow brings."

"I mean about me coming out or whatever."

"Sheriff, you don't need to make a public announcement to be out of the closet. You just have to stop caring what anyone else thinks. You ready?"

Jackson thought about that and nodded. "Yeah. I'm ready."

CHAPTER 34

CAM WOKE up early the next morning and was downstairs scrambling eggs when Jackson came thumping down to the kitchen.

"Morning," Jackson mumbled as he slumped into a kitchen chair. "So you don't even use an alarm in the morning?"

"Nah." Cam grinned over his shoulder. "The sun usually wakes me up."

"Yeah, no chance of sleeping late in that room. Hadn't gotten around to buying curtains or something?" Jackson scrubbed at his eyes.

"I like it that way." Cam scooped eggs onto two plates, then topped it with a few slices of bacon. "You like to sleep late, Sheriff?"

"Sometimes." Jackson nodded and reached to take his plate.

They each took the time to shovel in a few bites before continuing. Around some bacon, Jackson asked, "You said we should go on with our lives like normal, right?"

Cam nodded.

"Then I have church tomorrow." Jackson sighed. "That's going to be fun."

Cam was pretty sure Jackson didn't think it was going to be fun at all, and Cam had to agree with that assessment. He shrugged. "Then don't go. I wouldn't."

"But I love church. It's part of who I am." Now Jackson looked pained, and that set a burn going in Cam's stomach.

"Then go, Sheriff. Don't let anyone take that from you."

"Go with me?" Jackson looked hopeful, with big puppy eyes, and Cam cursed to himself.

"I—that's just not my thing."

"Please, Cam? I know you don't believe, and I'm not trying to trick you into anything. But it would mean a lot to me."

Cam huffed but finally nodded. "I'll have to do some ironing, though. And I don't have a suit or anything."

Jackson grinned. "Yeah, no problem. Thanks, Cam."

AFTER BREAKFAST, Cam went out and sat in one of the rockers on the porch to call his mom. The morning was still cool, but the day looked like it had the makings of a hot one. He propped his feet against the railing and dialed his aunt's number.

She answered on the first ring, as if she had been waiting for him to call. "Cam? Is that you?"

"Yes, ma'am. Is Mom still there with you?"

"Well, of course she is. Doug says it's just shameful how you've put your mother in the middle of this and then left her here for us to take care of. And after all she's done for you."

Cam opened his mouth but then closed it again and took a deep breath. He had no need to explain himself to anyone. "Can you put my mother on, please?"

"Well, all right, but you should know how much this is stressing her and...."

"I get it, Aunt Mary. Can I speak to her?"

There was silence, then he heard what sounded like a sliding door opening and some mumbling. Tommasina hopped up in his lap and nudged at his hand until he scrubbed behind her ear a time or two.

Finally, his mother came on the line. "Cam?"

"Mom, hey. Listen, everything is okay now. You can turn on your phone again."

Cam heard his mother blow out what he assumed was a huge cloud of cigarette smoke before answering. "Well, that's good, because I'm ready to go home. They won't even let me smoke in the house here. I'm living on their back porch so I can have my cigarettes, and Mary's husband even complains about that. And lord, you don't want to hear him when I ask him to run me to the store when I'm out. Makes me realize how nice it is not having your father around." Her voice sounded like a gravel crusher, and Cam could imagine how utterly unenjoyable it would be to have his mom staying at his house. If they weren't such assholes, he might feel bad for his aunt and uncle.

"Other than having to smoke on the porch, are you doing okay, Mom?" Cam asked.

"Well, about the same. I was worried about you. You told that man to stop calling me?"

"Yeah, Mom. He won't be calling you anymore. I got that straightened out." Cam rubbed his forehead. There was no need to tell her all that had happened. "You gonna go back home now?"

"Yeah, I may go today. Can you send me the gas money? I could be home in time to watch my stories tonight on the TV. You know, they don't watch the shows I do and they get all huffy if I ask them to change the channel. And if they do let me watch, I can't smoke, so what's the use?"

"Yeah, Mom. I can send you money. I'll go do that this morning."

"Make sure you do so I have time to get home before my stories start."

"Sure thing. You drive safe, Mom." He hung up and stared out over his front yard.

A few minutes later, Jackson strolled out, freshly showered and dressed for the day. "Everything okay with your mom?"

"Yeah. Fine. I was just thinking how much I like it here."

Jackson sat in a rocker and nodded. "Yeah. Country life is nice. We gonna sit and enjoy it all day?"

"Nah. I gotta go wire some money to Mom. You want to come along? We could grab some stuff for dinner tonight and I could stand to get some more supplies at the hardware store. Whatcha think, Sheriff?"

Jackson shrugged. "I got no other plans for the day. Let's do it. Maybe we could head by Ruby's too?"

Cam nodded. He wasn't really ready to see that yard again, but checking on the kids was more important than that. "Yeah, definitely." He stood and headed back inside. "Give me ten and I'll be ready to go."

CHAPTER 35

AFTER WIRING money, Cam and Jackson headed to the back of the grocery store to browse the selection of steaks. Cam was in the mood for a big hunk of meat. And that sounded good for dinner too. He snickered and Jackson nudged him with his elbow.

"What's so funny?" Jackson asked.

"Just thinking about hunks of meat I want to eat." Cam waggled his brow at Jackson to be sure he got the joke.

Jackson choked and glanced around to be sure no one was watching. "People are already giving us the stink eye. Don't make it worse."

Cam shrugged. "We're just living our life and not worrying about them. Right?" Cam picked up one of the packaged steaks and poked at it. "Do you know how to pick one of these?"

As he asked, the butcher stepped up to the counter and asked, "May I help you?" His expression seemed to purposefully communicate how much he didn't want to help them.

Cam put on his biggest smile and held up the steak he'd been poking. "I need a course in how to pick a steak."

The butcher frowned more. "It depends on what you like."

"Right. And I would like you to explain all those variables and what steak is best in each circumstance and how to pick just from looking." Cam kept the smile on his face, but Jackson was fidgeting beside him.

"That would take a lot of time, but if you tell me what you like, I can pick one for you."

"Oh, we are in no hurry. Please, explain."

Jackson wandered off as Cam learned all there was to know about steaks.

AN HOUR and a half later, Cam slid behind the steering wheel of the truck. Jackson was slumped in the passenger seat surfing the Internet on his phone.

"Have fun tormenting that man?" Jackson asked without looking up.

Cam placed a few bags of groceries on the seat between them and closed his door. "Oh yeah. That was a blast. The angrier that butcher got, the more I fucked with him."

"You like to stir the shit, Cam."

Cam canted his head to the side, then nodded. "I guess I do." He reached to turn the ignition and froze, staring out the windshield.

Jackson looked up and followed his line of sight to discover Grant just climbing out of his car where it was parked in front of the vet office. Jackson glanced back over at Cam. "I don't think—"

"I think I need some advice on cats."

"Cam, come on. Let's don't—"

But Cam was already out of the truck again and strolling in Grant's direction.

Cam heard Jackson slam the passenger side door and then his footsteps as he followed quickly after.

Grant glanced over his shoulder after unlocking the door to his business, his eyes widening as he caught sight of the two coming in his direction. He hurried into the shop and was nowhere to be seen when Cam made his way into the waiting area.

Regina gave them a smirk from behind her desk. "HIV testing is done at the clinic. We can't help you here." She flipped her hair and flounced into the back.

Cam growled, but Jackson touched his arm and murmured, "No scenes, Cam."

Cam nodded but headed to the back where the exam rooms were. Jackson followed.

"Oh, Grant! Come out, come out wherever you are," Cam called.

"Cam, if he calls the police…."

Suddenly a door jerked open and Grant stepped out into the hallway. "Please don't hurt me. I didn't do it!"

Cam and Jackson both froze in midstep. Was he telling the truth? But if it wasn't him, then who?

Obviously seeing an opportunity to state his case, Grant went on. "Come in and sit." He waved them into his office. "Regina, you too." This was said with more force, and Regina soon followed them in and took a seat.

Grant's office looked more like an upscale doctor's than a small-town vet's, with leather chairs and overly expensive appointments. Grant took his place behind a large teakwood desk, but he didn't seem to be in the mood to gloat as Cam imagined he usually was. Grant slumped in his chair.

"This fucks things up for me too, you know. Who is going to hook up with me if they're afraid I'm going to gossip about it to everyone afterward? Have you thought of how all this affects me?" There was definitely a whine in his voice, enough to make Cam roll his eyes.

"Then who—" Jackson started.

"Regina." Grant seemed quite eager to throw his gal pal under the bus.

Cam's mouth dropped open in shock, and he turned to glare at Regina where she sat off to the side. She didn't appear all that penitent. Her expression was hard as she said, "My boyfriend said I should."

Grant's brows went up. "That creepy guy you went out with once? Now he's your boyfriend?"

Cam was getting a weird feeling about this. "How creepy?"

Grant turned away from Regina. "Super creepy, like he was some serial killer or something."

Cutting to the heart of the matter, Jackson asked, "Name Harold by any chance?"

Regina seemed shocked that Jackson knew him. So that was what Harold had been doing since Monday. He'd been working to destroy Cam in the town. He'd said everyone would hate him before he was done.

"How do you know him?" Regina asked.

"He murdered Junior Watson yesterday and was killed right afterward. He was in the town to hurt Cam and used you as a way to do it." Jackson stood and turned to go. He looked tired, and Cam couldn't much blame him for it.

"No!" Regina yelled out. She obviously hadn't known he was dead and began weeping in her hands when it sank in.

Cam shook his head and stood too, following Jackson out. They wandered back across the parking lot, both in sort of a daze.

"I'm sorry, Sheriff," Cam said after climbing back into the truck.

Jackson shrugged after putting on his seat belt. "That man was evil, Cam."

"Yeah, he was."

No doubt about it.

CHAPTER 36

WHEN CAM and Jackson arrived at Hog Mountain First Baptist Church on Sunday morning, all eyes were on them. A few people with familiar faces waved, but most just stared. Pamela Rhodes frowned when she noticed Cam was with her son, but Walter hurried over and clapped both Jackson and Cam on the back.

"Glad you showed. This'll all pass as soon as the new scandal hits, you wait and see." Walter led them through the crowds. He was smiling, but there was a glint in his eye telling anyone who dared to speak negatively that he wasn't above coming to blows.

Cam glanced over at Jackson. He looked miserable, and Cam could understand it. These people had always been like family to him, and they were rejecting him just as he'd known they would. It pissed Cam off, and he would have let them all have it if Jackson hadn't made him promise not to stir the shit while at church. *Dammit.*

So instead, Cam smiled and tried to appear happy with the fact he was about to spend an hour or more of torture with a bunch of people who didn't want him there. Since he was restricted from telling any of them off, he decided his only course of action was to kill them all with kindness.

Cam's smile spread wide across his face, and he stepped away from Jackson to shake hands with a man who had been giving them the stink eye. "Camden Sanders," he greeted, shaking the hand with enough liveliness to rattle the man's brains.

"Kenneth Matthews," the man replied and pulled back his hand as soon as possible.

Before Cam could introduce himself to anyone else, Jackson grabbed his arm and guided him toward the open doors of the church. "I said no stirring," Jackson murmured.

"That was more shaking than stirring," Cam quipped, but Jackson didn't even snicker. Boy, this was going to be a hoot.

A man Cam felt sure to be the minister was positioned at the open doors, greeting people as they entered. It occurred to Cam then that all preachers had a look to them, although he couldn't quite pinpoint what it was that made them recognizable. There were all kinds of preachers, just like with anything else in the world, but good or bad, they still all had some quality that made their vocation apparent. *Huh.*

The pastor seemed to have something personal to say to everyone that walked by him, shaking hands or patting shoulders in welcome. He had an honest face and his smile appeared genuine. Although Cam had never thought of preachers as someone he would like to know, this guy didn't seem so bad. But that opinion could change, depending on the next couple of hours.

When it was their turn for the meet and greet, the pastor's eyes widened, as did his smile. "Jackson! So good to see you today." He shook Jackson's hand and slapped his shoulder, then turned his attention to Cam. The smile didn't falter even a bit as he grabbed Cam's hand and shook. "And you must be Mr. Sanders. I'm Jimmy Brown. So good to meet you. I've been remiss with coming to welcome you to the town. Welcome to Hog Mountain First Baptist."

Cam was a little shocked by Jimmy's enthusiasm but smiled back. "Glad to be here." While that wasn't necessarily true, he figured God wouldn't smite him for that little white lie. He hoped.

He followed Walter and Jackson farther into the building and through another set of doors to a room full of padded pews surrounded by stained glass windows. People were already seated throughout the auditorium, and Walter and Jackson seemed to know where they were going as they headed down the main aisle. Maybe members were assigned seats or something.

Walter turned into one of the pews about six rows from the front. Jackson followed right behind, and they traveled across until they were almost at the outside. When Walter sat, he left room for another person on the outside end, Jackson dropped down beside Walter, and so Cam took a seat too, glancing around to see others finding their places as well.

"So what happens now?" Cam asked Jackson in a hushed tone.

"Have you never been to church?" Jackson responded.

He sounded so incredulous that Cam felt the need to lie. "Well, yeah, but this could be different. Right?"

Jackson appeared not to completely buy his answer but didn't argue, instead shrugging. "It's pretty standard. We sing some songs, have some prayers, the pastor gives a sermon, and then some more singing and praying. Nothing crazy."

Cam nodded. "So an hour?"

"About," Jackson said. "I don't think they have any baptisms scheduled for today, but Mom would know better."

That seemed to be Pamela's cue to slip into the seat left open beside Walter. She didn't lean forward to acknowledge Jackson or Cam, but took Walter's hand when he offered it.

The rest of the pew to Cam's left was empty, and while other pews were filling up, no one seemed eager to sit with them. Cam was about to mention that development to Jackson when an older couple turned into the pew and Cam smiled as he recognized Ida and Charles. Charles wheeled a small canister of oxygen behind him as they made their way over.

They both returned his smile, and Ida patted Cam's leg as she sat down beside him. "I am so pleased to see you here, Cam. We love you so much." She then leaned forward and patted Jackson's leg too. When she sat back, Charles leaned forward and shook their hands. He appeared a little out of breath from the trip into the church and huffed a bit as he turned his attention to the front.

Just as a group of men walked up the steps to the podium, Cam felt a pat on his shoulder. He turned to see Dotty was just getting situated in the pew behind them. She smiled and winked, then pulled a hymnal from the back of the seat and looked to the man now waiting for everyone's attention.

Cam followed Jackson's actions, and for the next half an hour, he stood and sang, sat and sang, stood and prayed, and sat and prayed. He wondered if all the movement was just to make sure everyone stayed awake. It did keep a person from getting too comfortable.

Then Jimmy Brown stepped up to the pulpit and looked out over the congregation. Cam wondered if they weren't supposed to do something, since the man appeared to be waiting on something, but he sure wasn't going to be the first to make a sound in the quiet that suddenly surrounded him.

After what felt like an eternity, Pastor Brown nodded, as if finally seeing or hearing what he wanted from the crowd, and began his sermon. "You know… each year, I try to touch on all the topics I think we need to remember. I am blessed to lead a strong congregation, and I feel most of my messages are more like Post-it notes, similar to what my wife leaves me. 'Remember to take the trash out' or 'the electric bill is due on the tenth' or 'daylight savings starts this weekend.' But in the past week, I have been struck with the fact that even in a godly community like our own, there is still a need to preach the basics. I have been lax with my responsibility, but I will make it right today."

There were a smattering of replies from those in the audience. "Amen" and "Yes, Lord" came from all around Cam, and he began to worry at what the preacher might be about to preach. It hadn't crossed his mind until just then that this would be the perfect opportunity for a sermon on the evils of homosexuality and that could account for why the pastor was so pleased to see that he and Jackson had attended the service. *Well, shit.*

"Rarely do I teach an old-fashion come-to-Jesus sermon, because this flock is so strong, righteous. But today, there is a need for REPENTANCE AND RENEWAL, and I KNOW that those I speak to will accept the Lord's word with an open heart." When Jimmy emphasized certain words, they echoed in the high-ceilinged room.

"Praise God!" came a cry from the back of the auditorium, and Cam looked back over his shoulder but couldn't identify who said the words. This might get awkward right quick. In fact, there might be a stoning immediately following the service. Did they schedule those too?

"From this day forward, the blackness at our door will be washed clean." Pastor Brown got quiet as he opened his Bible and flipped a few pages. In the crowd, people nodded and smiled. Cam bounced his leg nervously and glanced over at Jackson. Maybe they could make a run for it.

Jackson sat with his lips pursed. He looked nervous too, and didn't that make Cam want to beat someone's ass. Fuck 'em all. He'd just have to stay and make sure no one messed with Jackson.

"Acts 16:31. 'Believe on the Lord Jesus Christ and thou shalt be saved.' Romans 10:9. 'If thou shalt confess with thy mouth the Lord Jesus, and shalt believe in thine heart that God hath raised him from the dead, thou shalt be saved.'" The preacher paused again and looked around. Cam did too, and this time he saw much confusion on the faces in the crowd. Cam had to admit, he wasn't sure what point Jimmy was going for anymore either.

"I want everyone to open their Bibles and look up Romans 10:9." There was the sound of many pages flipping, and Cam was impressed at the control Jimmy had over his audience. But if comic books had taught him anything, it was that with great power comes great responsibility.

When the page turning quieted, Pastor Brown continued. "Read that scripture again. I'll wait." And he did before adding, "Is there an asterisk at the end of that verse?"

The crowd mumbled, "No."

"Does the next verse start with the word 'except'?"

"No."

"And do you believe? Do you believe this is the truth?"

Louder now, the crowd answered, "Yes! Amen!"

"Then I have a surprise for you," the preacher said, leaning on the pulpit as if about to tell a juicy secret. "Whether homosexuality is a sin or not, if a man or woman believes that Jesus is the son of God, he or she is going to be in heaven right beside you, sitting at the Lord's feet. And if God loves them enough to welcome them into heaven, who do you think you are to turn them away from your own home or community?"

Cam's eyes widened, and he turned to Jackson, who also seemed flabbergasted. Ida patted his leg and Dotty patted his shoulder. Cam was liking this church stuff more by the minute. The rest of the crowd appeared to be as shocked as he was. He couldn't work up the nerve to lean forward enough to see what Jackson's mother's reaction was, but he could tell Walter had put his arm around her in a protective way. The crowd was now eerily quiet after being so boisterous at the beginning of the sermon.

As the preacher went on to talk about casting first stones and how love was the greatest among these and gossip being a sin, Cam leaned closer to Jackson and whispered, "And you told *me* not to stir the shit."

Jackson shushed him, but there was a grin threatening at the corners of his lips.

"So when Jesus says to love your neighbor, does he mean only the ones that go to church? Only the ones we think are good enough? We are all sinners, and the road we walk on this earth is a hard one. We don't need to waste our time making sure everyone else is doing what they are supposed to. We need to keep our eye on the path we walk in order to keep from stumbling. Sure, we should encourage each other, help one another along. But can anything that has happened in this town in the past few days be considered as encouraging? Helpful? As far as I have seen, it was nothing but a disgusting mess. And we should be ashamed. Hate has never been what this town is about."

Charles's voice rang out louder than Cam had ever heard it when he said, "Amen!" Cam felt his eyes sting with the threat of tears at the conviction behind that one word.

"As far as I can see, we have not done unto others as we would have them do unto us, have we? No, children, we have not. Our behavior has been shameful. Shameful and unworthy of the people we hold ourselves to be, both to the Lord and to each other. If we judge, then should we not be judged?" Pastor Brown pointed out into the audience. "What if your son or *your* daughter should grow up to be different? What if *their* child sees love in a different way? Will you disown them? Damn them as something unholy?"

Cam was getting uncomfortable again and began squirming in his seat. To his surprise, Jackson reached over and placed his big hand on Cam's thigh, giving a squeeze. He didn't pull it back, just left it there, a strong weight that felt warm and reassuring. Cam glanced over and Jackson smiled, a smile full of confidence that made Cam's heart break a little.

With a rumble, the crowd rose to their feet, and Cam realized they were going to sing again. He'd been so distracted he'd missed the end of the sermon. He was surprised when, as soon as the singing began, people exited the pews and started walking to the front. Cam glanced around in confusion. Jackson hadn't told him about this part.

Jackson leaned over and Cam realized Jackson's eyes were watery. He whispered, "They're going forward to confess their sins. We'll just stay here."

Cam nodded. "You okay?"

"Yeah," Jackson said and sniffed. "Real good."

Then Pamela leaned over and touched Jackson's arm, whispering, "I'm so sorry." She nudged Walter out of the way and pulled her son into a tight hug, holding there for a minute before reaching farther and pulling Cam in to the embrace too. "I'm so, so sorry," she whispered again, then turned and stepped out of the pew, heading down the aisle with the others going forward to confess their sins.

Jackson crumpled into the seat, his shoulders shaking with his sobs. As he slumped there, Walter and Cam sat beside him, although Cam wasn't sure what to do other than rub his back in small circles. That seemed to help, and Cam was happy for it.

The rest of the service went by in a blur, and after dismissal, Cam shook hands with more people than he would ever be able to remember. He would have grabbed Jackson and made a run for it, but Jackson appeared to be enjoying being right where he was. So Cam backed up against the wall and just watched. Cam wasn't dumb enough to think that sermon had changed how everyone thought, but it seemed to have changed enough to make Jackson feel better about things, and that was what mattered to Cam.

After a while, Dotty sidled up beside him with a grin. "Are we going to start seeing you here every Sunday?"

Cam smiled but shook his head. "I doubt it, but it wouldn't be so bad to visit every once in a while."

She nodded. "Jackson would like having you with him and we'd enjoy seeing you." She patted his arm. "I need to get home and heat up some lunch. You boys have a nice day."

Cam waved, and as he was watching her make her way down the front steps of the church, Jackson stepped up next to him. "Ready to go?"

"Yeah," Cam said. "Wanna go eat at the diner?"

"That sounds nice." Jackson took Cam's hand as they walked out the door, and Cam had to admit he was surprised. But it was a nice surprise, one he could definitely get used to.

CHAPTER 37

TWO DAYS later, Junior's funeral was held at a small funeral home off Highway 365, not far from the hospital. It looked as if the entire town showed up, which Cam was pretty impressed with. Although Junior had been a man with an addiction, not some monster or anything, Cam got the feeling death kinda wiped people's memories of all the bad that had gone before. In the last few days, Junior had risen to saint status, which Cam thought was good as far as the kids were concerned but odd otherwise.

Speaking of the kids, they all seemed so small and lifeless, dressed up in clothes that made them almost unrecognizable, their hair tamed into styles Cam had never seen on them. They hung their heads as they sat next to their mother, nothing like the boisterous kids he'd come to know. Ruby was trying to be strong for the kids, but she looked crushed as well. Cam wondered if they blamed him for all that had happened, because there sure was a part of him that did.

After sitting through a service at the funeral home and then standing through another at the graveside, he and Jackson headed to Ruby's house. Death was another occasion that called for food in Hog Mountain. Since they couldn't go empty-handed, Cam and Jackson had learned to make a roast and veggies in the Crock-Pot. Dotty had given them a list of ingredients and they'd gone shopping for both those and the appliance to cook it all in. Then the night before, Dotty had talked them through mixing it all together and turning the thing on. It'd smelled so good as it cooked that Cam planned to do the whole process again the next day, only for their own dinner this time. Since Jackson had been staying with him while his house was cleaned up following Harold's rampage, it would be nice to have a home-cooked dinner together.

Cam had always liked his own space, but for some reason, having Jackson around wasn't cramping his style at all. Their only problem so far had been Cam's lack of drapes in his upstairs bedroom and how it let in far too much light for Jackson's taste. Cam had agreed to tack up a blanket over the window for the time Jackson was there, but he already missed his view and the morning sun waking him up at first light.

Cam carried the Crock-Pot with the cord wrapped around the handle. It felt surreal walking across the lawn where everything had happened. All the cars parked throughout the yard made it look different, though, and that helped Cam deal with it. Jackson seemed to understand and laid a hand at the small of his back as they headed for the front steps. The weight and warmth of his touch did the trick, and Cam put on a smile as he passed through the open front door.

The living room was filled with people chatting in small groups, some sitting, others standing. A few of the visitors paused in their conversations to stare in a decidedly unfriendly manner as they entered, but for the most part, they were greeted with at least acceptance. Sounds of dishes clanking and cabinets closing could be heard from the kitchen, and it appeared the crowds extended into that area as well. Cam nodded toward the kitchen, figuring they would at least go in there long enough to hand over the Crock-Pot of food, but they made it no more than a few steps before Jackson was clapped on the back by one of the visitors. Cam smiled a greeting but decided to move on without Jackson. He could always find him later, and it sure wasn't like they were connected at the hip or anything.

There were lots of smiles and nods and waves as he made his way through the crowd, and that made the frowns and turned-up noses less of a problem. He was glad so many had turned out for Ruby, but he imagined the silence would be all the louder when they left. He wondered how she would handle everything without Junior, and decided to make sure to talk to her about it.

At the door to the kitchen, he paused and looked around. The room was much like his, only bigger, he decided. It was filled to the brim with ladies in dresses, moving efficiently around each other as they worked and talked, the sound much like that of a busy henhouse. Only one in the crowd appeared to be motionless, and that was Ruby Mae. She stood against the counter, holding a plate with a few dabs of food on it, but she looked as if she had no idea what was in her hand or even what was going on around her. Cam looked around again but didn't see any sign of the kids.

When he was noticed, stalled in the doorway, a cry went up, and Cam was greeted happily by the gaggle of women. They swooped in and took the Crock-Pot, raving over how delicious the roast looked and how nice it was of him to bring it.

"Jackson helped," Cam interjected, then felt like some kid in a Shake 'N Bake commercial.

The ladies trilled over the news and began flooding him with questions about his relationship with the town's golden boy.

"Will you two be moving in together?"

"Don't you think they should marry first?"

"Have you considered children?"

"All right, ladies," Pamela said loudly as she entered the kitchen. "Don't scare off Jackson's new love interest. He's not here for an inquisition." Pamela wrapped her arm around Cam's shoulder and gave him a pat.

There were giggles as the women went back to their work in the kitchen, much to Cam's relief. Marriage? Love? Children? Good lord! They'd never even fucked each other yet. The revelation was quite a shock to Cam, and he decided it was about time to change that. He'd have to chat with Jackson when there was time.

Cam heard sounds from the backyard and stepped over to the door to look out. The kids had changed out of their dress clothes, and all of them but the two youngest were now standing around the yard, not so much playing as they were moping. Cam sighed. They all looked shell-shocked, and he guessed that was about as close a way to describe them as he could come up with.

Cam glanced around, but everyone was busy making plates and slicing cakes and pouring drinks, so Cam slipped out back and sat on the steps. "Hey," he said, and they all turned. Smiles quickly appeared and they hurried closer. Cam didn't know the little ones as well as the older ones, but they seemed just as eager for attention. Cam realized that everyone's focus was on Ruby at the moment—what she needed, how she was going to get by—but the kids had been a bit forgotten in the mix.

The six of them found places on the steps around him, and Cam spent the next hour or so listening and talking. He made jokes but didn't try to keep the kids from having the opportunity to talk about what happened or how they felt about it. They seemed happier for the attention, and Cam felt better for having given it.

When the back door opened, they all craned their heads around to find Jackson along with a guy the kids appeared to recognize and Cam was pretty sure worked for the police department. The kids greeted both men and then they wandered off to play in the yard.

Jackson came down a step and then sat next to Cam. "Cam, this is Brian. He's organizing a group of people who are going to help Ruby out."

Brian nodded at Cam's greeting and took a seat on the other side of Cam. "We aren't trying to make decisions for her or take over her life. We just want to make sure she doesn't go under, you know?"

Cam nodded. He totally understood. "So what do you need?"

"Well, we think we might have a job for Ruby, but then there's finding places for the kids while she's away from home. I know you've been spending time with Galen and—"

Cam nodded. "Yeah, and Luanne and Tony. They're welcome to my place anytime. They got bikes there."

Brian grinned. "I was hoping you'd say that. When school starts, the bus can drop them there in the afternoon 'til Ruby gets off work. Sound good?"

Cam grinned. "Sounds great. But...."

Brian raised his brows. "But?"

Cam shrugged. "I don't know how well I'll do with helping on homework."

"If they need help, maybe we can get someone to come over and tutor them?"

"Yeah, okay," Cam agreed. He glanced over to Jackson, who was smiling like Cam had just done the greatest thing in the world. That made Cam smile right back, but when he looked out to the kids as they wandered around the yard, his smile faded. "You know, they are hurting bad and everyone is focused on Ruby. They may need to talk to someone."

Brian and Jackson turned to stare out into the yard too. "I think you're right," Brian said. "I'll make sure to put that on the list of things they need." He pulled out a notepad from his pocket and scribbled a note.

"Do they need any bills paid?" Jackson asked.

Brian sighed and looked up from his pad. "The house is paid for, so that makes things easier. We already paid six months on the electric bill, and Matt Gordon and the church are providing food. The Dairy Queen has made a big donation toward the funeral costs. But if Ruby gets a job, that old station wagon is going to need work and gas in the tank in order to get her back and forth."

"I can do the work," Cam said.

"I'll pay for the gas," Jackson added.

Brian nodded and grinned, then went back to scribbling on his pad. Cam looked out at the kids again and thought of how different it might be if they hadn't lived in a small town like Hog Mountain where everyone came together and helped each other.

They stayed about an hour more, having a plate of food and chatting with the other visitors. Cam got plenty of claps on the back and numerous mentions of his garage. Several people set up times to bring their car by to be looked at, and when they left, Cam was feeling optimistic about the garage becoming a sustainable business.

The drive home was mostly quiet, both men lost in their thoughts. With Harold dead, Cam didn't have to worry about testifying against him. He was still instructed not to leave the town and there might be more needed from him, but Cally had disappeared according to what the police were saying, so for the time being, things were quiet. Cam felt like a dark shadow had been wiped away with the removal of Harold from his life.

When they stepped in the front door, they were met by Tommasina, who meowed and rubbed their legs as if they had been gone for days instead of hours. Cam went to check she had food and water, while Jackson turned on lights and got comfortable on the couch.

Cam came back with two glasses of iced tea, which he set down on the coffee table, then started removing his tie and button-up shirt. Jackson had already kicked off his shoes and had his tie draped over the banister to take up when they went. He then began unbuttoning his own shirt, and soon they were both down to just their dress pants.

Cam sat beside Jackson and leaned into him, taking a sip of his tea and enjoying the feel of skin on skin. "I thought about something today, Sheriff."

"Oh yeah? Just one thing?" Jackson grinned and sipped from his glass.

"You know me and my one-track mind." Cam winked.

Jackson put an arm around Cam and got comfy, his cast hanging over Cam's shoulder. "Tell me what you thought."

Cam looked over into Jackson's eyes and said, "We've never had sex. I mean, you know, like *let me plow your field* kinda sex."

Jackson laughed, and Cam smirked.

"Well, we've both been kinda beat to hell and back," Jackson said.

"True. But I'm feeling better," Cam assured him.

Jackson nodded. "I could probably live through it." He was still smiling.

"You sure, Sheriff? I wouldn't want to do any permanent damage or anything." Cam was grinning right back and started unbuckling his pants. He was all in, no matter who was topping. And speaking of which... "Who does who?"

Jackson shrugged. "I usually top, but...."

"Same here," Cam agreed. "So whoever gives it up needs to be careful, I guess."

Jackson nodded and stared at Cam as if waiting for him to decide.

"So here's how I see it going. We do it standing so bones don't get crushed and bumped."

Jackson nodded and waited.

"And you plow me like a farmer with a vengeance."

Jackson laughed and stood. Cam stayed where he was, watching the show as Jackson began removing his dress slacks and underwear. Yeah, the guy was built like a brick shithouse.

"I'm kinda looking forward to this," Cam said, standing and dropping his own pants to show a hard cock pressing against his own underwear. He kicked off his shoes and pants, then headed for the first-floor bathroom to retrieve lube and condoms.

When Cam returned, Jackson was naked and pumping his cock as he stood near the end of the couch. Jesus, the man was hot. Cam had to stop and simply take in the magnificence that was Jackson Rhodes. All that golden skin and hair, the thick muscles, the equally thick cock with a big bear paw of a hand wrapped around it. Cam dropped his own underwear and joined in the stroke fest. Just thinking of having Jackson pounding into him had his cock ready to burst.

Jackson stepped closer, his focus running the length of Cam's body, letting Cam know that Jackson was just as pleased with what he saw. They came together in a rush, and Jackson rearranged his grip to take both of their cocks into his hand.

Cam groaned, his hips thrusting of their own accord. "Oh God, Jackson, yeah." Cam was already deciding that they could do anything else they had planned later. He was happy right where he was.

But then Jackson stopped and took the lube. He pushed Cam toward the armrest of the couch and then stepped behind him, kneeling and spreading the globes of his ass wide.

"Mmmm," Jackson hummed. Cam had never really worried about if other partners were pleased with his body parts, but with Jackson, it definitely mattered, and it felt good for him to offer even that small bit of approval.

Cam leaned forward and closed his eyes as Jackson placed a lubed finger against his hole. He circled the finger and then pressed until it popped in, sinking slowly and ratcheting up Cam's excitement. He groaned as the pad of Jackson's finger put pressure against his prostate.

Jackson pulled back, then pressed in again with two fingers this time. "Yeah, you're pretty tight." He sounded out of breath with anticipation.

"Feels good," Cam assured him, pushing back to meet the thick fingers.

Cam glanced back when Jackson's ministrations ceased, watching with piqued interest as Jackson rolled on the condom and added some additional lube. When he stood, Cam pushed his ass out in offering, enjoying the feel of at least one of Jackson's hands clamping down hard on his hip.

"Might be a little awkward with only one hand to guide," Jackson said, his focus on his cock as the tip touched against Cam's asshole.

Cam didn't answer, just closed his eyes and waited. He'd never particularly cared to bottom in the past. It had happened and he'd enjoyed it when it did, but he'd never thought he'd be this excited about getting a guy's dick inside of him.

Once Jackson had bottomed out inside him, they both held still for a moment. The feeling was incredible, but his need for Jackson was growing exponentially. He finally rocked his hips, eliciting a moan from Jackson but also getting him moving.

After that, it was mostly sounds and feelings and movements, needs and wants and a lot of fulfillment. The couch creaked with each deep thrust, but Cam couldn't have cared less if it crumbled to bits beneath him, as long as it didn't put a stop to what was happening at the moment.

When Cam yelled with his release, he heard Jackson huffing at his neck and then a deep inhale as Jackson arched and held himself deep. Cam slumped over the arm of the couch, sweaty and out of breath and totally sated. Jackson came down on top of him and the couch protested.

"Sheriff, this couch can't take much more. Let's take this game upstairs."

"Yeah." Jackson pulled out, then turned to dispose of the condom.

Cam swiped at the cum on the couch arm, then shrugged and figured he'd deal with it later. He was halfway up the stairs when he heard Jackson's footsteps on the bottom riser.

Their room was almost fully dark with the thick blanket covering the window. Cam fumbled his way across the room until he felt the edge of the bed, then followed it around to his side. The bed shook as Jackson did the same thing, heading for his own side, and then they were lying next to each other.

As they were fluffing pillows and getting comfortable, Jackson commented, "I heard you getting some business for the shop today."

"Yeah. Some sounds like it will be pretty pricy work too," Cam responded. "I was beginning to think there wouldn't be enough traffic around here for a full-time garage."

"You're gaining their trust." Jackson rolled over on his side to face Cam.

Cam looked over and could make out the shine of Jackson's eyes. "A few weeks ago, that would have been my cue to strike. But I don't want to be that snake anymore, Sheriff."

Jackson nodded and leaned in for a kiss. "You're just one of us town folk now."

As he listened to Jackson's breathing even out, Cam stared off into the black of the room. He wished he could look out at the moon but figured it wasn't as important as having Jackson beside him. The bed shook when Tommasina hopped up and got comfortable. Cam reached out and petted her, listening as she took up a rumbling purr.

Yeah, life was good. He'd finally found his home.

JASON HUFFMAN-BLACK could be described as the porn star alter ego of the mild-mannered editor for several LGBT publishers. By day, Jason edits and writes in a cozy chair, while Mr. Huffman-Black travels the globe on such adventurous excursions as wrestling the one-eyed spitting serpent of Tangiers, ass-spelunking into the hidden tomb of King CockTut, and most recently, sharing a prison cell in a small third-world nation with a rather sweaty fur-covered hulk of a man named Javier.